T0157297

A HOOP FABLE

HARVEY A. KAPLAN

ARCHWAY
PUBLISHING

Archway Publishing books may be ordered through booksellers or by contacting:

Archway Publishing
1663 Liberty Drive
Bloomington, IN 47403
www.archwaypublishing.com
844-669-3957

Because of the dynamic nature of the Internet, any web addresses or
links contained in this book may have changed since publication and
may no longer be valid. The views expressed in this work are solely those
of the author and do not necessarily reflect the views of the publisher,
and the publisher hereby disclaims any responsibility for them.

Any people depicted in stock imagery provided by Getty Images are
models, and such images are being used for illustrative purposes only.
Certain stock imagery © Getty Images.

ISBN: 978-1-6657-1769-4 (sc)
ISBN: 978-1-6657-1770-0 (e)

Library of Congress Control Number: 2022900898

Print information available on the last page.

Archway Publishing rev. date: 05/26/2022

INTRODUCTION

This is the story of Larry Evans, and how his engagement in play, in this case basketball, changed his character, gave his life its purpose, and changed the world around him.

Play is not only a dimension of knowing, but also a dimension of living and feeling and willing—in short, a way of being. It is said of Zarathustra that when he was born, instead of first crying, he laughed. The laughter of the child expresses the joy of freedom, of the sense of adventure, of delight, of pleasure. This must have been what Jesus meant when he said: "Truly I say to you, unless you receive the kingdom of God as a little child, you cannot enter into it."

Play, however, has its own seriousness and even inspires fanatic passions. Some games are played, literally, to the death. Even little children, one observes, do not play as adults glowingly remember, in carefree innocence, but with bitter and combative intensity.

Man is most nearly himself when he achieves the seriousness of a child at play.

–Heraclitus

The soul that has not established aim loses itself.

– Montaigne

You must listen to your own heart. You can't be successful if you aren't happy with what you're doing.

–Curtis Carlson

Desire is the key to motivation, but it's the determination and commitment to an unrelenting pursuit of your goal – a commitment to excellence – that will enable you to attain the success you seek.

–Mario Andretti

Success comes from knowing that you did your best to become the best that you are capable of becoming

– John Wooden

If you find a path with no obstacles, it probably doesn't lead anywhere.

– Frank A. Clark

There is no security on this earth; there is only opportunity.

– Douglas MacArthur

When you discover your mission, you will feel its demand. It will fill you with enthusiasm and a burning desire to get to work on it.

-- W. Clement Stone

Your first obligation is to carry out the mission you are meant for, not what your father, mother, mate, or friends say you should do. Your mission will manifest in you when you decide to listen to your heart's desire.

– Naomi Stephan

CONTENTS

CHAPTER ONE

Childhood

Dreams & Aspirations

When we are young, we think like youngsters, and when we become adults, we think as grownups. There are many people who straddle these two worlds, so that as adults, they retain the lively, enthusiastic moods of childhood, and as children, they adopt a keen sense of their purpose in life.

Larry Evans developed into such a person. He was the younger of two brothers born five years apart into a Jewish family, in a quiet and comfortable neighborhood in the North Bronx. This was a section of rather well-constructed apartment buildings and with a train line that ran directly into Grand Central Station. The neighborhood was quite attractive and was removed from the noisy part of the Bronx. But in other ways it was cut off from Manhattan and remained somewhat isolated from the rest of New York.

As a young child he showed a moderate interest in school and did what was required to pass his subjects. He was a bright seven-year-old who was a middling success in school. He read at an early age, was able to grasp mathematics, and showed an interest in geography. But aside from that, he just put up with school, the way many youngsters do. They go about their business satisfying the requirements of each course, but not doing much more, nor are they interested in doing much more.

He enjoyed playing different games after school; stickball was his favorite, but that he just tolerated, and he reacted to sports as a pleasant way of passing time and hanging out with his friends. The goal of winning or losing was not a premium for him. The boys did enjoy each other, laughed, played, and horsed around a lot. Once he came home, he changed and became a different sort of a kid. He was more sullen and withdrawn around his family.

His older brother Bill was more studious, and much more serious, and they rarely shared similar interests. They didn't have much to say to each other and in fact they seemed like night and day. Often, relatives would remark that the two brothers seemed as if they came from different parents. Their five-year age difference appeared to span two continents. Underneath it all, Bill cared for Larry and tried to help him when he could, especially in math, but Larry was not always receptive to his aid and at times tried to avoid him. One time Bill was explaining particular mathematical concepts and finally gave up when he saw that Larry was ignoring him, which almost turned into a fight between them.

Bill had a group of friends much like himself and they rarely went out of their way to engage Larry; and Larry had two particularly close buddies who followed him throughout his life. The chemistry was terrific among them and it lent him strong support.

Luckily each brother had his own bedroom so that they were able to keep to themselves. Yet even with that, Larry yearned for the day when Bill would go off to college so that he would be spared the few moments that they did interact. His parents were another thing. They were closer to Bill and somehow seemed to ignore Larry–or possibly they really didn't understand him.

This was the 1980s, and the Evans family lived in a small enclave of Jews in the northern part of the Bronx. It was not so much isolated as cut off from the main borough of Manhattan, but there were many perks that went with that: cheaper,rents and generally a more moderate life style. Ronald Reagan was elected U.S. President in 1980, and the country progressed according to his hardline policy toward Communism and the way he stood up to the Soviet Union.

But more important, as we will see for Larry, was how the American basketball player Michael Jordan burst onto the scene in the NBA during the 1980s, bringing a surge in popularity for the sport and becoming one of the most beloved sports icons in the United States. In addition, Magic Johnson and Larry Bird faced against each other in three NBA Finals. As our story progresses, the last two events had a tremendous impact on Larry.

Larry's father David was a lawyer who grew up in the Bronx, married, and then stayed in the Bronx, getting a large three-bedroom apartment that would have been prohibitively expensive if it were in Manhattan. He married Janet, a girl two years younger than he, from a nearby high school. When David went off to college, Janet, who graduated two years later, went to a community college, so that they graduated from their respective schools at the same time. They married soon afterward, and Janet took a job as a secretary in a Wall Street firm in order to support David, who was now entering law school at Seton Hall. After finishing school and passing the bar exam, David started working at the New York City Board of Education, where he eventually advanced to a senior legal position. He loved the job, the free time, the prospect of a future pension, and the security that the position offered. The thought of working at a law office almost frightened him.

When David was 30, he and Janet had their first child; and five years later they had their second. They both loved being parents, although Janet had quietly hoped to have a girl. However, they then decided that two children would be enough to bring up and provide for. While they took an interest in their children, they rarely showed concern for their individual futures but were always attentive to the importance of their children's grades. In many ways, Janet was not always comfortable around her two sons, and David tended to be deeply into himself. They rarely discussed what they envisioned could be the future of each child. Maybe this threatened them too much, considering they weren't overjoyed at what they had accomplished in life.

One particular April, when Larry was 8 years old, the parents made their usual preparation for Passover, a holiday that they had observed since childhood. Their own parents were invited, along with David's brother, who was referred to as Uncle Sol. Larry never liked the holiday and the rituals that went into it especially the reading of the *Haggadah* that could go on, he felt, for an eternity. He was proud to be Jewish but couldn't take the same story being told over and over again, yet he did love to read about the Israeli-Arab wars starting in 1948. He had an intense interest in memorizing details and he could talk about the dates of each encounter and the resolutions that took place. History was his favorite subject and he knew all the wars that America had entered and could recite the names of most of the presidents.

This love for recall shifted to movies, whereby he could recite the names of five actors or actresses in all the movies he saw. He was part of a group of kids who hung out and played these quiz contests, especially when it came to baseball, but none had the interest or skill of memory that Larry had, nor did they seem to care that he could recall these names. Most of his friends felt as if it were just an oddity of his. They found it a bit peculiar for a boy of their own years to be so interested in unimportant facts. Of course, when it came to school it gave him a slight advantage in spelling and history.

The two sets of grandparents came to the seder with David's brother, which made for an intimate dinner setting. Sol had recently moved to Israel for half the year, where he had set up a successful business. For some reason, Sol never married; but he did travel a lot and regaled the family with stories of his sojourns. Now he seemed to be entering into a new path, living halftime in a foreign country. He had always been involved with Jewish causes and with the politics of Israel. In fact, he started taking Hebrew lessons after his bar mitzvah when he became so curious about the different alphabet and pronunciations, and little by little gravitated more toward the cultural and secular aspects of the Jewish religion. As a teenager he went to Israel and from that day on became very enmeshed in anything with an Israeli theme. This included folk dancing, singing, and Klezmer music. He only dated women who shared these interests, but nothing seriously romantic ever developed.

As Sol never had children, he took a special interest in Larry and took him to baseball games, but he could see after a while that the game seemed to bore Larry and often they left after six innings. Then he switched and took Larry to basketball games, where they both found their real interest and excitement. They hung out a lot and it became evident that Larry was the son that Sol never had. His parents wholeheartedly approved of this. The older son Bill was more aloof and never had that much to say to Sol. Bill seemed to come from a different breed altogether. He was much more studious and serious and never could get close to Uncle Sol. His personality did not mesh well with that of either Larry or Uncle Sol. As often happens, the two brothers, while fond of each other, never really had that much in common. They seemed to prefer it that way, even though Bill hoped he could provide some kind of guidance or direction for Larry; but this was not destined to happen.

On this particular evening, when Larry was 10 years old, something happened that would change his life forever. Sol brought two gifts to the house. He gave Bill a science set that very much interested him. And then he brought out this rather large item and handed it to Larry.

Uncle Sol said as he handed the gift to Larry, "Well, I hope you like this. I had you in mind when I bought it for you." Larry slowly opened it and saw this enormous backboard. As he was looking at it, Sol handed him a medium-sized rubber ball. Now Larry had watched a lot of basketball games in his schoolyard, as well as the games that he and Sol attended, but without that much interest. As Larry watched intently, Sol took the backboard and fitted it over the door; then hooked on the rim and net. Larry stood still in amazement. Then Sol took the ball, arched his arms, and tossed it toward the basket and broke out in a huge smile as the ball went in. He then turned to Larry and said to him, "You see, you can toss the ball, or hook it and lay it up just as we saw when we went to a Knicks game."

Larry took the ball and attempted it, but missed the three shots that he took. Then he grabbed the ball, stopped to observe the net, took special aim, and shot it toward the basket. When the ball went in he broke out in this huge smile. Something had touched him deeply. He picked up the ball and tried again, but with no success, so he tried over and over again. By this time the adults were moving into the dining room, and Larry was left alone to play his game.

Once seated, they broke into their usual family conversation, where they caught up on what was going on in their lives. The two sets of grandparents were retired, and as they both lived not far from one another, over time they had become quite friendly. When there was a break in the discussion, Sol turned to David and told him of his latest adventures in Israel and the goings-on in that country. While David had a great deal of knowledge, he rarely offered too many of his views; he tended to listen to his older brother. The women took a back seat in these discussions, waiting for subjects more akin to their own personal interests. Now it became time to recite the history of the Jews and each had his or her own book to read from, while David appointed his son Bill to lead the reading. As David looked around, he saw immediately that Larry was missing. They had to call him in a number of times to join them, and finally Larry went into the dining room, resenting it because he wanted to stay with the ball and hoop.

The group read over the passages while passing the matzoh and it was evident at one point that they had enough of the service and just wanted to get on with their meal. Larry saw the moment when he could leave the table and quickly took the opportunity. He motioned Sol to come with him. Larry was quite serious when he said to Uncle Sol that the board had too much spring to it and the ball bounced too sharply off it. Sol went about trying to fix it so that the spring was softened. By then David came over and tried his hand, and together they were moderately successful. The ball didn't bounce with as much action and it became easier to get it into the basket.

In the days to come, Larry couldn't wait until the evening meal was over so that he could resume the basketball game. After the boys went to sleep one night, David turned to his wife and said: "He really loves this. I've never seen him so serious about a game, maybe there are things about our son we never noticed before." Janet had barely noticed this attachment of her son's, as she was really made to be a mother to a girl and to share her interests. And she rarely engaged Larry in conversation, but would ask him about school and the subjects he was taking. She had never considered probing his other interests; she grew up with an older sister and it was all girl talk in their house. In fact, her father removed himself from the family of three women so that male interests never gained much attention. She was not indifferent to Larry's interest, but rather the idea had never entered her mind. But she agreed with her husband about this Interest.

A month later, Larry continued to pursue the game; his interest did not diminish, and in fact he expanded the game by including all sorts of different moves. He jumped while shooting the ball, hooked it, laid it up and shot from a standing position.

Finally, Dave, watching this repetitive activity, finally confronted his son, "What gives with this game?"

"I don't know," Larry shot back, "Is there a problem? I just find it so exciting and it gives me so much pleasure; and I want to get better and better."

Dave began to wonder whether the fine line had become blurred between fantasy and reality. Was the game replacing Larry's interest in the everyday pursuits of his life? It was play, but it was more than that. He knew how serious kids could be, including himself when he was younger, and how they could fight over who was the winner in board games. He knew that for all children, games are played with a similar seriousness. It was Larry's obsession that bothered him, and it seemed to have become more than a game – too many misses haunted him and he acted as if his one aim in life was sinking one shot after another. Was the game actually acting as a metaphor for life, with the challenges, difficulties and barriers that everyone faced in growing up? Were the obstacles in life rolled up into one intensive game?

Larry could no longer just treat it as a fun pastime; his preoccupation excluded that possibility. And this is what changed him and would point to a very particular path that he would choose to follow. In short, the game for him represented life itself.

After another month, Larry brought the contraption into his room where he was able to practice in isolation without any interruption. Then he worked on improving the mechanism. This took quite a bit of ingenuity, as he inserted all kinds of material that would soften the spring even more. By then his father realized that he should participate in his son's obsession. He surprised him one evening and brought him a real basketball that he could take to the playground. By then Larry was close to eleven years old and certainly strong enough to throw the ball at the basket.

Dribbling was a bit more difficult, but he managed as well as he could. He then tried to enlist his friends in the game, and he had to motivate them to join in. By now Janet was a bit concerned and wondered why he did not come home right after school as he usually did. Finally, Janet went over to the playground to see what he was up to. She saw Larry playing with two of his friends and he was dribbling, shooting and passing the ball. He stood out from the rest of the kids; he was decidedly more efficient, and he played with greater solemnity. When she walked back home, she told herself that it was a good athletic activity that could only make him stronger.

One night, three months later, Janet turned to Dave and told him some of her concerns. She had never seen Larry so preoccupied and possessed. It wasn't just for a few hours; even after he finished playing, he read all these basketball books and then the posters of various players were plastered all over his room. "We need to get some handle on this," she pleaded. Dave was not that concerned, but he agreed and told her that he would talk to the school psychologist, and the next day made an appointment to see him.

Dave entered his office and took a seat; he then explained to him his concerns. What did this compulsion mean? "It's one thing to play, but I wonder if this really is just playing anymore. He is constantly practicing different moves, different shots, dribbling between his legs and then he just repeats it over and over again. He never misses a game on TV; but, more than this, he has an understanding of the game that seems beyond his years. I have heard him discussing the game with adults, and I can tell you he does more than just hold his own—he starts to argue with them until they back off. This is not usual for a boy his age, so I wanted to talk to you about your take on it."

The psychologist took all of this in and tried to make some sense of the fixation. "Kids do get obsessed with sports but maybe not to this degree, but many are taken by baseball and get very involved with Little League, and then they get caught up with statistics and that kind of stuff. They all have their heroes and can recite all kinds of stats about them. But I can see that this is not answering your question. Maybe there is something different about basketball, something that has a sexual meaning. You know the idea of putting a ball into this hole they call the hoop."

The psychologist wanted to make a definite point to Dave and he paused at moments and then stared directly into Dave's eyes and continued on about his thoughts having to do with Larry's preoccupation.

The father looked doubtful but nevertheless inclined his head in some kind of agreement. "I take it you are a Freudian and, if I understand you, that you think that there is something sexual about the game. I think that is your point, something I feel is a bit way out, I mean, do you really think this?"

"Well," the psychologist continued, "I think there may be a better explanation, but I still would consider the possibility." The psychologist could see that what he said annoyed Dave, so he quickly switched subjects and said: "Look, let me think about this and get back to you. I am sorry, but I have another appointment. You know kids are always involved with solving one conflict or another. Your son may be trying to make himself more effective in overcoming some tension in his life. That's how it starts; and if the activity become so pleasurable, well then, it takes on a life of its own. Unless his marks are falling and I take it that this is not the case, I wouldn't worry about it. We both know kids can get involved in activities that we may wonder about, yet we know it makes sense for them. And in the end it may turn out to be both positive and satisfying. What he is doing is hardly negative and actually could be constructive

Dave walked out of the office a bit perplexed and started to think that maybe he ought to see Larry's activity in a different light, but the total seriousness of his son's behavior really started to get to him. He then thought that maybe it could be part of his own inner problem; he had never gotten passionately involved in sports and could he be envious of his son? Maybe he had been too passive as a child and should have had stronger interests. He remembered that he was on the debating team, but never possessed the drive to win over the other team. Okay, he thought to himself, you'd better tolerate your son's intensity and be patient and see where it leads. That would be a better compromise than just being negative about it. Maybe the kids who get so involved in these kinds of activities make better adjustments later in life? Dave started to feel better about the whole situation and realized that it would be better for him to provide support and encouragement rather than criticism. His whole attitude shifted and now he was able to view what his son was doing with a more wholesome attitude.

One weekend when Larry was out, David went into his room and caught sight of the books that Larry was reading. They seemed mostly to do with basketball: Rick Pitino, John Calipari, and one by Bobby Knight. Well at least he reads, but it is all skewed in one direction. "Probably all kids do that," he reasoned to himself.

At the dinner table, Larry seemed uninterested in family conversation, more so than usual. In fact, there was not a subject brought up that Larry attempted to take any part in. So his father thought it best to draw him out.

"You seem uninterested in our conversation, is there something on your mind?"

Larry shot back, "It's not that I am uninterested but sometimes I don't see the point of what you are talking about. It doesn't seem to take on any importance. I mean if it were politics or history... but not the saga of our everyday life."

The father reacted to this: "And what do you consider as being important?"

"Let's say some outstanding action, something that is unusual or that really gets to us. I have been reading about the history of basketball and I can't believe some of the wildest shots that have been attempted, but I don't know if anyone is interested." His brother, Bill, in a rare attitude of friendliness, said that he would certainly be interested.

"Well," Larry shot back, "There was this guy Ernie Calverley who played for the University of Rhode Island and hit a shot from behind the midcourt line to tie the game against Bowling Green State University and then won in overtime. Unfortunately, they eventually lost to Kentucky in the NIT final. Can you imagine someone making a shot from that far out?"

His older brother feigned an interest in this that Larry picked up on immediately but decided to ignore. His curiosity about statistics and all facets of the game were written down in notebooks piled up on his bookshelf. Each notebook was labeled carefully so that he could easily consult it when he wanted to locate a particular statistic. When not doing his homework, he was reading about basketball or glued to the TV watching game after game. He moved from college stats to professional players and their coaches.

When he watched games on TV, he found the behavior of the coaches so impressive as they pranced up and down the sidelines yelling and motioning for all kinds of plays. He would have loved to overhear what they told their players during time-outs or half-time. But this was certainly the stuff that excited him and made life eventful. The rest of his schoolwork was done with much less fervor. In math he loved to study about percentages and ratios. Then he remembered one quote from Karl Wallenda, spoken on the occasion of his going back up to the high wire after his troupe's fatal accident, when he is supposed to have said: "To be on the high wire is life; the rest is waiting." Larry was so impressed with that remark, it described his interest in the game.

Now a year had passed since he had gotten the hoop; and Larry was now twelve years old and he had put on weight and filled out. Little by little, his relationship with his family changed, as it did with his friends. His father, who worked for the Board of Education, seemed to have reached the apex of his strivings, even though he wasn't even fifty years of age. He never moved very far from where he grew up, thinking that the modest rents would enable him to provide more stability for the family. At times, Dave had envisioned working for a high powered law firm; but somehow his fear of competition interfered with that thought,. He was more suited to the job he had now and knew that it was the right fit for him.

Janet stopped working as soon as she gave birth to Larry. She never really had any real career in mind and was perfectly willing to be a stay-at-home mom. In fact, much like Dave, she felt that she had attained happiness and success in life. She was certainly willing to support Dave in his everyday work life.

Maybe the one thing that they felt they missed was a more stimulating social life She maintained an intimacy with the few friends she had been close to throughout the years. They did enjoy a bimonthly bridge game and would meet some of their friends for dinner at the local Italian restaurant. But it looked as if both Janet and Dave enjoyed their lives in a moderate way but could not say that their existence was a great deal of fun.

Bill, the older brother, fit in much better with the family. Somehow he shared more of their values and wanted to be appreciated by them. Larry felt like the maverick who had found a unique path for himself, and anything anyone would say to him would bounce off him. At times, his father would ask him about his friends, Paul or Phil, and Larry would say that he really didn't know what they were up to but he valued their friendship a great deal.

Larry did realize that he needed to make his parents feel as if he took what they said seriously. He would listen attentively to his parents, but he really put up with them, not really taking anything they said with much seriousness. He felt as if they really didn't try to understand him and he wondered to himself, "What am I, a different species? He told them once in a solemn tone : "You should be happy for me. I have this interest that keeps my grades up and I find so much in life that excites me." What could they say to this? Basketball was an honest pursuit and he did seem more alive and serious than a lot of other kids his age. It was evident that basketball was creating particular character changes. It gave him a purpose to this whole affair we call living. But the gap between his family and Larry widened and he didn't really want to share much of this with them. He wanted it to be a private matter; otherwise, he felt that they would feel sorry for him on some level and would try to humor him or reduce the seriousness that basketball had for him.

Then one day Larry came home from school feeling quite excited. At dinner he told his parents that the school wanted to enlist parent volunteers and he had offered their names. He told them that they would get more involved in the school's activities and could really make a difference. His father was puzzled at the possibility that this would be of any interest to him and his wife, and thought that maybe they really weren't suited for this position. But Larry prevailed, and in the end they went to their first meeting. In the weeks that followed, they invested their time in planning to make the school a better place for learning. And after a while, both he and Janet took on a more active role in the lives they led. And they were impressed with how Larry was subtlety changing their lives.

At dinner, their discussions started to center more on the school's activities and Larry showed them what activities would make the school a better place for learning. They could see how their son really got involved with life and took an active interest in what was going on around him. And they wondered "Could this all have happened because of basketball?"

When Larry passed his twelfth birthday, he decided that he ought to get out on a court and play with other kids. He would go down to one court near his house which was usually empty during the week and start his regimen. This would entail picking particular spots on the court and then starting to send up shots. He would stay in one spot until he made eight shots in a row, and then he would move on to another position. After moving around the court, he would then practice his jump shot. He would start by taking the ball out at midcourt, dribble up the court, and jump and shoot. Of course, he spent endless time dribbling the ball, especially between his legs, and then streaking toward the basketball for a layup. He never seemed to tire of these practices and time would just fly by. He was in what could be called a state of flow. In this state individuals typically feel strong, alert, in effortless control, unselfconscious, and as if they were performing at the peak of their abilities. Both the sense of time and emotional conflicts disappear. There is an exhilarating feeling of divine existence, a state of pure pleasure. That is why Larry would find practicing so rewarding.

On this certain Saturday, he went down to the courts early, hoping that he would have one basket for himself so that he could practice for a few hours. But there were a number of guys there already playing a game, three on three, and all the baskets were taken. He wondered what he wanted to do, so he said to himself that this was the moment of truth. He took a place alongside the guys who were on the sideline. Two players next to him who were waiting in line for the next game asked him if he wanted to get into the game together with them. "Sure!" he blurted out; but he did feel anxious underneath it. The first guy asked him if he had played much before, to which Larry assured him that he was tried and tested. "Okay," remarked the guy, "I just hope you are not one of those guys who shoots every time they get the ball?" "Not at all. I'm a big passer, a team player," he said with assurance. They guy was about 5'11," a bit bigger than the other players. He looked friendly and upbeat, the kind of a guy you would want to be with. The second guy was a bit shorter and seemed more quiet, as if he weren't sure about his place in the world. But together they looked damn good. Then they introduced themselves: the first guy's name was Frank and the second was Howie.

The game they were watching was over and now it was their turn. They took the court as the first team threw the ball in, and of course the first guy who got the ball sent up a long shot that bounded off the backboard and Larry grabbed the ball. The rules of the game dictated that if you grabbed a rebound you had to take it out behind the foul line, so he threw it out to his teammate, who threw it right back to Larry. He held it a moment, then dribbled on the right side and caught the guy cutting to the basket with a sharp pass. In one motion he got the ball and laid it up for a score. The first guy nodded his approval, "Good pass."

This was the first play that Larry had ever attempted, except with some of the kids from his class who were pretty bad. But these guys were a bit older and bigger and certainly more seasoned. As the game continued Larry got up the nerve to try a shot, and, lo and behold, he banked it perfectly. These countless hours of practice finally paid off. Now he was off and running, so he tried a few jump shots and twist shots, always remembering not to hog the ball. Frank stopped the game for a moment and called his team together.

"Listen, Larry, you've got the makings of a good shooter. Certainly you must have practiced a lot but I have to tell you that you look like you are in your own zone. I mean it's not that you don't look to pass, but you seem to be in a personal zone and I think you would have more fun if you felt freer and just let the game flow as it is. Let's see if we can work this out, and Howie will try and keep focused on your shot. Sometimes I get the feeling when you jump and attempt to shoot that you take your eyes off the basket, or maybe it's something else, but I'd like to see you more focused. Get it?" When they regrouped to take the ball out, Larry thought that he really liked this guy. Frank was a kind of born leader who took charge, and he was the kind of guy you would want to play with because he was positive, patient, and had a winner's instinct.

Larry's team won that game and Frank patted him on the back, "Not bad for a small guy. I like the way you play and pass the ball, and I especially like the way you take direction. You opened up your game and it gave us an edge to win." But Larry was at first hurt by that remark about his height, even if it were meant to be humorous. Yet the total expression made him feel wonderful, as if his lifelong fantasy could really come true and as if the mountains of success that had filled his imagination could be climbed. Life is grand with the right actions; and those lofty horizons might be within reach, he thought.

The team won the next few games and then decided to call it quits. As they left the court, Frank asked him he was available tomorrow because they were good together and should follow it up. "Why yes," Larry said, "I would love to get together tomorrow." "Okay you're in, see you tomorrow, same time and same place." Larry liked Frank immediately, in fact, he felt as if he adored him. There was something so wholesome and caring about him and he felt that the Irish kids were more alive and adventurous and in some ways tougher and scrappier than the Jewish kids.

Well, this was perfect, but as he was walking home he realized that he may have talked too soon. His family often made plans on Sunday to get together with the family, his cousins, aunts, uncles and grandparents. He didn't want to start a rift between them, but he did not want to disappoint the guys who expected him in the game. He was angry with himself, but he knew if he didn't show up they could be turned off to him in the future and alienating them was the last thing he wanted to do. "How old do you have to be to graduate from this family commitment?" he thought. More to the point, he had really never liked his family and would find most of the afternoons boring as hell. Obviously, he may have been growing up too fast because he felt too old for this kind of stuff.

He came home and greeted both his parents. David smiled as Larry walked in, and asked, "So how did it go?" Larry replied eagerly, "We won and we played well and fought hard. I really like those guys; I didn't know them before today but I think they like me a lot also." His father put down the newspaper. "That's terrific, your practicing is really paying off. You see, practice makes perfect." Their interaction was touching, they were forming a better bond, and Larry was feeling more and more that he had a real father, one who cared. His mother was getting some food together in the kitchen.

"So what are you making?" he asked as he stepped inside.

"Same thing I do every Sunday, making some potatoes and

goulash. Everybody seems to love it so why not continue a good thing." "Is this for tomorrow?" Larry asked,

"Well of course, like every Sunday."

"Well I don't think I can make it tomorrow, I made other plans."

"What kind of plans? Your cousins will be there and they expect you to be there also."

"You know," he said, "I really don't have that much in common with them. I am old enough to do what I want to do."

Janet then called in Dave, and related their conversation. The father wrinkled up his forehead, "We're a family and we go together. This isn't like you, and we can't disappoint the rest of the family. Come on, let's keep the date at least for now."

", I am just talking about tomorrow, not all the time. I have a chance to gain some valuable pointers about high school and college from this counselor who is going to talk to a bunch of us," he lied to them.

"What kind of pointers?" the father asked him.

"Well this guy has been a coach and teacher for years and he wants to tell us about the best high school for us to go to and then how we could make plans for college."

"But you are not going to college for over four years."

"Yes, but you have to make plans way in advance especially if it involves a possible scholarship for basketball. You know, dad, the cost of college keeps getting higher and higher and in terms of money, any kind of scholarship would reduce our financial burdens."

As he went on making up this whole situation, the father began to feel guilty. How could he deny his son this opportunity to further his education, especially if it involved reducing their costs? He knew Larry had gotten the best of him, and he certainly respected his son's ability to put an argument over. He thought that this would serve him well in the future.

"Why don't we take a moment to talk about your future?"

"Okay," replied Larry. The father then asked him what he

thought this heavy focus on basketball would get him. Larry sat down, thought a moment, then went on. He shook his head and went on to explain.

"I feel a lot of things about it. I wonder if I were playing chess whether you would feel the same way? You know, in what I have read about chess, one player really wants to kill the other player–that's what they mean by checkmating the king. I don't want to kill my opponent; I just want to win; and I am able to appreciate good moves on their part. But as for me, I am beginning to feel as if basketball is giving my character a certain zest for life."

The father listened quietly, then replied. "It's just a game, how can you feel that it is doing so much for you?"

Larry smiled and he went on almost reciting something he had read. "But then life is a game. Practicing law is a game and when you find the game you enjoy playing, then you should play it with all your might. I thought about what you just asked me. I just don't go out to the playground and willy-nilly throw the ball around. I take what I am going to do with a serious perspective. And I think that my playing can help me get through life. Maybe it can center me in my life. And you know it gets me to focus more on what I am doing especially in school and with some of the courses I am taking." I just want to be as good a player as I can, and I want to understand the finer points of the game."

As he went on, Dave had to be impressed by the boy's ability to express himself and present such a clear picture of what he wanted to do at this point in his life. He shook his head and thanked Larry.

Larry left his house early the next day, apologizing for not being there and yet so relieved that he could do what he wanted. There was a kind of freedom in this, a feeling that his life was going to be built around his interests, his plans, and his own ideas of what was best for him. He walked over to the courts feeling as if he had the world in his hands. "I'm a big guy now, and I want to be treated like a big guy now". But the realization hit him, "What am I going to do about next Sunday and all the Sundays after this? This excuse may hold up this time, but hell, I'd better come up with something better next time. I don't want to get into a fight with them. But I'd better start thinking about this. My cousins don't understand me, they really don't have any interest in what I like and do. In fact," he confronted himself, "You don't even like them, they are nerds always trying to be so nice and sweet. I can't stand the way their parents point out their good traits, what nice sons they are—and then they look so proud instead of just telling their mother to shut up. But they get off on this, and I could throw up with their performance." By the time he had run through this speech, he found himself at the gates of the playground, where he saw his two friends from yesterday waiting for him. They waved at him and he felt so damn good that he was wanted and appreciated by them, even though they were a bit different from him. "Maybe they are Irish. But they are good for me and I think that we could become good friends."

The games even went better the second day: they were more used to each other and for some reason the competition got better. Frank, the first guy, was taller than most of the other team, so he could grab the rebounds. The second guy, Howie, was a great playmaker who kept the action going and now Larry could really get into his groove, reminding himself constantly not to shoot too often. But he could feel that he was getting hungrier and hungrier for winning, playing a satisfyingly sound game that was more than just beating the other team. And it was just a wonderful inner experience for him— and he started thinking about those adults who strive so hard and those who just want to take it easy.

He remembered thinking this thought yesterday about his father and why he had ended up in the Board of Education making peanuts, while those lawyers in the big firms were pulling down carloads of money. "But it is the same in basketball," he reasoned, "especially with those coaches who would do anything short of murder to win a game, while others retreat to calmer and trouble-free environments."

But he knew he was drawn to those coaches who ran up and down the sidelines yelling and motioning what his players should be doing. "That's the kind of guy I want behind me, pushing and yelling at me to get better. I know a lot of players don't like it, but I think I would shine with that force behind me." Larry thrived on these lectures that he gave himself. "You have to be hungry, you have to want it really bad. Then nothing should stand in the way and that includes Sunday get-togethers with the family." Now he was already giving himself some vital messages to carry him through life. Although he knew that he could call them pep talks, for him they would become his mantra for superior success.

Yes, he went on, what is it really that makes one guy accept his own mediocre performances while the next guy is always striving to do and be better? He knew at that moment that unless he was driven to succeed he would make all kinds of excuses for why he wasn't getting ahead. And he had these excuses tailor-made, but he knew also that he just had to push himself harder and rule out or blot out all the physical minuses that he could use against himself. There will be no excuses from now on—he would discard them from his psyche as well as he could. The one thing he knew is that he had to have a ferocious coach pushing him or even bullying him on. If only Bobby Knight were still in the game. That was the kind of guy he wished for. Otherwise one could just as well settle for mediocrity like his father had. Why are we living in the Bronx? was another puzzle for him, when he knew that lawyers and other professionals moved to Manhattan. Yet he actually loved the neighborhood in which he was living. It had open spaces and he never loved how crowded other places could be. "No," he said to himself, "I am happy that they picked here to live."

These were the thoughts that filled his mind as he walked to the playground to meet his teammates the following Sunday. This was the second time they were playing together. They formed a cohesive team and they were really settling into a nice groove. Larry was hitting some great outside shots. By now he could master the pump fake, where the opponent would jump when he made a motion to shoot and then when the defensive player came down, he would then jump up and deliver the ball into the basket–that is, if he were lucky. When he didn't think of shooting, he was focused on passing the ball to the guy who was cutting. Another strategy he developed was the screen, where he would block out the opposing player so that his player could dribble by him. They won most of the games that day and decided to pack it in after four hours. They really played well together and Larry could feel the warmth from these guys. When you win as a team there is always good cheer; losing isn't as much fun "Hey," Larry blurted out, "Winning isn't everything, it's the only thing!"

"Who said that," asked Howie.

"Are you kidding," Larry responded, "Vince Lombardi of the Green Bay Packers." He realized that his friends now never heard of Lombardi and he knew also that a lot to things separated them but what held them together was basketball and winning and hell, that was the only thing that counted.

Larry's playing had a decided influence on the other parts of his life. In fact, his whole attitude toward life began to change radically. He saw the need to engage life with a particular vigor, a new addition of intensity, a keen interest in participating, whereas before he had been bored with most things. His attitude changed, as if he had suddenly awakened and realized that there was a world out there to be challenged and tackled. The game that captivated Larry helped him discover a clearer identity of himself. He developed a dynamic wherein he felt more of a performer and could establish a role in life. Playing this game enabled Larry to become more socialized while he became part of a group of guys.

In short, what Larry did was to undergo a major reconstruction of his way of approaching life. Is the child who plays games practicing how to become an adult, or are children who do not play enough or do not play properly have their development arrested? Something surely will be missing. The engagement in sports provided an opportunity for him to work on developing an idea of a future for himself. Of course the aim of these thoughts is to develop a plan to win. In this way he started to think more seriously of working out a plan to accomplish his goal.

His classmates started noticing that Larry was changing; he evinced a new kind of assertiveness, no more a child but a different kind of player who was involved in this new game for himself that assumed a role he had never had before. His approach to himself was different, not just as a kid, but as someone who understood more and more the importance of planning and achieving. He took himself more seriously and rarely attempted to joke around as he had done before. And, odd as it may seem, he approached his homework assignments with more thought and diligence.

CHAPTER TWO

Adolescence

Striving to Separate

When Larry was a bit over the age of twelve, his father asked him about his thoughts of preparing for his Bar Mitzvah. "Dad, I looked into this thing and I just feel it would be a joke to recite these sacred words in Hebrew when I wouldn't understand what any of them meant. I saw this when I went to my friend's Bar Mitzvah and they agreed with me. It would all be phonetic and that ain't honest But I would like to talk to you about other ideas." Larry was settling in to becoming his own man; he stood up for himself and pursued his own interests with a persistence and self-reliance that impressed his parents. They often would talk about him and express their respect and admiration.

He told them that he would go through the whole ceremony, but he wanted to go to a Yiddish school where learning the language would be more practical. In fact it is close to German, which he could later study in college. He hoped that his parents would go along with him, since he had really researched the whole issue. As much as he understood that Hebrew was an important issue for all Jews, it just didn't make sense to him at this time. And actually his parents were impressed and went along with it. They realized that Yiddish had more of a practical value.

Then he realized that he had better take a greater part in planning for his Bar Mitzvah, the last requirement that would come from the family, or so he thought. But he wanted it to be a happy, fulfilling day, as he had practiced for it for over a year. He couldn't hide the fact that he was proud of this day, the one that would proclaim him as a man. And he had mastered enough Yiddish to make him feel as if he were more than ready for the service.

Dave asked him how he felt and Larry replied: "I feel that this is an important moment for me. I think that it is an achievement when a boy reaches 13. And there are so many other feelings I have."

"Like what? Dave inquired.

"Well, I feel fortunate to be where I am. In fact, I can rightfully say that I am happy with my life and how I am leading it. There are many kids I see who don't have an idea of what they are all about or where they are going, but I feel as if I am following in a direction, wherever it may lead me. But more than that…" he went on, and paused so as to capture his further thoughts.

Larry then thought of what he was going to say.

"From what I have read, I think that this period of my adolescence is an important marker for how I will greet the rest of my life. Those of us who feel down or depressed as an adolescent will face the same problems as adults; but those of us who feel excited and see life as one magical encounter will become better adjusted adults. This is more than a thought for me: I think you will read about it in psychology books that treat the subject of adolescents. It is an important phase of my life and I am so appreciative that you haven't burdened me with your expectations, but let me become my own person. I wake up in the morning and I feel good about the coming day, like there are so many things I want to do."

Dave broke in for a moment. "That is such a wonderful thing to hear from you and I think this is the way all kids should feel, although we know that they do not. But we are so proud of you and how you are doing in school and now with the Bar Mitzvah."

Larry smiled in response, "Thank you."

The day went splendidly. Larry went up to the stage in the synagogue and read from the Torah in a lively and literate manner. He had invited a group of friends to share the day with him, and afterward his parents had reserved a space in a nearby kosher restaurant where they had some music and just engaged in games and good times.

After his Bar Mitzvah when he turned 13, he began to feel stronger. His body filled out and he asked for a set of barbells as his gift. Now he began lifting weights every other day with the expectation that he would be in a better position to face opponents on the court. He felt that it was a requirement for him to make an impression of presence, to better look the part that he wanted to play and have the strength and power to prevail.

Larry did not develop an arrogance that would have cast him at odds with adults; he just felt more sure about himself. He actually enlisted his parents in his pursuits and his hopes for himself.

"If I can play well enough, I may be able to get a scholarship to a college and you wouldn't have to put up a dime for me. And I think I can go in that direction. It just takes a lot of work and a lot of believing in yourself, the kinds of things that Rick Pitino talks about. It may sound like hokum to you, but there is a lot of truth in gouging out a successful path in life starting at my age. I have seen so many classmates who have no idea what the world is all about, nor do they have any direction or idea of their role in life."

His parents couldn't really contradict him; and maybe in the end he would be good enough to tackle a basketball scholarship and yes, that would free up a lot of bucks for his father, especially when so much money was being spent on his older brother in California. And then his father, sensing his son's seriousness, made special efforts in engaging him in thoughtful conversations about life with all its complexities. Their subjects ranged from girls to money to future plans. His father realized how important it would be to embrace his son's interests, draw him out, and have him express what he wanted in life. He realized that he never had gotten that from his father and maybe that resulted in his inability to pursue his interests with the kinds of persistence that would have result in tougher challenges.

It was around this time that Larry realized that his body was changing. It was firming up and he began to see the payoff for all his work. He shot up a few inches and now stood 5'6", not huge in his eyes, but certainly big enough to take on most of the guys on the court. He was getting a bit tired of playing the same guys week after week, so a suggestion from Frank really interested him.

As they packed up their stuff and started walking in the direction of home one day, Frank said that he thought they ought to move on to another court where the action would be more competitive. He told them that if they walked about a mile further south, it would take them to a playground that had tougher opponents.

"Do you mean black guys?" asked Howie.

"Yeah, that's what I mean, you got to rise up in this game if you are going to get anywhere." They discussed this among themselves for some minutes and realized that they weren't going to get any better unless the competition got stiffer. The only point in competing and hopefully winning is that it should make you better.

"I would go for that," reacted Larry; but at the same time he said this, he felt a quiver in his stomach. He knew it could be a tougher game, especially if those guys would be more physical. Yet he knew he had better face this test, otherwise he would never improve himself. And then he reasoned that it would be the same game, only harder and maybe more rewarding.

So they met early the next Saturday and started walking over to the other court. They were talking in a rapid cadence, masking their underlying anxiety about this impending opposition. They avoided talking about what they would anticipate in meeting these new opponents. And then after all the talk and joking around, they finally arrived at the other playground. It looked like the one they were previously playing on, except the faces were different as well as the bodies. But it was not totally black, which was a relief, as he retained the idea that white players were a bit weaker. Then they ambled over to a spot where there were a few players waiting to get into the next game, and they took their places.

As they watched they became a bit relieved. The game was certainly more physical, but these guys weren't all that good – they tended to heave shots from way out on the court. And, in addition, there wasn't that fine meshing together. They tended to play individually instead of in the team effort that Larry and his crew had worked out. After the next group of guys took their place on the court and then they lost, it was time for Larry's squad to face up against the winners. They greeted each other and shook hands as if they had been friends for a while. There were two black players and one white guy and they looked stronger and sturdier. There wasn't much to say to each other, no introductions and no formalities.

The previous winning team took the ball out at half court and moved toward the basket, and then got off a shot that hit the rim and bounced out, which Frank retrieved. He threw to Howie, who got it off to Larry, cutting to the basketball, and Larry then laid it up and scored. On the next play, Frank scored on a short hook. The other team didn't like what was happening and they showed their wrath at being scored against. Then in the next play, Larry drove to the basket, but before he could attempt a shot he was pushed and he lost the ball out of bounds so the other team took it out and scored. Then they took the ball out, threw it to their big man, who barreled to the basket, knocking Frank out of the way. Normally this and the play before it would be considered fouls, but there are no referees in playgrounds, so there is no one to call the fouls and there are no foul shots taken, so that if one player calls a foul they just take the ball out. But the members of Larry's team were not comfortable calling a foul; they wanted to come across as tough as they could.

Larry got off a few good shots and after some time the score was pretty close, but his team was being manhandled. This began to get to him, and he knew he just couldn't let this go. Before the other team took the ball out, Larry waved his arms and started to address this issue.

"Look, I know the game can get physical, but really you guys are pushing us around. I go for a shot and you hack me and then Frank gets knocked out of the way when his offensive player is going in for a shot. I don't think we have much of a chance playing this way. Can't we come to some kind of a compromise?–this really isn't any fun for us." Oddly, Larry couldn't believe he could express his thoughts without appearing tentative.

"What do you mean?" shot back one of the other players.

"You know what I mean: you are fouling us and it changes the game. I only want to play fair and square."

"You can't take it," this one guy stared him down. Larry replied quickly: "Ah come on, let's play the game and not fight. It's no fun this way and we don't stand a chance."

Finally their big guy interceded after considering whether he wanted to get into this.

"I know what he is saying, and he has a point to it all. Maybe they annoy us and we play hard, but he is right, we should beat them if we can in a fair way. We could be more careful." He was such a commanding personality that Larry's team was very much impressed by him.

His team seemed a bit stunned that he would take Larry's side, but they certainly all felt that it was reasonable. "Come on," this guy goes on, "we'll beat them fair and square."

"Maybe," pipes in Larry and then they all smile at each other. "Okay let's play the game!"

Larry saw in this fellow some of the traits that he liked in Frank.

Someone who could assume a leadership role and who exuded a confidence in directing his team. There was also something about his smile and attitude that was compelling and forceful, as in someone you wanted to get close to because of his persuasive attitude. He picked this up after the guy interceded with his team to back off from the physical stuff. He was a guy who was able to show more concern and caring while at the same time being a true competitor.

"Hell," Larry thought, "I would love to be his friend." And then he wondered whether that could ever happen, but it stayed with him.

But even without resorting to fouling, the other team was better. Better meant they were more driven to win. This was more than a game to them, this was a kind of minor warfare where the strongest come out on top. Maybe it had to do with the position in life to which they felt they had been relegated, and winning at a basketball game would partially make up for it, especially against three white guys. But could it ever really make up for it? It could only make up for it if the dynamics of the game were able to be carried into life itself, which would be a major proposition. Larry saw immediately that they had a different attitude. It had nothing to do with fun, it had to do with conquest, the stronger over the weaker. And the weaker had better be the white guys. The whites and the blacks lived only a mile apart, but they were many miles apart when it came to their feelings about success or moving ahead in life. This game was more than just a game to them; it represented rising above the oppression of the ghetto and the prejudice that had permeated American society for so many hundreds of years. Now for once given a chance to finish on top, they were not going to let these white guys roll past the finish line ahead of them.

Larry picked this up very quickly, but no one else seemed to have this kind of insight. In a way Larry would become a kind of compromiser, a negotiator, or conciliator. His attitude on the court and his consideration of the other guys enabled the two teams to forge a closer relationship. Much of this had to do with his comments,

"Good shot," or "Wow" or "When you got it you got it." It did bring out smiles from the other team and during the game they began to feel as though they were playing against friends and not enemies. Larry had this social knack which would come in handy later in life. He could read the other guys' minds so sensitively that it all came naturally to him; and in return he managed to get their respect and good will. He refused to let any game become too much of a fight, and he always interceded in the name of good sportsmanship. He never could figure out where he got this from, but he valued this in himself. He took it as a present from the gods above.

When the game was over, Larry's team decided to pack it in for the day. The other team decided to skip the next game and take a quick rest. Larry walked over to the leader of the other team.

"How are you, my name is Larry and I was impressed by your playing and the way you can take over the game."

The guy smiled broadly and introduced himself. "My name is Sherman and I liked the way you play also, I hope we meet again." Larry would have liked to follow up on this but he didn't know how he could. He didn't think Sherman would enjoy hanging out with him and he figured Sherman may have been at least a year or two older so he would have different kinds of interests. He knew he would like to pal around with him, but they seemed worlds apart, or was that so? Larry wondered.

Larry decided to extend himself. "So what do you do when you are not playing basketball?"

"The same thing everyone else does, listen to music and study for school. You know I'm in a band now, I play drums and we really raise a storm on weekends."

Now he was getting friendlier and invited Larry to hear him and his band play somewhere in the East Bronx. Larry shook his hand and thanked him, but he knew he wasn't going to the East Bronx while he was living at home. More than that, he wondered what the scene would look like and whether he would feel out of place– but he knew he would have to put all thoughts of this kind of socializing off to the future when he was a few years older.

As he walked away, he thought again about the game and how he had brought the teams together and the best thing about it was that he liked this in himself. He never became so angry toward the next guy that it rendered him unable to approach him or talk it out. Black and white relationships had always been a problem in most areas. In many ways the two cultures don't understand each other with the needed kind of sensitivity that could bring them closer. He had read about the civil rights confrontations in the South where blacks and whites did bond and form a strong unit, especially after the murders of Chaney, Schwerner and Goodman, two Jews and a black. After that the divide between them started again, but soon when the political field was open for the blacks the two sides came together once more.

But in any sporting event, there has to be a strong alliance between the two races. It was clear after the 1970s that no team would win without blacks' taking a strong presence on the team. But he knew that this had happened way before his time, at least in New York City, where Sherman White from L.I.U. was the best in the country. And then he could recite the story of the coming of Bill Russell in 1955 in San Francisco, where he won two NCAA titles; and then the supremacy started with Wilt Chamberlain, Elgin Baylor, Oscar Robertson, and continued with Magic Johnson and of course Lew Alcindor, whose team at UCLA dominated basketball in the 60s and 70s.

He had heard about the scandals of New York City basketball in 1950 but why had most New York teams other than maybe St. John's receded to the background? It is odd, he thought, that with the greatest concentration of players the Eastern teams achieved very little, and even across the river in New Jersey with that large university, Rutgers didn't add up to much.

He knew why the two teams at the playground would come to

be battling each other because there were no moderators or coaches to hold things together. Most of the stuff that went on wouldn't be permitted in a real game with real referees, and before in the other playground none of this existed – it was when the blacks confronted the whites and had to show them who were the strongest and that they needed to come out on top.

He would give anything if he could play on a championship team. The glory and the esteem of it would just be out of this world. These are the dreams and thoughts he often had when he left the playground and walked home by himself. He wondered what it must feel like to play in front of huge crowds that kept yelling you on and cheering at every shot you made…and the time-outs where the coach pointed out the needed strategies to win… and of course what it must feel like to be coached by the likes of a Pitino, Calipari, Williams or Mike Krzyzewski.

He tried to keep all other thoughts out of existence. For example, he knew that he was never going to attain the height or maybe the strength that would go into becoming a true basketball star. Of course if he had been born 50 years ago this might not have been the case; but he wasn't, so he had better make up his mind to live with it. He knew that he would be content if he could reach 6'2" or 6'3", but how would that ever happen when his father was 5'9" and his mother 5'5" and then his brother was a little over 5'9". Nope, he had better come to terms with this or become one of the great sharpshooters in the game.

Now it was nearing the summer months, when school would be out. His parents called him in for a talk about summer plans. They wanted to send Larry to camp for the summer, and he wanted to know what kind of camp it was and something about the activities they would have there.

His father collected himself, managed a smile, and then faced Larry and said: "We can't be totally sure about it, but it certainly has a lot of activities, like swimming and stuff like that." Larry wanted to know about its basketball program but his father couldn't tell him directly.

"Look," said Larry with his arms extended, "This is my last year in junior high school and I really have to work on my jump shot or I won't make the team in high school. Because of my genetic inheritance I am not going to grow much taller than I am, so I will be at a disadvantage unless I really have a great outside shot."

The father was now getting a bit annoyed at this whole analysis. "I am sorry," he said, "that we couldn't endow you with the right equipment to play the game."

"Come on," Larry shot back, "You have given me the stuff of winners, I am happy with my brains, my drive, my understanding of the world. I couldn't ask for much more except that I wished I could reach 6'9" but that never will happen to Jews anyway so let's just compromise, you save your money with camp and I will get out and practice so that when I go to high school, I will have that edge. And I think that you would want me to have that, wouldn't you?"

The father shook his head, for he knew by now that once Larry made up his mind there was no way of changing it. He could turn most situations to his advantage. His drive and persistence was really a big plus and his basketball enthusiasm was certainly enabling him to get better marks, so why make a fuss over it and of course he said to himself: "We are saving money, so why contradict that?"

Another facet in Larry's development that made his parents wonder a bit about him was related to his speech patterns. Not that he talked in clichés, but rather he captured and recited phrases that could have come out of a self-help book. He wouldn't say "It will all work out" or "It is what it is" or even "That's the way the cookie crumbles." No, Larry was more into stuff like, "It's going to take hard work, but it's worth it" or "Losers always have excuses." The one they couldn't stand was the phrase, "Winning isn't everything, it's the only thing," and "If you could have won, you should have."

They talked among themselves about his reading habits,

especially the stuff that had been attributed to Vince Lombardi, the former Green Bay Packers coach. Sayings like, "You don't do things right once in a while. You do them right all the time." But then they could see that these words of wisdom really were only innocent reflections on life and what constitutes success. Maybe Lombardi believed that all of this pumped-up stuff about winning is a habit and so is losing, yet they couldn't put their finger on what about it really bothered them. Dave usually turned to Janet and told her that this is not the substance of girl talk, that it seemed to grab guys more. And when asked why, he would tell her that guys have to pump themselves up because of something that Freud called the castration complex. She would look him in the eye and ask him whether he is reading Freud again or talking with that school psychologist with all those screwy ideas.

"No," Dave felt a bit serious, "The problem, Janet, is that I really think I believe this and if Larry can believe his sayings, I guess I can believe mine." But Janet was never convinced; moreover, she seemed to evince little interest in these ideas and that is what kept her apart from her son. She wasn't able to take an interest in the psychology of kids or even adults. It seemed that Janet was uncomfortable with the seriousness of ideas and therefore it was hard for her to get the point of Larry's detour in his development. Dave realized this in her, but he brushed it away; he adored his wife, even though he wished she could dig a little deeper into her ideas about life.

In school, Larry's teacher told the social studies class that they would each give a talk to the class that reflected on some aspect of the way they viewed their lives. It would be a five-minute dialogue and the important thing was the way the students constructed their ideas. It could be called a recitation in public speaking and it was important in life to clearly bring your ideas to the marketplace and express them with vitality and wisdom. Then he asked who would want to lead it off, starting next week. No one volunteered but Phil, one of Larry's friends came up with the idea that since Larry was always talking about sports, he should lead off with his ideas of the importance of sports in our lives. At first Larry was taken aback, but he quickly regained his focus and then nodded and agreed that he would like the challenge. So the first talk was scheduled for the following Tuesday.

The teacher saw immediately that Larry rarely backed down. He had a sureness of purpose, something like an inner gyroscope, that pushed him forward and made him his own person. It was clear that he certainly savored the opportunity. After class Larry went over to Phil, the guy who had volunteered him, and actually thanked him. Larry told him that it would give him a chance to collect his thoughts and make a presentation. "Yes," he reiterated, "This is a good opportunity to have you guys listen to me and see what I am feeling." In fact he became more animated. "I like the challenge.," he said in a lively manner. "I really want to thank you for putting me out there." Phil nodded, accepting the kind words.

In the week that followed, Larry read through many of his books, and started outlining what he wanted to say, what points he needed to express, and how to forcefully compose his ideas. Actually it gave him a lot of pleasure, because he was getting into the gist of his life, the things that were guiding him, and what he was reaching for and striving to attain. These are wonderful exercises, he began to think, especially if you know deep down what the major principles in your life Are. He thought to himself: "What were the models on which you are building your life? Then he kept continuing to think about the beliefs that had become the substance of his world, and what were the sustaining principles that guided him. These were the items that he started to outline and it kept him deep in thought.

When the day finally came for him to deliver his talk, Larry was stirred up and found it hard to sit still. When the teacher introduced him, he rose in his seat with a determination and walked slowly to the front of the class, almost as if he were receiving an award. He thanked the teacher and the class for giving him this chance, then took out the paper with his speech.

He then began his talk, looking up to make sure he had the attention of the class: "I look forward in the coming days to listening to others express their thoughts. The question I am addressing today is why I love sports, especially basketball or what sports offers me. How do I explain it to myself, let alone to you and especially to those who are skeptical? What really is the excitement in all of this? So let me begin with my prepared talk."

I feel that the basic reality of human life is the way we play and the games that involve us. This is where our metaphors of life are drawn. Our work, politics and history are the misleading false world. Our ideals, beauty, truth and excellence are grown in the soil of play, and wilt in the sand of work. Play belongs to the Kingdom of Ends, work to the Kingdom of Means. The more primitive among us play in order to work, while civilized man works in order to play. What grabs so many millions? What is the secret power of attraction? How can we care so much about the world before us? I probably concentrate on basketball because of all the sports I love it the most. There is no substitute for the squeak of sneakers on the court and the sound of the ball slipping through the cords. Or the sight of an artistic jump shot or a pass that hits its mark to the driving player.

So many games are played every year in grammar schools, high schools, colleges and professional stadiums; all the routines are thoroughly known. Athletic achievement, like the achievements of the heroes and the gods of Greece, is the momentary attainment of perfect form; a great play is a revelation. The curtains of ordinary life part and perfection flashes for an instant before the eye.

The teacher listening to his talk realized that he had copied some of these phrases from particular books and probably did not understand them fully, but then thought that it was a fun exercise and this kid should be encouraged.

Larry went on:

If you have not played the game, you may not recognize how difficult it is to launch a successful play, how much more difficult it is to sustain a series of successful plays without a mistake. But even if you do not understand the game, and suspend skepticism for a moment, at least you will see or sense a dramatic resolution. Will is pitted against will; skill against skill; one team emerges the victor. The drama – beginning, middle, end – is resolved. It mimics life and offers a purpose of its own. Our human plans involve a great many paradoxes. Our choices are made with so little insight into their eventual effects that what we desire is often not the path to what we want. At times, the decisions we make turn out to be major turning points. What we prepare with flawless detail never happens, but sports are structured so that the breaks *may intervene and become central components in the action. That is, we see our major human conflicts played out before us on a huge stage with earnest performers.*

To have a purpose in life, to strive and to achieve, you need to have heroic forms to try to live up to: patterns of excellence so high that human beings live up to them only rarely, even when they strive to do so; and images of perfection so beautiful that, living up to them produces a kind of exhilaration

"And toward fulfilling this purpose, you need to have a way to delight the human body, and desire and will, and the sense of beauty, and a sense of oneness with the universe and other humans. You need chants and songs, the rhythm of bodies in unison, the indescribable feeling of many who together act as if they were each members of a single body.

All these things you have in sports. Michael Jordan touched something vulnerable in the hearts of millions. He seemed to acquire some form of magic, some miraculous power, some beautiful achievement like the deeds of dreams. Some truth about life, some deep vein of ancient emotion and human imagination – this is the chord Michael Jordan's performances happened to strike.

Larry was getting moved by the words he was speaking even

though he couldn't fully understand everything he said but it moved him nevertheless. He plainly got off on the phrases he recited.

To conclude, sports represent something of our world that the vast majority of Americans understand. They form the essential bedrock of our intellectual and emotional life. The world of sports contain all of the virtues, experiences, and interests, as well as the relation between body and emotion and intelligence, as through it we are in a better position to understand the many twists and turns of our everyday life. Thank you.

With that, Larry put the paper he had just read from into his pocket. He looked up and smiled at the class, almost feeling as if he just scored an amazing jump shot.

When he finished, the class remained silent; they were touched by these most moving of words and sentiments even though they didn't catch it all. They realized also that this guy was not kidding – he believed all this hype and in many ways it all made sense. A bit poetic, a bit dramatic, quite romantic, and very uplifting and profound. After this talk, Larry was no longer looked upon as some jock who proceeded to show off his testosterone level. No, this was a student who had found a deeply moving metaphor for living life. Maybe that's what is behind Lombardi's saying about winning and competing. It is meant to inspire and fill our minds with the deeds of heroes and the actions they take. It is meant to lift us up above the usual or tiresome occurrences of our everyday life. Where could we possibly find the excitement in our lives that could equal the tension of a close basketball game, or the dramatic scene between a pitcher and batter? Larry was getting at something that would overshadow the ordinary actions of his classmates' lives. Such ideas expressed in words had the power to transform their fantasies into striving and hope. The teacher thanked him and said that she was certainly taken with these words.

"But where did you find these ideas?" she asked him seriously. Larry thought a moment and then said to her that he had some books on the wisdom of sports and took them from those books and he hoped that she didn't think he copied them without understanding them. "No," she answered him, "I think you did a wonderful job of melding your ideas together with what you read and I think we all are impressed with that."

A day or two after, Larry found himself in the company of a few friends during lunch. One of them smiled and asked him if he believed all that crap that he presented to the class. "Of course I do, why would I lie to everyone? We are talking about the will to win and why athletes can give us a clearer picture of this. I was trying to emphasize, without ever spelling it out, the importance of desire. I have seen players who in practice seem sleepy and unimpressive, who can't seem to find themselves except in the excitement of the game; there are players who seem to have every talent and perform efficiently in practice but fall down in the real game. This is why coaches and scouts seek out what I am calling desire. There are athletes with lesser talents, but those with great desire are better fitted for actual contests than men of vast ability who have some reluctance."

Larry saw that about four other guys were listening intently to him and he knew he had better show off a couple of his ideas.

So he went on: "If you listen to me you will see why I stress that desire may be a purer gift than talent. Physical skills may be improved by hard work, but there is no way of improving one's desire. If a man lacks desire it may be impossible for him or anyone else to rouse him to play to his capacity. When the game is underway, being 'up' for the game—fit, passionate, and totally attentive – is indispensable. Maybe you are annoyed at what I say because you question your own desire – your will to win?" Now Larry was getting a bit confronting.

Bobby, who was listening to him, became visibly disturbed, a bit ashamed of being addressed this way in front of the other guys; and then to defend himself he went on the attack: "You don't know what the hell you are talking about, all this bullshit about desire and winning – this is really a figment of your imagination."

Now Larry was calm and he knew he had the advantage. "These words don't bother me, a good athlete does not judge by external standards. He measures his performance against his own ideal. He sets his own goals for each season. He sees his career as a whole. His takes his eyes off how others are doing and even off outcomes, and limits himself to playing each game with maximum concentration. He becomes his own man. Remember the career athlete keeps in his mind an image of his own ideal performance. Bobby, I get the feeling that you have a very shaky adjustment – you always worry about being liked and that seems to define who you are but this isn't going to get you where you want to go – you will be liked when you do it your way. Then you will be respected and appreciated. You had better get over this if you want to succeed in life."

As Larry walked away, Bobby was left with a shiver that enveloped his body. Something that was said to him hurt because it struck him in the deepest recesses of his mind. This had been said to him before but he had tossed it off. Now he was forced to come face to face with it, and now he didn't want to relegate it to the bottom of the garbage can. No, he knew that Larry was on to something and he liked Larry more than he was willing to admit. This guy could be more than a friend to me, he thought—he could be a kind of mentor who would lead me out of the desert of indecision. At least he realized they would be going to the same high school and he promised himself that he would put all annoyances to rest and come to Larry for his advice and counsel.

Larry's pronouncements started to fill the hearts and minds of many of his fellow students. They started to see that even if he was tooting his own horn, there was truth to what he was alluding to. There was a ring of reality that coincided with the emergence of their adolescent awakening and all of the doubts that went along with this. What adolescent is not baffled by the conflicts that fill his life, by the appearance of sexual tensions that disrupt his reality? And all adolescents have many questions about their identities and mistrust of their strengths and weaknesses.

In the beginning, the class looked at Larry as if he were an oddball, as if he were really walking to a different drummer. They discarded much of what he would say and wondered at his inflated talk; however, over time they became drawn to his expressions and the forcefulness of his rhetoric. As a group, they were going through all the usual turmoil of their changing bodies and their struggle with separating from their parents, so now Larry's voice started to strongly permeate the very core of their existence. His message started having a profound effect and it wasn't just about sports—there was a more important lesson in his exhortations.

Some weeks before, the teacher had assigned, *Catcher in the Rye* by J.D. Salinger. Though Holden the main character is 17 years old and the students in the class were closer to 14, the book had an impact of deeper meaning for most of them. Holden doesn't know what to do with himself; he is a malcontent, uneasy from thinking of his future and, worst of all, dreading to grow up to be like his parents. When Phoebe asks him what he wants to do when he grows up, he can't really answer in a clear fashion, he can only describe a dream of his. He tells her that he sees all these kids playing in this big field of rye and that he is standing on the edge of some crazy cliff. His main purpose is to catch as many kids as possible if there is a chance that they may fall over the cliff. And that is all he would do all day. He would be the catcher in the rye and oddly enough that is the only thing he'd really like to be.

The class discussed how the crazy cliff represents growing up, and what Holden wants to do is to keep the kids in the field, which represents childhood. Holden finds it so painful to grow up because he dislikes what he is meant to grow up into. But he is 17, and childhood is no longer available. His way of helping others is to protect them from the same fate. The children are so carefree in the rye because they are children and the field must therefore be threatened, simply because childhood is temporary. And the children in Larry's class knew that high school awaited them next year and big changes were going to take place.

Intertwined with this fear was a burst of growth that propels the adolescent toward the future. A wave of vitality that expands every appetite and interest pushes them away from childhood, opening the way for new solutions. However, the child in us will not give up so easily. Playing in the playground is a lot of fun and who really enjoys giving up fun for the seriousness of becoming an adult?

Heroes and heroines are appealing because of their glamor, sexual prowess, wealth, or prominence in politics, art, science, or crime. Many of the ideals of the younger adolescent are merely in the service of self-aggrandizement. Raw and vulnerable, they feel worthwhile and powerful only through their association, real or fantasized, with those they worship.

Their walls and closet doors will be covered with posters, photographs, and other mementos of their current super-heroes and heroines. One sure way for parents to know that their children are finally on their way to more realistic self-aspirations and less glorified moral standards will be the gradual clearing of wall space in their bedroom. As they grow more into adulthood, a few treasured possessions will remain. One or two of the heroes will be immortalized. The rest will vanish without a trace.

With this in mind, it was easy to see why Larry's lofty catch-phrases and buzzwords could capture his classmates' own dreams and imagination and fill them with excitement. Larry was sure of himself; he told them the importance of having ideals and striving to live up to them. This would ensure a firm and genuine adjustment in later life. Even redefining that language of ambition and quoting significant individuals could be the best tonic of the day. And now the world was being filled with female sports figures where before it was all a boy's world. But women's basketball was emerging on all campuses and in professional sports as well. The female basketball stars could now take center stage; they were not so big or powerful as their male counterparts, but they were damn near as impressive.

Everyone wanted to engage Larry in conversation, wanting to understand how he sized up the world and how he came to terms with particular conflicts and clashes in life. They wanted to appreciate and comprehend the drummer that Larry was following. And Larry was all the more cooperative in answering these questions; in short time he was called upon to give speeches and express his thoughts about the world that spun around him. Initially, his classmates harbored resentment toward him because of his self-assurance, but now they approached him as a guy who maybe could answer some of the more difficult questions and take them on like a jousting match. He attacked the very foundations of their doubts about themselves, about life and choices and which professions to choose. He was a minor celebrity and it all rested upon his intensity to play and enmesh himself in the game of basketball. He had all the hallmarks of success, talking about what a team effort meant, the value of practice, conditioning, of keeping your body in fine condition, eating healthy, and treating yourself as if you were meant for some aspect of greatness. This is the term that he loved to incorporate in his talks as well as winning, competing, and standing the test of time.

Larry easily became the class president and continued to dispense his words of wisdom. He never missed an opportunity to launch into short speeches or fiery dialogues about the substance of life or the pursuit of victory, and often he would just substitute the value of good grades for field goals or three point shots. What was so impressive was that the grades of the class soon showed clear improvement and most students were now invested in doing their best. Teachers started to remark how Larry lifted his class to a higher interest in getting better, how he infused them with a need to succeed and achieve and imbued them with a winning mindset.

How he managed to hold himself steady in this fashion without incurring resentment from his classmates was hard to understand. They felt that he was not just inflating his ego, but rather truly wanted the other students to move ahead. He was doing it for them. He liked them and wanted them to get the message. This was the stuff of all great coaches. Their teams played for them and all members wanted their coaches to feel the state of triumph. But isn't this the intent of all successful managers and teachers?– except that a good coach has this trait in spades. It all unfolds before them, right before their eyes on the playing field. Instead of criticizing your team you encourage, goad and spur them on. And here in the eighth grade Larry was on his way.

It was during his last year in junior high school that Larry entered a new phase of his life. He began to understand his need to engage more of his classmates in discussions of their lives and the importance of planning for their futures. Even though they were all only 14 years of age, he told them that they needed to think about themselves with a new commitment to understanding what was in store for them, what they felt they did, and how they wanted to improve their lives. Toward this end, he started small groups that met after class in which he tried to get everyone into a discussion about their lives. Most of the time the discussions didn't really get anywhere, but on some occasions the group could touch on serious issues and, in fact, everyone who attended felt that he was justly rewarded. His classmates noticed that Larry's talent as a speaker had improved over the years. Initially they had found him more reserved, but now he freely expressed his thoughts. Some of his classmates felt that he could become a salesman, because he was good at selling things and could talk anyone into anything. But now the junior high school class moved on to high school. In a way he became a bit of a celebrity.

CHAPTER THREE

High School

Test of Character

The end of the school year came, and while Larry and his classmates felt a kind of freedom because they would not be returning to this school again. While many felt the free spirit that often goes with change, they were also a bit apprehensive. Larry's thoughts focused on how high school would work out and how would he get along with everyone. He felt good that his two closest friends, Phil and Paul, were also attending; but he knew the real problem that gave him all this anxiety was whether he would be able to make the basketball team. At this high school a player would have to make the junior varsity for a year and then there would be two years of varsity ball. Larry felt a bit anxious at the thought that he would have to wait until they announced the dates for the tryouts, which took place sometime in September.

Paul's parents invited him for a week to come up to their country house in upstate New York in New Paltz. Initially he did not feel comfortable going; however, his friend pressed him into keeping him company. And since he had decided not to go to camp, this could be a good break in his summer plans. It was an odd occurrence for Larry to feel the way he did. He could move away from his parents and feel more independent, but he had more trouble in moving away from the schoolyard and all that it meant to him. He wondered why some people become intertwined with their neighborhoods or their surroundings, and he figured that it acts much like an anchor that gives them security. You walk down the same street and pass the same places over and over again but it doesn't get boring; rather, there is some inner satisfaction that acts as if it's a personal security. Move a person to the country and he or she feels a pocket of loneliness when night descends as a quiet spreads out across the sky. Yes, for him the nights would be the hardest part of the day, but then he knew he had his friend with him.

But for a number of reasons, Larry just felt out of sorts. He had established a good position at school, having forged a bond with his class, especially after they found him interesting and full of wisdom. Now he had lost this support, there would be no more school, and his only refuge would lie in the playground, where his fellow ball players valued his presence. He thought to himself, "Could I play basketball every day and why not? It may look odd to a number of people but it sits just fine with me." A few days later on Sunday, Paul's family picked him up and drove upstate.

It was a pleasant drive; Paul's parents rarely intruded into Larry's life and they were very generous toward him, knowing that he was Paul's best friend. They wanted to nourish that relationship, as Paul was an only child, so they knew he needed friends very badly. On the drive up, Paul and Larry went over their fond memories of the public school they just attended. Paul turned to Larry and told him how popular he was and how everyone got off on him and his passion for sports. Then he asked him if he had ever thought of college after leaving high school.

"Who doesn't think of college?" Larry replied, "But the question remains, where would I like to go? My brother is going to a school in California and I don't think I would want to go that far. You know my parents went to schools close by and that is always a thought. But what about you, do you have any idea?"

"I have some thoughts that I have discussed with my father." His father overheard this conversation and replied to his son, "You both know why college is so important, it can have a tremendous influence on the way your life turns out. You can make connections in college that last a lifetime. Just ask your mother, she doesn't know one person from the college she went to but I have stayed in touch with the guys I met at Vassar. You know I was on the tennis team and we loved the game and then we got to know each other; and here we are riding upstate where a number of these old friends have places near us."

The two boys in the back seat did not pick up on his remarks, they felt as if they had little to add; it could never convert into a conversation which happens often when adults are out of touch with what their kids are talking about. They are always imparting their wisdom, which feels like an invasion of their kids' privacy. So Paul quickly said that they ought to discuss it later.

Once up in New Paltz, Larry was shown his room, which was big and nicely furnished with a bed and a chair with a reading lamp over it. It had all the feel of country furniture. He looked around and felt quite comfortable and yet he knew that one week would be enough up here, especially since Paul's father had the week off, so that he would always be around. Then Paul asked Larry to take a walk with him so that he could show him around. It was beautiful country, a hint of summer was in the air, and then Larry began to feel as if this empty hole was beginning to percolate into his insides. He knew the signs immediately and they expanded when he left the city. In one of his criticism of country life, he expressed the idea that he preferred to have pavement under his feet and the swirling of activity around him. The country is a bit too quiet and the nights feel creepy. But this was quite beautiful while still being rustic, and Paul's parents were very friendly, warm and gracious. They made strong attempts to make Larry feel comfortable. They told him that the refrigerator was open to him all the time and for him to feel as if their house was also his. He had known them for a long time and always enjoyed their company. They were more involved in their son's life than were Larry's parents.

That night over dinner, Paul's father attempted to make conversation with the two boys. He turned to Larry: "So you seem to know what you want to do in life? I realize that is not an easy question especially when you are only fourteen." Then Sam, Paul's father, went on. "Paul told me that you are quite the leader in your class and that you try to get your classmates involved with themselves and their future. I feel that this is such an important trait and I hope you carry it along with you wherever you go." Larry picked up on the question, paused a moment and then went on: "I am in no rush to come to any answer, you know after high school we still have four years of college to get through. And most people make their decisions then."

Larry had some hesitancy about telling them his thoughts. It's like a kid telling adults that he wants to be a major league baseball player when he grows up. It sounds too childish and certainly unsophisticated. He remembered a workshop he once attended where the girls said they wanted to be nurses or actresses and the boys talked of firemen, policemen or baseball players. This struck him as so juvenile until one girl said she wanted to be a doctor and try to cure the world of disease. This impressed him because there was something profound in this. He wished then that he could have had some thoughts that would have sounded as deeply mature. But now it was different and he felt strangely funny about sharing any of this with Paul's father. He wondered what he would think of him and whether he would come across as juvenile or appear as an immature adolescent. Over the years, Larry had become very sensitive to the way adults reacted to him. Of course, if he would tell them that he wanted to be a movie star, he could understand that; but his dreams never took on such a childlike expression.

He started to talk of his hopeful future with his usual gift for explanation and justification. "I feel as if I am a bit different from many of my classmates. I read a great deal and try to absorb the substance of what is being expressed. There is a term called 'games' but I don't mean it to be games like bridge or poker or stuff like that. For example, you can call what you do the economics game, or the money game or whatever. In this sense a game is a pleasurable activity that is played according to certain rules, boundaries or limitations. For example, if you want to be a lawyer there are certain criteria you will need to address. In all of these games, you would hope that there is pleasure being derived and then comes some fun, otherwise what you would be doing would become burdensome. Many people do not realize that pleasure is an important item in all of this. If we then call what we do games then we have to understand that we play at these games." Larry went on as if had he memorized the whole presentation.

"I remember reading about the importance of children's games and what they learn from them, and we know that children become quite serious in playing their games. I feel that what people really need and want from life is not necessarily wealth, comfort or esteem, but a game worth playing. And once you have found the game, play it with intensity– in fact play it as if your life depended on it." Larry then looked Paul's father directly and continued. "I am sure that in your experience with your work on Wall Street that you are knowledgeable about the rules of the game you are playing. I am sure that the rules have implied meanings and you have to learn them first before you can play them. The quality of the game depends also on our own innate characteristics. Great chess masters are born, not made. Great football players are bound to have certain physical characteristics. So a game that a person plays is determined by his type and the person who tries to play a game for which his type does not fit him violates his own essence with often terrible consequences. I know from my own studies I could not be a doctor or scientist. Ask Paul and he will tell you that there are certain kids in the class who are phenomenal in mathematics. So that each of us must come to terms with our natural abilities and of course our passions."

So far, Larry had not really answered the question asked him, and he knew that, but at times he enjoyed hearing himself talk almost as if it were a kind of lecture. And he had a peculiar knack for memorizing strong phrases and sayings and then reciting them back without any hesitancy. Now he went on exuding a kind of assurance that what he was saying had been seriously thought out. "Now I love basketball and I want to treat it as more than just a game, but a master game that hopefully would absorb my whole life. I can do this as a player or in some other capacity, but this is what I would like to pursue and this is where I would like to go. I have fun with it and I can play it over and over again without losing interest. So can many other kids, but I have something a bit more. I am also interested in strategies, plays and a host of other elements that go into the game. The major problem I have is that I am physically limited. I do not think I will grow beyond say 5'10" – this is not a great height for a basketball player, so I will have to wait and decide what I am going to do. This looks like a limitation that I will not be able to overcome but I certainly will give it a try in high school. Oh, I know that there are many players my height and they usually play a guard position, but they are quick and agile and can pass like a demon. Now could I be that person, only time will tell."

He paused and Paul chimed in: "You should see Larry in action, he has one of the best shots I have ever seen. His jump shot is awesome." Larry smiled, and then said, "Well thank you very much, that was such a nice compliment."

Paul's father was a bit flabbergasted, he didn't remember a kid his age talking like this, quite precocious, he thought to himself.

The father then asked him, "So you think that you would pursue this dream from now on."

Larry replied, "Yes, I think I am not going to let this dream elude me. I feel that it will lead me to a life of adventure. Success is important, but it is not always the issue. I think that the crucial thing in life is to play the game and be a good sport about it. You know about people who climb mountains and face the possibility of getting hurt. The adventurer knows this full well. His trust is not in the naïve promise of a successful outcome, but in the value of the adventure for its own sake. If this leads to some kind of fulfillment, then the player has no need other than to allow himself to fully pursue a life as full of adventure as possible.

"I know also that the adventures of a player may not appear exciting to the person not playing, for they are the result of some inner feelings rather than outer circumstance. Even the simplest play activities of young children may be as remarkable to them as some dramatic stories are for adults. At the end of a child's play, children will tell great tales, for that is the only way such experiences are communicated to outsiders. Not all the games played by adults are visible to those who are unable to participate. So I know that maybe what I am telling you about and what I hope to do may not seem so exciting or adventurous to you, but I can state positively that I find it to be that way."

Later, both parents agreed that Larry was a hard act to follow, he could certainly dominate the conversation and he knew exactly where he wanted to go in it. Sam then said, "Maybe he is a bit anxious about his life and this is the way he controls it by lecturing you." His wife agreed. Yet they were both impressed by a fourteen-year-old who could talk this way.

The next day, Paul informed Larry that they would be going to a country club that they belonged. He told them that this was a really cool place where there were tennis courts, a golf course, and a large swimming pool and then –he saved this for last– basketball courts.

Larry was impressed; he had never seen such posh surroundings. He did tell Paul that he wasn't much for swimming and never had the chance to master tennis.

"So what do your parents do when they are up here?"

"My father plays golf and my mother plays bridge. You should see the bridge room, it is filled with maybe fifty or so women, some play

canasta and they really get into it."

Larry could detect immediately that this might not be the place for him yet he really couldn't put his finger on what made him uncomfortable. Possibly it was the change of environment, making him feel a bit like an outsider or someone who came from another planet. Even the term "country club" bothered him. Sometimes you know immediately when you feel as if you don't fit in: maybe it is a bit too posh or it spells a kind of privilege or wealth. "It's a wonder," he thought, "how some people can move to different cities or to towns without any hesitation and what is unfamiliar does not present many problems. Growing up in an apartment house seems to limit your ability to move elsewhere, and yet so many people he knew wanted their own private homes. He could understand that, especially when it came to raising a family. He knew many of the people he had gone to school with who moved away, but he never could grasp how those people could move so easily to a private house or to a smaller city or village. He knew that it was the nights that gave him the most trouble; they were so serene, quiet, almost spooky. Where was the action?

And yet across America this is how most people live out their lives. Sam drove the boys to a place called Emerson Country Club. It was quite imposing as if it just had grown out of the surrounding woodland. Larry knew that it made a statement, something like that all who entered had money or were able to afford such lavish surroundings. When you walked through these old oak doors, an accompanying expression was sent forth, "You now have made it."

But he tried to put all that negativity out of his mind. Sometimes you know that you're in an environment that speaks of fun and pleasure, and yet for some reason you just can't submerge yourself into it. "This should be fun," he thought, "so why do I feel so damned uncomfortable? Why can't I take advantage of what this place offers and why become critical? Do I have to only feel comfortable in someplace that duplicates my present home? Why don't I just make believe that I am at college and am going to have a great time?" He had this strong sense of imposing insight into the thoughts that were giving him trouble. Down deep he was able to realize that what he was feeling or experiencing was not always so reasonable, and it could even be weird or peculiar. He was always able to come to grips with these negative thoughts.

Paul led Larry into the locker room and they changed into their bathing suits and went out to the pool. This was an enormous pool that spread out into a huge area that looked as if it could accommodate an army of people or could be the site of an Olympic competition. There were about twenty people in the pool who were just standing and talking, and Larry wondered where the kids were, and then Paul told him that there was another area that was reserved for the younger children. On one end of the pool there were two diving boards that jutted out into the water. The higher one really looked high and was frightening to him, while the lower one was well within his capability. Larry never really mastered swimming but he knew he could if he put out any effort. So he jumped in and swished around in the pool. Paul went to the lower diving board took a deep breath and made one great-looking dive into the pool. "Very graceful," Larry thought. Finally he could see the strengths of Paul's athletic ability, but certainly not in any team sport. Then Paul showed Larry the right kind of moves he needed to make if he wanted to swim. Larry picked this up very quickly and the thought came to him that maybe this could be fun.

He showed him how to arch his arms, kick and breathe in the

water. And Larry found the instruction to be cool and rather liked the idea that he was being taught a new game. He liked it so much that he continued to practice in the pool until he found that he was able to master the swimming strokes that would propel him forward. The longer he practiced, the more fun it became. He thought that breathing was the real skill and key that needed to be mastered and with that and the movement of his arms, Larry found himself getting better and better.

"This is a great place you have here," he told Paul. "Yes, it is, and I think that I may try my hand at golf one of these days, although it is so slow-moving; but they say that there is a lot of technique that goes into the game."

Larry came out of the pool, grabbed a towel, slung it around his shoulders, and reclined on one of the *chaise lounges* that lined the pool. As he looked around he began to understand the meaning and the allure of this place. It helped people live a life closer to their dreams, a life nearer to their ideas of grandeur, a more affluent life… and it rewarded those who have made successes of their lives. It was that prize that was dangling at the end of a feeling of triumph: "You have made it and now enjoy it." He began to think better of Paul's parents and appreciate them more. They really were able to absorb the pleasurable things in life. But with their money, they never moved too far from where they were raised. He said to himself that this had better not happen to him, that he had to be prepared to change locales – that's if he wanted to move forward in life. And he said emphatically that he had better come to terms with this country club atmosphere. Then he thought of the many basketball coaches who had moved around at the drop of a hat. Pitano was born in Long Island and now resides in Louisville, Kentucky. The same with Calipari and so many others. The same with the multitudes of entertainers. This prevailing conflict between career and locale is the stuff of many works of fiction. And then he thought of those who have moved to other countries, with different languages and cultures. They have to be my role model, as my parents never moved much further than where they were born. But I bet most people die within a 10-to-20-mile radius from where they grew up, as if life were circumscribed around the diner that they went to as adolescents. In his mind, Larry took on the issue with a vengeance, and he finally pressed Paul to show him golf.

"Why is this game of golf, o hard to pick up and yet when you look at it, it seems so easy?" he asked Paul. "Well, why don't we give it a shot tomorrow, I will talk to my dad," his friend responded.

But at the same time Larry knew he didn't really want to take any part in the game; it had to be for older people because it was so slow. Yet so many former basketball players go in for it, so it must have some fascination. Paul interjected, "Do you want to shoot some hoops?" But Larry knew he just being kind rather than interested; and Larry was on a different roll at that moment, so he declined and asked him to give him a once-over tour of this majestic country club. So they picked themselves up and Paul walked him around the place. He stopped at a huge room with the doors shut and told him that he had better be prepared for what was inside. He then opened the door and Larry looked in and saw a huge assembly of women playing cards. There must have been close to a hundred. He had never seen such an amazing collection of women involved with the playing of cards before. They were all enmeshed in the game and didn't notice that they were being observed by these two boys. Larry was so impressed with this spectacle that for the next few weeks he couldn't help telling friends and his parents what he had seen. Of course he knew about bridge and even canasta, but he had never witnessed their being played with such grandeur.

The day had proved eventful, not of course for Paul, who had seen this drama many times before and knew his mother could play bridge all day long. He often wondered why there were so few men who played. They usually played poker in another room, but there weren't that many of them. And the guys would puff on their cigars and the place would stink to high heaven—that is, until they banned smoking at the club.

The week at Paul's country house actually was a wonderful break for Larry; he was able to settle in and enjoy the many amenities and Paul's parents were just great. But he was happy to get back to the city. He wanted to concentrate on his jump shot and dribbling, and now he could focus on this feeling refreshed. He was sorry that Paul would be away for most of July, but he had a few other friends with whom he could hang out at night. Still Paul was kind of special and all guys and girls have their particular best friend, and Larry felt that way about Paul. At night up in New Paltz they had such stimulating conversations about their hopes and plans in life. And Larry knew that there were not too many people with whom he could share his most intimate feelings. There was something that existed between Paul and himself that provided a stage for closeness and intimacy, one in which he could unburden himself about so many of his doubts in life. And Paul was such a good listener and was always so patient, someone who could pay attention to Larry's unwinding about himself. He knew that girls did this so much more easily than guys, and often he was envious of that ability but at least he had found the one guy with whom he could do this.

Larry knew that he had to get back to Sherman and find out how things were going for him. He called him and they made a date to get together the next day. He was sorry that Sherman rarely showed up at the basketball court and he was not able to get a sound answer from him.

They met in a coffee shop and Sherman told Larry what was going on.

"I have a job for the summer," Sherman explained, "and it doesn't give me that much time to get to the yard, but I am going to make a special effort on Sundays if you are going to be there."

"Of course I will be," shot back Larry, "I miss you're not being there and besides, how are you going to work on your game?"

"Well, I just have to do the best I can. I really have to help out my Mom with some of the finances. You know it is not easy for her and now my sister is going to college, so even with the college load it is going to be a long haul."

Larry felt uncomfortable with this talk, as he knew that his family's finances were not a problem, but he hated to see this in Sherman. They sat on a bench and Larry started asking some more intimate questions about Sherman's family.

"I guess it is not easy to talk about, but my father left the house when I was about three and I really haven't seen much of him since then. He kind of abandoned the family, as you would say. But I am so lucky that my mom is so dedicated to us and she always wants the best for us. She is so strong and is always right behind me so I feel lucky more than anything else."

Larry felt odd talking to Sherman about his family. He knew the high incidence of divorce among his classmates and yet this seemed different. In most cases that he knew, the father, though leaving, contributed to the family and was involved with the kids. Here was a case where the father had got lost somewhere and he felt so sorry for Sherman. Yet, he was envious of his mother who was so involved with her children. Unlike his mother, he thought, who took a back seat to her children's education.

"It puts a heavy weight on you, doesn't it?" inquired Larry.

Sherman thought a bit: "You know, honestly, I don't feel that way. I know families where the father can be such a drag and hostile. You think that all fathers are so supportive, but that's not the way it is. When he was around he created an awful atmosphere and my mother was always miserable, and when he left there was a freedom that we never had before and if he were around today, I would be a different boy. I think I would be unhappy and maybe miserable. So don't feel sorry for me."

"Actually, I don't when you put it that way. I guess after talking to you I appreciate my father even more and yet I am impressed with the way you adjusted to things. But I don't want to lose you as a friend–you really are an important part of my life."

And Sherman paused for a moment and then went on; "And you are an important part of my life. Maybe there are miles between us, but let's make an effort to not let it interfere with our friendship." With that they got up, shook hands and then embraced.

Larry walked away feeling a bit teary-eyed and hoping that he would never lose this guy; and then he said to himself, "This is not going to happen. In spite of whatever gets between us, I am going to be close to him. He really gives me courage, and I know he likes me and wants me to be successful in life. So I must do the same for him." He wished that they were going to the same high school, but Sherman got into a parochial school that his mother felt would provide better education for her son.

The summer was finally over and high school beckoned. The first day of school was much better than he had anticipated. For one thing, there were older students from the grades above him and he felt more comfortable that way. Secondly, the subjects seemed to be more interesting and he was satisfied with the schedule that he was given. But the really important day for him would have to wait a few weeks.

At last he saw the announcement for tryouts for the junior varsity, at 4:00 PM the following Tuesday. The initial twinge of excitement soon became infused with fear, a worry that he might not make the team. Sure, he had been practicing all summer and playing almost every Saturday and Sunday for the past few years; but how could one ever predict who would turn out for the team? How tall or burly the other guys would be, how much weight he would give away, and a host of other unrealized questions. But hell, it was better to face the competition than to have to wait any longer.

On this Tuesday, Larry arrived at the gym a few minutes early. He looked around and from what he could see the competition was not so bad as he had feared. There were about thirty guys, mostly black, but he had figured that. They were taller, but there were some short guys as well. Now the coach gave them a welcoming speech and laid out the plans for picking the team. They would be divided into two teams that would play a full court game, and then at the end of the day he would announce his selections. Quite reasonable, everyone thought.

Now Larry launched into this speech that he gave himself. "Play with focus, don't take stupid shots, look for the open man cutting, set up screens, act like you know what you are doing, and try to impress the coach that you know what the game is all about. Coaches like careful players and they frown upon the guys who heave the ball." He had practiced some shots over and over again so he knew what he wanted to show off. He could almost have taken some of the shots with his eyes closed because he had taken them so often.

The game started after the coach asked each player to don a shirt with a number on it so that he could more easily identify the players. Larry found comfort in the team he was playing with. The ball was brought up, and he handled it and passed it off to a guy who lurched up the ball that bounded off the backboard. The other team grabbed the rebound and moved it up court. Larry got into place and defended the other player with his arms out to the side, something he had seen countless times. As the player he was guarding tried to jump and shoot, Larry was there to block the shot and then his team recovered the ball and moved it up court. When they got into place, Larry received the ball, feinted to the left, then spun right, jumped and scored. The rest of his team nodded with smiles on their faces.

The game moved back and forth and then in one play Larry spotted a guy cutting to the basket and bounced a perfect pass to him that he laid up for a score. In a later play, Larry got the ball deep on the side and put up an easy shot that was all net. He began now to really find his rhythm and he was so pleased that his teammates wanted him to shine. The envy that he had expected was not evident. Finally, the coach called the game to an end and then put the second team on the court. Larry had scored 10 points in this limited play, made about two assists and grabbed a rebound. He was proud of himself and knew at least for that moment in time, the gods were on his side.

At the end of the fourth game the coach called a halt to the activity. He then told them that he was going to call out the numbers of the selected players. Larry wore an 8 on his back and he almost couldn't breathe as the numbers were called out. As the coach shouted out the numbers, Larry heard him signal the number 8 and he felt a heavy burden lift and then held back his tears of joy. The coach then made a speech that told the ones who didn't make it that there would be a chance to try again in the next semester. This didn't make much sense to Larry if the team stayed intact, but maybe a few players would quit. Certainly he would not be among them.

He couldn't wait to tell Paul, who was in his class about the good news; and Paul almost jumped for joy and hugged Larry. Then he got to tell Phil, who broke out in a huge smile and wrapped his arms around him. Then he came home to tell his parents, but their reaction was a bit more muted than he had expected. His father grinned from ear to ear and said that he was so happy for him and then said that he hoped that he would have plenty of time for his studies. "So that's what they are worried about." And Larry realized that his parents really never accepted his prime interest in life, but then, he thought, why push it if it would only end in some sort of argument?

Larry had a glorious year as a freshman. He had a high percentage in shooting, his passes improved, and he was able to grab a few rebounds from time to time. What enabled him to shine was the amazing chemistry of the team. He attributed this to the coach, who was just the nicest guy he ever met. He yelled once in a while, criticized them when he had to, but generally tried to bring out the best in everyone and was very successful in getting the team to play as a group. And in the process the team won most of its games, and some with big scores, unless the opposing team just had some big bruisers who dominated. At the end of the season, Larry emerged as the leading scorer, all the while remembering the importance of his shot selections. But the best news was yet to come. The coach of the varsity team retired and the junior varsity coach took over. Larry had formed a very warm, close relationship with him. They almost became friends and often would talk about strategy and tactics. At that point, Larry had no fears of moving on to the varsity team and after the season, the coach, Tim Parker, informed Larry that he had definitely made the team.

Larry remembered walking out of his office that day with the secret feeling that someone was looking out for him. His doubts about believing in an Almighty was encountering some serious argument. Why else would fate have become a special friend to him? Here he had spent so much of his time worrying that he might not have the stuff of varsity basketball material. He had to laugh when he thought about that, but he also felt keenly that with enough resolve, hard work and a strong belief in himself, nothing would stand in his way for him to get where he wanted to go. Yes, when all was said and done, Vince Lombardi knew what he was talking about. Hard work does pay off and so does planning, with the ability to keep your eye on the crystal ball that predicts a bright future.

The coach called Larry into his office. "Look, I told you that you would make the varsity team and I will keep to this promise. However, there are a number of issues that we need to address. I can promise you that you will make the team but as far as playing minutes go, I don't know about that. So far, the team that is going to play range from 6 feet to 6'8". I know as well as you do that short guys sometimes do very well in the game, and they bring to the game something a bit different. They are more aggressive and they move in a hard-hitting fashion toward the basket. In fact, they usually stand out in the game because they have made up for their lack of height with a determined, forceful manner. I could pick out five outstanding short guys in the pros that highlight what I just said.

"Yes, you will make the team, but I know you want more than that, you want to get your minutes and you will, but you are going to have to change some of your game. You are not going to take short jump shots against the guy who is 5 inches bigger than you but if you shoot quickly you will make up for that. You are going to have to say to yourself that you will go crazy on the court; play like a mad man, and torment the other team. Now I know some of this will not be easy for you but if you don't change your game you will be sitting on the bench. You should take a look at a former player, Allen Iverson, who tormented his opponents. You tell me that you look up to Bobby Knight, so just take a page from his book. He coaches with so much venom, determination and hostility, but he wins and wins big. Now what do you think?"

Larry was thunderstruck. He hadn't expected this, but he so appreciated it because it was honest and he also felt it was loving. Larry paused to think: "Yes, I know it is one thing to strike an aggressive mode when talking and it is another to take this hardline approach onto a physical part of yourself. Wow, no one has ever talked to me like you have. In fact, I thought all along that I was playing the game just the way it should be played, but now you have thrown in another hurdle, which is how I have to make up for my deficiencies. Yes, you are right, some guys are just more talented than me, some less; and some tower over me. But I have to tackle this issue and I believe with all my heart that I can do it, especially with your words of encouragement. It won't be easy but I can play like a mad man and I think I could get to like it, in fact, I am starting to feel it in my bones already."

Tim got up, signaling that the meeting was over, and extended his hand. "You have made the team; now you have to decide how you will fit in." Larry took his hand, pumped it, thanked him; and left. When asked how he was doing he could now say, "I am on the varsity team at Roosevelt High." Wow! Life had certainly shifted around – there was so much to it now. So much striving, so much determination. Life had taken on a new dimension and he felt privileged to be among that select few. He guessed this was the feeling of high school football players as well, the chosen few: the ones where their classmates attend games and cheer the team on by yelling and shouting. And the player comes back after the game a hero, a true warrior. He was so deeply proud of himself, so enmeshed in the glory of the moment, that he wondered if he walked back to the gym, took a ball and shot it from one end of the court to the other, would it go in the basket? That's how high and crazy the feeling was.

Larry started making up scenes in his mind. "Larry Evans the terrific guard at Roosevelt High scores again and wins the game!" He finally had to stop himself, because otherwise there would be no end to his fantasies of greatness, fame, and prominence – the thing that legends are made of. Then his heroes started to pass through his mind, much like a movie of some glittering sky, the sun burnishing its light and the scene captured in 3-D to lend more of a glow and shine.

Yet, underneath it all, he knew he had to be a different guy on the court, someone who was going to electrify the crowd. This nut who shakes things up and wins games for his team. But this would have to be a new Larry; and he knew it was within his grasp, because he really didn't care how he came across to others, as long as he satisfied his quest to make the starting five.

Otherwise, the school year turned out to be a bit uneventful for Larry. He liked his classes but he was not the big cheese that he was before in Junior High School. The kids in his class were bigger than before, and now he had the presence of girls who were more mature. Thank heaven for his two friends, Paul and Phil; because it was not so easy making friends as it was before. He studied hard and analyzed every game that he played as well as the varsity. He didn't want to pull too much into himself, but he knew that he did not share a lot of the interests of his classmates.

One good thing was that his brother, Dave, was off to college so he had the apartment more to himself, and he liked that a lot. In fact, his relationship with both parents got better. He talked more about history with his father, and discussed the makeup of his classes with his mother. He decided to keep his keen interest in basketball to himself. And that worked wonders.

School was just about over before the summer break. And Larry was told that he would move on to the varsity. Was this not a moment of good fortune that his coach would be moving on also as he had always felt as if the coach was looking out for him, wanted him to succeed and excel. What a break! and he knew he would miss Tim Parker during the summer months, when his life would wilt and diminish without the action to sustain it. But that was all right, he figured, the future prospects will make up for it. And he had the playground to form teams and play for the whole day especially on weekends.

And then Paul told Larry that he had to tell him something important.

"Okay what gives?" asked Larry. Paul smiled for a moment, "My parents have decided to move to Manhattan. My father felt that the commute would be easier and they always hoped to live there. Unfortunately, I will have to change schools, not that I have to but it would be too hard commuting up to the Bronx."

Larry felt kind of sad at that news. He figured that they would go through school together. He said to Paul, "Well we can always get together on weekends."

Paul replied immediately, "Of course, I am not going to lose you as a friend and I don't want to lose Phil either."

Yet Larry felt as if a wedge had been driven between them. Certainly, he would miss their friendship and he had doubts whether he could be so close to someone again. He used to think that Manhattan was another world from the Bronx, but he knew that this was silly. His parents brought him there so often, to plays and movies and concerts. Then he took a page from one of his reflections, that his life would have to move on also. Maybe it would be better for him to hang out with the guys on the team. This would give him a good chance to move his life forward if he wanted to operate in a different orbit, the exalted position of an athlete, and maybe Paul would have harbored resentment toward this, or his position on the varsity would have created bitterness between them. He didn't think so, but who could tell?

Larry felt much trepidation when he decided to approach his parents with his plans for the summer. In a casual manner, he asked them to listen to what he thought was a good idea. "I would like to go to camp, not the one that you think about, but one that would be focused on basketball. I have been told that it is a terrific way to size up the caliber of play that is going around the country. I mean, the best of players attend, and I have saved up enough money to pay for it. So what do you think?"

His father seemed impressed at his son's striving to get better and he let him know immediately. "Sounds like a good idea, and it could put you on the right road." Larry's mother picked up on this and remarked, "Yes, I agree and I think you could only get better with this training." Larry smiled broadly and thanked them both for their support. He was off to Five-Star camp and felt damned proud about it. And the experience at camp was just terrific. Just being around other players was so exciting, to find out what others were thinking and how they sized up their game and how they envisioned their future. Yes, this was a wonderful idea that he had pursued.

When he got back from camp he found that the summer went by like a lark. His father attempted in the beginning to bring some clarity to his life, but Larry would just listen, nod his head, and then extract these talks from his mind. He justified his behavior as feeling that these people, especially his father, just did not understand, or that they really had strikingly different values and tastes. The world of basketball was the world of life; and the people that inhabited that world were really the only ones that counted or made sense for Larry. There was an array of people who tried to get Larry to understand that what he was doing was over-determined, but then he would counter this argument with the response that if it were not over-determined, how could he emerge as a success? That it was the attitude of over-determination that made successful doctors, lawyers, and even politicians. Otherwise, failure or mediocrity would seize the day, would they not?

But now the countless hours of practice, the charts he studied, and even the statistics he memorized as if they were his Bible, were going to face the ultimate test – would he have a successful season? Would he be able to apply the things Coach Parker talked about and put them to a test on the basketball court?

The varsity team was called together before the season started and Coach Parker explained his plans for the coming year. It was a good meeting and everyone seemed pleased; and then the starting five were announced, but that was a foregone conclusion. Larry walked out afterward, chatting a bit with the rest of the team, but he really wanted to be alone. He felt anointed and blessed, as if the Pope himself had placed the hand of divine Providence on him. When he dressed and left he walked to the park that was close to his house, sat down, put his head in the palms of his hands, and cried. He looked up at the sky and muttered, "Oh God, You have looked out for me, and I will not forget what You have done for me and what You have given me today. You have touched my heart with Your love and guidance and I will not fail You."

Then he went on with a silent monologue and told himself that patience and hard work are the just rewards of a good life. This one act of making the team gave him such solace, as if it opened the gates of heaven and invited him in. He promised right then and there that he would be up to meeting the challenges of any ongoing limitations of life, such as his height. Talking to himself, he said, "This will not be your albatross, even if it were the plight of Jews, where only a few grew to 6'7" or more, but they were few and far between. No, you have a special mission in life to challenge the forces against you and that's what God meant for you." Now if he could only explain this to his father. But life at this point would be radically different. Hopefully, they would say about him: "Maybe he wasn't tall, but he certainly had a stirring jump shot," and all he needed was to put it into practice. He also knew that he loved the coach and he would do everything to have the coach like and appreciate him, the good and faithful son who honors the father.

He began to practice with the team in a different way, much more aggressive, slashing through defenders and smashing toward the basket. He knew that he must keep this new player in his mind before it actually became a part of him and he began to take on this new role and found it rewarding. He could see that the other players started to be impressed by this aggressive behavior on the court.

The team practiced hard and ran many different offensive and defensive plays. The starting five was in place and Larry realized that unless his team was way out in front or way back in scoring, he did not expect to get in; too few players graduated, so the varsity retained most of its players. But when he did get in, he would use every capability within his power. And this chance came with his team up by 15 points. The coach took out three players and sent three in from the bench, including Larry. Now Larry started to give himself instructions, "Don't be a wise guy and don't think you can just shoot all the time; pass the ball but look for the opportunity where you can shine and have the coach feel as if he can rely on you in the pitch."

His team, Roosevelt High School, was moving the ball up court. Larry got the ball and dribbled slowly but surely into the front court. He passed off, moved forward, and received the ball back. Then he feinted to the right, faking his man out, and drove to the basket for an easy layup. Boy, did he like that. On the next play Larry passed off a few times and then after receiving the ball drove to the right of the key and hoisted a three-point shot that whisked through the nets. After a few more plays between the teams, time ran out.

As Larry was walking off the court, the coach motioned to him to come over. "I liked the way you played, young man; and you certainly have earned a good place on our team. You were more aggressive and you really shone out there."

"Thanks so much," replied Larry, "That means a lot to me, I feel wonderful and we are having such a great season with you guiding us and we all are happy that you were made coach." "Wow," he thought, "I had my first challenge and met it head on. I think this will be one great season!"

The first question his father asked him when he told him about his playing time was how the game went. Larry told him of his success on the court and then added that he got the highest mark in the history exam. "Don't worry, my game as well as my grades are going to be fine. I have the divine Providence behind me, do you think I would do anything to screw that up?" By then he was shutting out his parents from his life: they had little to offer him, and his older brother was not into sports, but anyway he was off to college where he had a scientific bent that helped him get good grades in math and science.

Larry still had Phil from elementary school, who followed his every exploit on the hardwood floor.

For the first year of his varsity life, Larry continued to warm the bench, as they would say, but he knew that by his third year much of the varsity would graduate and hopefully he would find a starting spot on the team. And that did happen and Larry sparkled as a starter. He followed the designated offensive plays to the letter and on defense he guarded his man like a hawk, all of which brought him the satisfaction of the coach. "This guy pays attention to what I tell the team," thought the coach. And Roosevelt High was having a banner year. The team had the right chemistry and they played with determination and persistence. After each game, Larry would go over the stats with his one close friend, Phil, and he actually found a warm relationship with a guy from his class who also had this deep interest in working out strategy.

Phil explained to him: "Look, you scored 14 points with three assists and two rebounds. Not bad, and now you are averaging almost 12 points a game with four assists. In fact you are the second biggest scorer for the team. Who could fault this?" Larry needed friends to lend credence to his game, although he missed Paul. It was wonderful sharing these exploits with these stats with Phil. He knew he would always love Phil and Paul. And the sad part was that his parents rarely ever came to any of the games. They came once for a playoff game but said nothing to him afterwards, as if basketball were a foreign language. Larry thought, "I guess they see it only as ten guys running up and down the court with little in mind other than putting the round ball in the basket." Then he thought, "Maybe it's better this way; otherwise, they could be an interference, like parents meddling into your business. This way I feel as if I am on my own and when high school finishes I could find a college away from here, some place where I could be free of this whole section of the Bronx with its lack of excitement and hope. To grow up here can be devastating if nothing else enters your life so I must count myself as one of the fortunate ones."

Toward the end of the season the coach called Larry into his office. As Larry sat down the coach screwed up his face as if he were going to make some serious pronouncement. "I know we have one more year to go, but I thought it would be important for us to talk about your future. And let me tell you that I appreciate the extra stuff that you do around here. You stay late, collect the equipment, distribute the plays I have laid out, and so many other things. It's guys like you who make my job so much more pleasant and easy. So now we talk about you. What are your plans after your senior year?"

"I had hopes I could get a scholarship to a good school and of course continue to play basketball. I always wanted to play varsity ball here and I find that I can really make a place for myself. I am

confident of my moves, my shot, and even my defense. I just want to
keep going and you have really been my guiding spirit and mentor
ever since my junior varsity years. In fact you got me to see how I
had to change my game if I would have a chance to make the team."

The coach listened and then began to react. "Look, even if
you could find a scholarship to a strong team, let's say Michigan
or Louisville, or North Carolina or Duke, you would probably be
sitting out the entire season on the bench. These bench fellows rarely
get into a game, and these teams have a nucleus of six or seven guys
that play game after game. Is this what you want?"

"No not at all, but why do you feel that this will be my place on
the team? And if so, what really are the alternatives?" Larry replied
with deep seriousness.

"What would make more sense is that you try to get into a
smaller, less competitive college where hopefully you could be on
a starting five. I don't have to go over the persistent issue in your
life and that is your height. Take a look at the professional teams in
the 70s, you rarely find anyone smaller than 6'1" and at that height
these guys rarely start. And even in colleges thirty years before this,
you rarely have anyone smaller than 6 feet. Yes, we talked about the
plight of the Jewish player and before your time there was a Harry
Boykoff who was 6'10" but he was slow as molasses; and then Dolph
Schayes who was 6'8" and he was a standout; and then that crook,
Jack Molinas, who at 6'7" could have been colossal but he fixed
his games and ended up with a bullet to his head. So where does
that leave you? And this is what I want to talk to you about. I have
watched you over time, how you digest the plays I lay out; and this
is only high school. I think your way in this sport is with coaching
and you know as well as I that we have some great coaches who were
not that much as players. Here height really doesn't enter into the
mix. Oddly enough, most coaches are on the small side. So what
do you think?"

Larry shrugged his shoulders: "Well of course I think you are right, it would be a continuous uphill battle for me and I would probably face insurmountable problems at the end of it all. But what if I made it like a small guy with an aggressive stance – the kind of stuff you told me about? And what makes you think I could make it as a coach? I love the idea of it, but these college coaches are tigers, I watch them in the games and they prance up and down the sidelines yelling at the players. I mean, I have rarely seen Roy Williams smile even when North Carolina is winning. They focus on what the team is not doing. I am not sure that this fits my personality, but then again maybe you grind yourself into that. Maybe my character is malleable but then maybe it isn't. But what colleges do you think I could play and hone my skills as a manager? Do such places exist? Of course I feel a bit disappointed; but you know, I love to see you coach the team. I love to watch the glee in your eyes when we take the other team apart. I would want to capture these feelings for myself. But where could I do this?"

The coach nodded and went on. "I thought of some smaller schools that don't have such a competitive bent where you could possibly make the starting team. Let me see, there is Bowling Green, I thought of Bradley that used to have great teams but have given them up for some reason. And ah, University of Massachusetts or Vermont, and then some teams in the Patriot League, such as Colgate or Lafayette. These are just a small number of possibilities. I would certainly talk to the people I know and see what we can do. I have some markers I could call in and I would be very willing to do it for you. So what do you think?... and let me add that I think it would be good for you to go to a Five Star Camp where coaches will be evaluating the players."

Larry shook his head. "I thought of going to a camp and thank you for suggesting it to me. Now, of course I think you are right, it's just that when you set your sights on a certain goal it doesn't feel rewarding to lower them. There was always a part of me that knew my height would stand in the way, and I would pray that in my teens

I could shoot up a few inches, but that never happened. And I can't carry this hope around much longer. I go out and see a white team pitted against a black team and I cross my fingers that it doesn't turn out to be a massacre. When did this change happen? I mean it can't have always been this way."

The coach smiled and took the stance of a teacher lecturing his class.

"Well in 1967 there were two teams that were squaring off in the NCAA finals. I know you already have read about it and you know a lot about the history of basketball. But to go over it again, there was Kentucky who had always been a world-beater, and there was the coach of Texas Western, who decided that he would play only his black players for this game. Well the coach of Kentucky, this cantankerous fellow by the name of Rupp, whom they called the Colonel, told his players that no black team was ever going to beat his players, who fielded only white guys. Well what do you think happened? Texas Western beat up on that team and then the South realized that integration was the only way to proceed; otherwise they would go down like Kentucky.

"Now up north we always had some damn good players who were black. City College and NYU had a large contingent of Jewish players, but LIU had this one great black player, Sherman White, who was banished for throwing the games, but this also happened at City College, who never had a Division One team after that. The scandal demolished basketball in New York City even though NYU continued for some time and then went into Division Three. Yes there were Fordham and St. John's, but somehow they never could get their act together, much like Rutgers in New Jersey. The only Eastern team that continued to be competitive was Connecticut, or Yukon as they call them, and of course Syracuse. So I think we should focus on the schools where you could start. I want you to think about this and we can talk further when you are decided on what you want to do.

"Now look Larry, we had scouts coming down here, they usually go from one high school to the next and of course go to these summer camps where the cream of basketball players work out, and then they want to talk with me. I never tell you about players when they are sitting in the stands, because that could influence the game and the shooter."

Now Larry was getting excited: "You know I have gotten the chance to go to basketball camp and maybe if I could shine, I would have a chance that they would recruit me?"

Parker waited a moment until Larry finished then went on: "But here is an analysis of your game to the best of my knowledge and the most honest assessment I can make to you. I happen to like you a lot and feel that you strengthen the team and make them stronger. But let's get back to the issues of your playing. We know about your height or lack of it, but in ways you make up for that deficiency with some really good outside shooting and your assertive play. You have a good eye for the basket that I am sure comes from the amount of time you practice. And of course that is a great asset in this game. But I noticed another thing I want to bring to your attention. You tend to get a bit tired a little too early in the game. Now no one is expected to play the whole time, but let's say that in college or the pros the player is in the game three-fourths of the time, and he is expected to play as hard at the end almost as he does in the beginning. I noticed that you start to get exhausted after about 15 minutes and then your shot is not that sharp. There was a guy who played for Boston Celtics before your time. His name was John Havilicek and I would watch him drive to the basket after playing almost the entire game just as sharply and aggressively as if he were just starting. The energy and endurance that this guy showed was off the charts. In fact, there is a story that when he took a chest X-ray where parts of his chest went off the X-ray. Now this is something you have to born with; you can practice endurance but only so far. It won't take you to the head of the marathon."

Parker stopped for a moment to give Larry a chance to respond. "Yes, of course, I know what you are talking about. The players with poor endurance I guess usually drop out of the game itself, but I imagine that would go for tennis also. I remember witnessing a five -set match played on a hot summer day out in Queens. I couldn't believe that each of the players was able to muster the endurance that it took, but then it became a bit evident that one started to slow down when he chased the ball and his opponent, seeing this decrease in energy, took advantage and won the match. But this is something I have no control over. I imagine that this is a Jewish symptom also that inflicts many of us who want to play basketball."

"That's right," the coach responded, "but it will dog you the rest of your playing days. Sure they could play you for only 10 or 15 minutes, but who is going to want to take this into consideration when hiring or playing you? Believe me, I wish it weren't the case, but there are worst scenarios about players: for example, the player who can't find the basket or who gets easily rattled or even doesn't know how to guard his opponent. You must have seen certain players who are so easily faked out of their position that they become laughable. This isn't you, but remember in high school, we play 32 minutes; in college we play 40 minutes; and in the pros they play 48 minutes, and that is running up and down the court continuously. A lack of energy just can wear you down. I can tell you that one reason I gave up tennis was that I ran out of breath after 40 minutes or so. What happens is that I am in the game where we are going to play two out of three sets. I am up the first set and then my opponent wins the second set and we now play the third set for the match. But, after five or ten minutes I start to huff and puff and realize that I don't have much to give. My opponent sees this and does not show much empathy but, rather, seems a bit disgusted if not disappointed that we can't get competitively into the third. I tell him that I really can't continue and he smiles and shakes his head, but I know that he doesn't like it. Well at that time I decide to only play doubles, which really does not make me a happy camper. But you can't do this in basketball, so what are you going to do?" he smiled. "Take up badminton?"

"Oddly enough, I don't find that too funny. Look, basketball isn't part of my life, it is my life. I live for the game, I watch as many games as I can on TV, I memorize statistics much like people do in baseball, I redistribute players in my mind. I follow the draft with such intensity it almost begins to scare me. I could go on and on like this, but I think you get the picture. What am I going to do now? I am not stupid, I know I could never make it to the NBA; but there is so much going on in college, they have full schedules and college coaches are fabulous. I mean, who wouldn't want to play for Pitino, or Calipari, or an endless number of people; but you are telling me that even if I were taken by a good college I would be sitting on the bench most of the game. Well, I can't accept it, even though I know that it is a reality, but, what am I going to do about it?"

Parker then went on: "Look, if you are really serious, you may have to confront yourself with another kind of reality. Yes, you are not going to be 6'7" but that is not what you should focus on if that is what you must do—we talked about it before." Parker pulled out a folder, opened it up, and then looked straight at Larry. " Let me read a few statistics. There was a guy by the name of Spud Webb who was 5'7". Unlike you, he was born in poverty and used basketball as an inspiration. Although he was not tall he used his quickness and jumping ability to outplay the other kids. Throughout his life he was told that he was too short to play basketball. Well, he didn't listen and he could dunk the ball when he was 5 feet 3 inches. But people started to be impressed with him and he was offered a scholarship to North Carolina State by no other than Jim Valvano. Then he was drafted in the 4th round of the 1985 NBA by the Detroit Pistons. To get to the point of the story, he retired in 1998 after playing 814 games and averaging 9.9 points per game and registering 8,072 points and 4,342 assists in twelve seasons. Since Webb made his

NBA debut there have been two shorter players, Earl Boykins and Muggsy Bogues."

Parker stopped for a moment and waited to see if Larry had digested what he had just said. He could see that these figures impressed Larry, so he went on.

"The most amazing thing is that Webb was the shortest person to compete in the NBA Slam Dunk Contest, winning the event in 1986. Do you know who he beat?– the great Dominque Wilkins. Now let's see what the dunks consisted of. He had an elevator two-handed dunk, a reverse double-pump dunk, the off-the-backboard one-handed jam, a 360-degree helicopter one-handed dunk, a reverse double-pump slam and finally, the reverse two-handed strawberry jam from a lob bounce off the floor. In fact, he defeated Wilkins with two perfect 50-point scores in the final round. How could Wilkins have prepared for anything so miraculous as this? At 5'7" to dunk like this has to be seen as a gift from the heavens. Now what do you say?"

Larry managed a smile and shook his head. "I think you are telling me that I should value my gifts and not the things that I lack. I think this talk will stay with me forever, for it gets to the parts of my character that I want to expel from my life. To beat Dominque is certainly awesome but I wish I had the speed of Spud or the jumping ability; and he will certainly become one of my heroes. I want to thank you for this. I value both your friendship and guidance."

"Well I have said it before, the route would be in coaching. Many of these exalted coaches never were that great as players–some, but few and far between–and you would have come to this point in a few years and I thought it better that you take it up now."

Larry was quiet; his words were settling into his mind, not sinking to the bottom as yet but floating around like some loose debris rising and falling into the ocean. "Do you have some more time to give me, or should we continue at another day?"

"Please take your time, I'm patient but more than that, I want to help you find your way in this. This is part of the pleasure I get from my job. There are a number of your teammates that I counsel about their grades, but that is a private matter."

Larry went on, "I am proud to be Jewish, I am a strong supporter of Israel and all that it stands for; but this is not about being Jewish, it's about my athleticism, and what I gather is that I am too limited to really make it. You know, I have had this feeling for some time, but I rubbed it out of my mind for as long as I could and I want to thank you for getting me to confront it before my senior year. So what are my options?"

"I think what you may want to do is to see how you could become an assistant after college to a coach who could teach you about the business. I know that you follow the game in a very thorough way; and you know that some of these assistants who go on to become coaches come back and play against their former coaches and can haunt their lives. Why? because they have been schooled in their plays, their defenses and so on. Some of the coaches make recommendations to other colleges that particular assistants really have what it takes to become coaches. The game is replete with these situations. Some of the people who assisted Bobby Knight or Rick Pitino are now in charge of their own colleges. But this takes a certain kind of effort, a certain type of learning, and absorbing the elements of the game."

Larry looked him in the eye, "I feel funny asking you this, but why did you settle for a high school position if you could have gone on to college ball?"

Parker smiled, "I think you all have given this some thought throughout your stay here. And I don't mind answering it, although it is mighty complicated. And you know, you can put this same question to a whole lot of teachers. Of course we know that they have to get their doctorates, but that is not a major stumbling block. But that is for them to reply. As for me, I can tell you that I was not willing to start out in some small town in Nebraska, where my wife would have rebelled. And if I had a crummy season, I could get fired–you don't have tenure in these positions. I wanted to raise a family and I couldn't conceive of moving around too much. That would be one side of it; the other is maybe I didn't have the confidence that I could coach a major or even not-so-major college team. I really think you have to be ferocious, and so focused that winning moves you to another level of your mindset. You watch these guys walking up and down the sidelines. As you yourself said, have you ever seen Roy Williams when he wasn't yelling about something or other? This has to be part and parcel of your character – you don't just make it up as you go along, and I don't think that this is me. Of course, you have seen me rant and rave and lash out at certain times at some stupid plays, but these are exceptions. I think college coaching intimidates me in some ways, and I find this job preferable. I am not sure I miss not coaching in college; I am not sure whether this is any different from working on Wall Street. Some guys really don't or can't stand the pressure. Do you see what I mean?"

"Mr. Parker, I really appreciate you and all that you have done for me and how honest you have been. In fact, my mind is moving in another direction, and that is a good thing. I have to tell you about an argument I got into with one of my father's friends. He was asking me about my time on the team and how I felt about it. I told him I loved the game and that it added a real purpose to my life. Well then, he wondered whether I would continue playing. I told him that I would love to do that if I were good enough, but my height is a real stumbling block. 'Oh well,' he says, 'Jews don't excel in it because they prefer medicine or law.' I responded to that by telling him that Jews don't play because they don't seem built to play. 'What are you talking about – who is built to play?' I tell him that it seems as if the Blacks have the physique for the game– I don't mean it in a prejudicial way, but they seem built to play just as the Kenyans appear more suited for the New York Marathon. Well, he doesn't buy that, and I go on to show him that at one time most of the New

York teams were Jewish, but if those teams were playing today they would be demolished. He shakes his head and changes the subject."

Then Larry walked out of Parker's office and in the months that followed he realized that the things that he said to him were on target. Certainly, they had an impact on his dreams; he wanted to play in college and would have been sad if he didn't give his all to the game. Yes, he could see himself as a coach, but it wasn't the same thing as shooting hoops. He would never have the opportunity to do this professionally so maybe the best of all worlds has come to pass. He could play while focusing on charts and strategies, and he would try to get closer to the coach of whatever college team he is on. But if he had figured this out, why did he still feel this emptiness in the pit of his stomach as if he were being cheated? Since he had got onto the starting team in high school he had held out hopes of playing for a dominant team and getting into the NCAA tournament.

Parker called Larry into his office toward the end of the season. "I think I found a place for you. They are interested in you at Iona College, where they are ready to give you a full scholarship."

"Iona!" Larry blurts out, "that's like never leaving home. Isn't it a few miles from here?"

"So what, did you ever hear of Richie Guerin who played for the Knicks. He went to Iona."

Larry was all smiles, "Okay, name another player besides Jeff Ruland?"

CHAPTER FOUR

Entering College

Independence Achieved

Larry decided to look into the situation at Iona College and the first thing that impressed him was that he was not going to be the shortest guy on the team. There was a guy they recruited who was 5'9" and now Larry was 5'10" and maybe still growing, but he wouldn't bet on it. They play in the Metro Atlantic Athletic Conference and some of the competition isn't bad but not made up of world- beaters. However, they do well enough to be in the running for an NCAA bid. This would make Larry one proud camper; but now he had to wait to get a letter of acceptance. Tim told him that he already had an intensive conversation with the coach, who was excited about the prospect of having Larry on the team.

His parents had both heard of Iona and they knew it was a religious school and that was impressive; a lot of schools are religious, such as Fordham, Georgetown and Seton Hall, and they knew that they had high academic standards. And of course the best news was that the four years would all be paid for. The father heaved a sigh of relief but he did that privately. He did not want Larry to think that this would be such a big deal to him. Larry consulted with his two other friends. Phil, who had great marks, was going to Middlebury and Paul was attending Boston University. So all three were very satisfied with their prospects. Yet in some ways, Larry felt that he had got the advantage over them because he had got what he strived for. And then Larry received the letter detailing his acceptance and scholarship.

Larry immediately called Sherman to tell him the good news and Sherman then told Larry of his news. "I just got my scholarship to Providence and my family is going wild over it. My mom is so proud of me and I feel like floating in the air." They made up to meet in a few days to celebrate their hard-earned triumphs.

The coach of Iona invited Larry to come up and see his accommodations as well as the gym where he was going to play. He liked his accommodations and there was a nice feel about the school. It was situated not far from the downtown area of New Rochelle, which was a cute little town. Also, there was a friendly aura that permeated the school. He began to feel that he had made a good choice, not the one he wished for, but a good compromise nevertheless.

Once the team was established, Larry was told that he would not start in the beginning because they had three holdovers from the year before. But within no time he secured a starting position after posting some excellent numbers. He found that the competition was not too intense and winning did not take on the same meaning as it did in a larger college. He scored more and felt less worried and stressed, but he didn't feel the heightened drive to win that is really one of the main aims of playing. And during this time he used his social skills to become closer to the coach, and finally he was able to help both the coach and his assistants. In conversations with the assistants he got the immediate impression that they harbored fantasies about coaching their own team and this was a great way of starting on this road. He began to get a different focus on the game and realized the difficulty of planning an action but then putting this plan into operation. There is a big difference between working out something on paper and then getting the players to follow this plan. He began to turn his interests toward coaching.

Larry found that the courses at Iona were not so easy as he hoped. They required a lot of study and the instructors tended to be demanding. "But, hell," he thought, "this is college and it is a big difference from high school."

One of the highlights of his studies at Iona was the course he took in psychology. There was a section of the course that dealt with social psychology and in this study the professor went over the theories of the achievement motive. Larry became absorbed in the subject: the whole idea of why certain people keep moving on in life while others reach a plateau and then continue to live out their lives without any movement forward. He thought of himself as well as his father, and he knew that he wanted to keep progressing. So he made an appointment with the professor to discuss this in more depth.

"So why are some people more motivated to achieve than others, what's the hidden ingredient? As you know, I am on the basketball team and I wonder why certain coaches keep going higher and higher while others just stop in place. I don't want to give you the impression that I think happiness only lies in this forward drive."

The professor grinned at the question. "You know, as I told you in the class, this subject has been studied and researched countless times. There must be thousands of doctoral dissertations written about it. In fact, my own dissertation had something to do with this. But you ought to look into the writings of a Harvard psychologist, David McClelland. Motivation of one kind or another was his life's work.

Larry listened intensely and then asked him: "What exactly is it that motivates a person to achieve?"

The professor grinned at the question and then went on. "It has to do with what usually is on your mind. Do you think about getting better or is your mind usually occupied with other thoughts like what you are going to do on the weekend? In short, if you are consumed with achievement you stand a good chance of getting there."

The professor went on. "Someone in college who strives to be at the top of his or her class and get the best marks has a need for achievement, while those who seek out warm and friendly relationships have a strong need for affiliation. These people are socially motivated.

Larry then asked him more about coaches and he replied that those coaches who are highly achievement-oriented strive to attain better and better results and they are always looking for more effective strategies to win. These thoughts fill their minds during the waking state: in short, they are consumed and always thinking about more effective ways to improve themselves and the team."

Larry thanked him and walked away, thinking of his parents; but then his mind reverted to his Uncle Sol and how he felt so specially treated by him, and then his thoughts moved to his high-school coach. It certainly made more sense to him now. And then he realized that he was usually absorbed with ideas of achievement, that they filled his mind for much of the day; and in that moment really understood what the professor was talking about. But he promised himself that he would read up on this David McClelland.

Larry started to make friends, but they were mostly from the team. What bothered him was that he was no longer the celebrity that he was in high school. He took medium-level courses so that he couldn't be caught up with too much class work, and overall he found the atmosphere at Iona to be supportive and friendly. He tried to keep in touch with Phil and Paul but found that this was not so easy as each of them had developed his own interests. Larry was becoming even more focused on basketball, but he enjoyed every minute of it.

So the four years at Iona went quite well. On the basketball team, he was their leading scorer and gave the team a needed structure, while his attention gravitated more toward the coaching elements than actual playing. He was able to shift his thinking to more intellectual pursuits, and certainly coaching took on that frame. "Oh well, maybe that's what speaks to my flexibility. Why go down a road that will lead to frustrations?"

In one of his courses, a priest, Father John, addressed the class and discussed some aspects of spirituality. He was a gripping and compelling speaker who imparted words of wisdom concerning the spiritual self. After the class, Larry approached him and asked if he could talk with him privately. Father John was receptive and they made an appointment later in the week. Larry always wanted to get closer to those people who excited and impressed him.

Larry entered his office and after sitting down explained to the Father some of his concerns. "Basketball energizes me, in fact it gives me a purpose in life and I felt privileged growing up that I had this passion for the game." The father sat and listened attentively and Larry went on. "The big problem that I have to face is that because of my height limitations and my speed, I cannot pursue playing the game beyond college. The competition would be too strong for me and I was advised to consider coaching, but this is not what I really want to do and I have found myself withdrawing from life. I wish I had a better solution, but I can't continue fooling myself into thinking that I could move away from playing the game."

After Larry expressed what was bothering him, Father John took up the exchange. "Yes, I know you are on our team and I have watched a number of the games, and I was impressed by your playing. However, your concerns do seem justified. In some ways, the game has gotten out of control, but that is something else. Basketball takes in a whole array of different features; there is so much to it and I think that playing is only one part of it, as I am sure you already understand."

Larry interrupted him and wondered if he could find happiness in going in a different direction. Father John went back to his original point. "If we treat it as one game of life, then you could single out the one feature that would lead to your success and of course you put your finger on that feature, coaching. I am not sure that it isn't any less important than actual playing, and it may be even more important. I think the significant point is that you stay within the game itself. And if continuing to be part of the game means you coach well, that is not a bad solution. I see myself as part of the G-d game and it is a game to be played. Except here we are searching for a way that will lead us in finding Jesus. Being a priest keeps me in the game; why, even prayer is a form of playing, a kind of chanting that relates to what goes on with the fans as they watch a game – it gives people pleasure.

"Maybe you were meant to do other things than playing. There are those who fight wars and those who plan them. Without Eisenhower and the rest of his command how could we have ever won the Second World War?"

Larry laughed a bit. "That's such an interesting analogy. Those who fight the wars and those that plan them. I really like that one, because I feel it is so apt."

"Well, thank you," said the priest, "I would like to see you put the same passion you have for competing as a player to participating in another vein. Stay close to the game, and you will have a long and fruitful career because as we are talking I feel that you are blessed to have found such a purpose in life. God has certainly sanctified your existence and you are one of the more fortunate ones. Be well, my son."

Larry thanked him and left. He wanted to hug him but he thought it would make the priest uncomfortable and knew there would be other times. As he walked away, he felt better about the college. There was a profound structure, a reverence for principle, and a testament to man's higher objectives. He thought that the religious atmosphere provided a spectrum of seriousness and a thoughtful gaze at reality. He also saw a relationship between basketball and religion: they could both be seen as confronting the wonders of the game of life.

He remembered the times when he had doubts about himself as well as the path along which he found himself traveling. Would he be able to retain the same sense of seriousness or is it all a passing fancy that will fade away with time? He was worried about his resolve, and he always came back to basketball and the way it should be played. And here in this college, he realized that when there were doubts about one's position in life, religion could provide an access into the mystery of life that clarified the riddle of one's existence. Larry didn't want to be simplistic or naïve in relating the two, but he could always say to himself, "Should I shoot? Should I pass? Should I press my opponent?" Of course this was not the same and yet the puzzle was being challenged in an active manner.

One day he was reading through the sports section of the *New York Times* and came across a forcefully written article. "NYU enters into a very aggressive expansion program in Greenwich Village." There was a noted lawyer, Martin Lipton, who was steamrolling this expansion with the help of the university's president, John Sexton. While many of the faculty members were against this move, it did not deter Lipton from plowing ahead. The article went on to say that NYU is the largest private university in the country. Larry looked over the names of some of the individuals on the Board: William C. Rudin, Barry Diller, as well as Kenneth G. Langone, co-founder of Home Depot. The group wants to add roughly two million square feet of space in the Village and six million overall. The article affirmed that the cost of attendance is about $64,000 per year and it ranks among the country's most expensive colleges and universities. Since Mr. Lipton took office, the board has raised $5.97 billion dollars. At the end of the article it stated that the university had the approval to build a huge athletic facility on the West Side of Manhattan. This large building would house a basketball court with more than 10 thousand seats. Larry shook his head in wonderment.

"Why would they build such a place when they are a Division Three team? But I guess once a school gets started, there is no stopping it. Wow! This certainly puts it on par with any other school in the country, but why is it doing this?"

During his second year he had his first sexual relationship. As he was a prominent player, the students all knew him; and as his image as this jock became more pronounced, he found he was esteemed by many women. Usually, he ignored this attention; however, in one situation, he found the young woman unusually attractive and she invited herself to dinner with him. He gladly accepted and they had an intense conversation about life and one's hopes. When the night ended he asked her out for another date. This time she had other ideas and after dinner she invited him back to her dorm room. While he was sitting on a couch next to her she sort of snuggled up to him and the next thing he knew he was lying next to her in bed with no clothes on. And his genital desires just took over. He had this powerful attraction toward her and his sexual energy swelled over his entire body which led to his first sexual encounter. Afterwards he couldn't wait to see her again and they met early the next week and he found her to be just as amorous as the week before.

When he called for another date, she became hesitant, and said that she would have to call him back. He felt as if a strong wave had smacked him in his face; he couldn't understand her uncertainty, why she vacillated so. When he hung up the phone his heart sank like a lead balloon, he felt he was in the midst of a minor crisis. He wanted her so and yet she had changed before his eyes; he felt so rejected and she seemed so indifferent. He couldn't understand the transformation. Unfortunately, what he didn't know was her fear of her parents. They would never approve of her going out with some-one who was not Catholic; she was not sure if that they would have made an exception for a Protestant, but it did seem that way. And someone who was not Christian was considered an alien. How could Larry have known this when she never told him? What she did tell him was that she was not able get into a committed relationship, which didn't make much sense either. Larry never implied that he wanted such a relationship. What he did want from her was sex, pure and simple, but that was out of the question at this point. So he just suffered quietly and played basketball.

In the following year he entered into a relationship that became much more meaningful for him. Laura, who became his girlfriend, looked up to him, especially the fact that he was on the team. That made him a kind of celebrity. And she could see the two of them raising a family in the future. He told her that he loved history and found it to be a great major. She heard this in a different way. She figured that when a person majors in history he then intends to go on and get a law degree, which excited her. And she knew his father was a lawyer. Finally, she brought the matter to a head when she asked him his exact plans when he graduated. She felt as if it all was too vague.

He realized that he had to tell her his honest thoughts, hat he was planning to try to become a college coach. At first, she said nothing but shook her head in an affirmative manner. The next time they got together she confronted him. "From what I gathered from talking to people I don't think I would like to marry someone whose job would mean moving from one city to another."

Larry wasn't sure how she could jump from their dating to getting married. He wondered how she could come to this conclusion though he may have indicated that he really liked her, however, that is a long stretch to getting married. But then Laura was a determined woman who had the very sense of achievement that he had thought about before. She didn't leave much to conjecture.

Well she went on: "I was told that coaches keep trying to move up, and that means either leaving one college or getting fired from the college and then going on to another. This is not the way to raise a family. Do you want to take your kids out of one school and register them in another? I don't see the stability in this or in the permanence of your job. I always thought you would become a lawyer and we would settle down in a big city and live a good life. I think it is clear that our relationship could not survive this conflict. A woman who is married to a coach has to be ready to submit her life to her husband's."

Larry was a bit flabbergasted. They had gone out for less than a year and she was thinking marriage. Yet he could envision being married to her also; she had her two feet planted solidly on the ground and knew where she wanted to go. This could be a good thing for Larry, but not as she envisioned it.

Obviously, Laura could not see herself in that position. She was born in New England and would have moved elsewhere, but not often. She told him that she didn't countenance a life of coaching where there is a constant movement from one city to another. They had long discussions about their life together, but Laura was not impressed with anything he said about it. The life of a coach's wife was almost offensive to her. If you have children they have to keep entering one school after the other, she continued to say. Finally, by his senior year, they broke up – they both were relieved with their decision.

In Larry's last year, Iona had one of its best seasons. The team competed with Manhattan College as winners of their respective conferences. It was a well-fought game and Iona just managed to pull it out with two important free throws at the end of the game. The college team then received an automatic bid to the NCAA conference. Larry was ecstatic, as this was a dream that he had harbored almost all his life. And now he would play in the most exalted conference in all of college basketball. But Iona was placed near the bottom of its region which means that the team would have to face the top contender in that particular regional playoffs. He knew who the top teams were and he prayed that they could manage to get a bit higher in the standings, so that their opponent wouldn't be that tough. However, this was not meant to be.

When Larry looked at the opposition, his stomach fell, as did those of the rest of his teammates. They were to play North Carolina with that intimidating coach, but you play with the team you have and not with the team who want to have. And he realized that this could be the last game he ever played in college. So why did he have to draw North Carolina?– but then the players talked among themselves. Would it have been any different if it were Louisville, Kentucky, Michigan State, or even Duke or Kansas? No, it was just Roy Williams that bothered him; and he hoped he could muster enough mental toughness to play one hell of a game. That was his intent, the directive that he gave himself.

The regional final was in Philadelphia which was great for being so close to home. However, it also wasn't that far from North Carolina, which meant that there would be a lot of screaming fans from their school. Someone told him to wear ear plugs but he didn't find that too funny. Iona's coach, Cluess, brought his team together in practice and took time to point out Carolina's weaknesses and strengths. The team wished they could see more of the weaknesses because the power of the team seemed awesome. The players were bigger, stronger and faster. This is not a combination that is too easy to overcome. But they worked on strategies for holding down Carolina. In one of them they took a page from Pitino's strategies. They would pick up their men as they took the ball out and not wait until they crossed mid-court. Hopefully, this would slow them down and maybe wear them down.

Finally, the day of the game approached. They had come down to Philadelphia the night before to get the most rest they could. As they took the floor to have a shoot around, Larry glanced over at North Carolina's players. They looked like a bunch of bulldozers, but hell, when he looked at their season's record they weren't world-beaters but they had come up against some very tough teams, certainly tougher than what Iona had been pitted against..

"Well boys, it has come down to this. We have had one great

season and we are going to take it down the line and see what we are made of. North Carolina is a damn good team, but they are not invincible and they have been beaten quite often this year. One problem is, of course, their height advantage, which could mean a problem with rebounds and taking it inside. We have to pray that we can make our outside shots and I think this is where it brings us. As I said before, we need to pick them up as they take out the ball so that they are not able to set up their plays. Anything we can do to offset their offense will be one for us. Okay, let's get on with it!"

As Larry came out on the floor he remembered that his parents were sitting up there somewhere and that his friend Paul and his parents were also there at the game, together with other friends and, of course, his high-school coach. The arena was packed and the bands were blasting their team songs while the attractive coeds were dancing their different numbers.

"What a night," he thought, "this is the zenith of my career, playing in the NCAA tournament." A dream that he had all his life was finally realized. And then his mind raced forward to the possibility of what an upset could mean for Iona, for their fans and for the parents and friends sitting up there with their hopes so high that they would reach the sky.

As expected, North Carolina controlled the jump and swung into action. They were going to work it into their big men and take over from there, and that's how they scored their first basket, right underneath the rim. Iona brought the ball up, Larry got it at the top of the key and tried to dribble forward, but to no avail. He tossed it to his teammate, who threw up a three that went in and Iona led 3 to 2. But that was the last time they would lead in the first half and by that time the score was 31 to 20, not exactly a wipeout. In fact, he thought everyone should be proud with the way the Gaels of Iona were playing.

Now the second half started and Larry scored immediately after getting the ball, on a short jumper. He had already tallied 12 points which kept his team in contention. But North Carolina was just too strong and they wouldn't give an inch. He looked over at Coach Williams and as he suspected, the guy still didn't smile. The score ended as a 62 – 50 loss and Larry was the high scorer with 23 points. Not bad he thought, he wasn't really so disappointed as he thought he might be, because he felt as if they did better than predicted. "I guess," he said to one player, "might makes right. But we played one terrific game. It's the same issue all over again, the height advantage. I hope it doesn't plague me all my life."

As usual, the players lined up to shake the hands of the winners or the losers. As Larry was going down the line, he spotted Roy Williams at the end of the other line coming his way. "Well," he thought, "I finally get a chance to shake his hands but what do I say to him?" As Williams came down the line, Larry extended his hand, which was taken by Williams, and then he said quietly, "Great game, even though you were lucky." Williams evinced a broad smile as Larry muttered these words and then walked right by him. Larry thought the whole game was worth this short episode: he had got Williams to smile at him and then he wondered if he were ever to meet him again. "I hope so," he said to himself, "this is where all the action is."

Once in the locker, Coach Cluess congratulated his team. "You guys have nothing to be disappointed about, you played them right up to the end of the game. It was only at the end that doubt about who was going to win emerged. But before that we gave them a game we both won't forget. And remember we had one great season, tops in our conference and an NCAA bid. This has a lot of meaning for us all, and the sorry thing about this game is that we are going to say goodbye to three of you guys and we are going to miss you."

He came up to each player who was graduating and put his arms around him and then came to Larry, the last one, and hugged him as hard as he could. He had a special affection for him and now wanted to see what he could do for him, but that would come later.

Now in his last year, Larry was immensely popular and he knew that he had made the right decision in coming to Iona and was able to make the starting team. He was a leading basketball player and a guy who talked in this wonderful, uplifting language. By this time he had memorized so many platitudes and quotations from famous people. Also, most students found him a pleasure to be with: he had an all-around knowledge of politics, history and, of course, sports. He was asked to give one of the graduation speeches at Iona along with the valedictorian. At first he felt hesitant but then thought it would be a great privilege and thrill to speak in front of the entire student body and, in addition, to talk of his ideas of life to his parents and others who would be sitting there.

He began to plan what he wanted to say and in particular what themes he would use. He remembered giving a talk at his elementary school graduation. The more he thought of it, the more he came to realize that it would be better to refrain from delivering one of his sports-related premises or theses. No, it would be more inspirational and stirring to choose a topic that would arouse and stir a larger element of the audience: something that would give meaning and depth to both students and faculty. And then he thought further that it would not be a bad idea to weave in some features of a religious nature. This was a college founded by the Christian Brothers and it stood for solid stuff. Now he himself was inspired by this feature of the college. So he isolated himself quite often in the library and started to work on this speech. He decided that he wanted to give it depth, intensity and wisdom, something he had learned after four years of study. And he hit upon a subject immediately. He would talk about the meaning of life within the context of a mission to follow throughout one's existence.

And then came the day of graduation. It was a cool, rather wistful part of spring. The mood of the day gave rise to a reflective, almost melancholic aura surrounding the entire proceedings. Slowly and quietly, the graduating students filed into the stadium and took their respective seats. The president addressed them in a fine, serious and forceful expression of his faith in their success. After some other short remarks, Larry was introduced with rather glowing remarks. He got up from his chair that was positioned on stage and came to the microphone. A quiet, solemn mood descended on the audience. This was certainly a somber moment in the graduation. And Larry took out his prepared comments and laid them flat upon the lectern, then looked up, managed a broad smile, and began.

Throughout the four years that I have attended Iona College I have searched for clues into the mystery of how a successful future would look.

There is a book that I read when I first came here that has changed my life irrevocably and forever. It required great energy, patience and time to read, one with much meaning and very deep content. Then I put the book down and it sat on my shelf until now and then I picked it up again and took prolific amounts of notes.

*This book is about self, about becoming the true you and living your life optimally. This is not a pep talk really or a psychological breakdown of how to boost your self-esteem. The book is **The Seven Habits of Highly Effective People** and it's about understanding where you can and should be taking yourself in your life.*

The influence, the support, the understanding, the energy that Dr. Stephen Covey discusses comes from within yourself. You create it; you live it; it becomes you and you become it. You create yourself, you build upon yourself and you become an effective person in your life through learning to help yourself and others. You learn how to graduate from dependence to independence and then even further on to a higher level, interdependence—all by looking deeply within yourself and following seven sound principles that are laid out in a very logical, rational and emotionally sound manner. The principles behind Dr. Covey's ideas are based on faith in self, community and God. He helps you to understand the philosophy, "Love Me for Me."

In it he also talks about a Personal Mission Statement. This is a project that you create, write, rewrite over and over until it describes the person you most want to be. Then you simply spend the rest of your life living those beliefs until you become that person. It is probably the easiest, yet most difficult thing you will ever do in your entire life. Why? Because you must devote your entire life and energy to this task. How easy it is to become side-tracked into old habits of comfort. This is a difficult road to follow. It is also, without a doubt, the most rewarding activity you will ever do in your entire life. After all, the most rewarding things in life are often the most difficult. In this process you will find that you will be driven by a dynamic energy that promotes your personal calling in life.

The part of ourselves that embodies this calling has been given many names, and I think the term soul *best describes this invisible force. This soul guides us and serves as a blueprint for our destiny; it counsels, navigates and motivates us. It is composed of your particular DNA, talents, skills, and interests and propels you down specific paths, steering you in your travels on this earth. It cares for you, takes an interest in your endeavors, loves you if you'll permit it, and appreciates your struggles. If you pay close attention to its message, you will be repaid many times over. But there's a cost for listening and paying heed to your soul, for once you affirm its existence you have a responsibility to nourish it and follow its calling. And the way you can do this is by developing and pursuing a personal mission in life – that's the debt you're required to pay in exchange for being given this unique existence. You must give that soul a life through the pursuit of your personal mission.*

Life becomes an adventure when you're living out your mission, an adventure both striking and risky. It's a challenging event, a contest. Whether that contest is with yourself (such as learning to fly a kite), with others (when playing a game of soccer), or with nature (mountain climbing), the point is that you're playing your game and success comes in playing this game to the fullest.

We've all had moments when we've felt as if we were on an adventure. At various times and places we've strayed from our usual need for protection and trusted whatever was going to happen. Living the adventure became all consuming. And during those times, our actions told a story, one with purpose and vitality. As we are entering into adulthood, we will have fewer adventures than we did as children. If we are really fortunate, our careers, or marriage take on the nature of an adventure. But what if were able to live our entire lives as an adventure? That's what a personal mission is all about: putting adventure in your life, then playing your game as well as you can. It's the game you were meant to play.

Everyone can have a mission in life, but few people actually do. Instead of looking to the stars, many of us go through life carefully watching our feet to make sure we don't stumble on something. While that may be the safest strategy, when you're focused on your feet you're unaware of what lies ahead, be it an obstacle, a door to open, a vista, a delight, or a pathway to the heavens above.

It is essential to stop every now and then as you travel through life in order to take a look around. Only when you are aware of your surroundings, aware of the world you are walking through and of your place in it, can you choose your direction, your path, and, most important, your destination. You must stop now and then to read your map and make plans. Which trail will you choose? Will you journey east or west? How fast must you go to get to the good resting point by nightfall? If you head one way you will be forced to climb a steep cliff, if you go another you must ford that icy river. Or maybe one path leads to a beautiful waterfall, while another ends at a gorgeous and serene lake. Both are lovely, but you may only be able to get to one.

Do you know where you're going in life, why and how to get there? Have you ever asked yourself this basic question: What is my personal mission? You've probably asked yourself what you want to be when you grow up. But have you also asked who you want to be? How you want to be? How you're supposed to tackle your tasks, how you should think about what you do every day; and whether you're headed in the right direction? Or have you, like most people, simply been watching your feet stumble along some arbitrarily chosen trail of life, wondering why you haven't really found success?

Unfortunately too many of us allow ourselves to drift with the currents of our lives, and with the lives of those around us. But you need to make a conscious decision to choose your path and your destination; if not, you're at grave risk of getting lost along the way. On the other hand, if you successfully define your personal mission, you considerably lessen your risk of simply drifting through your life.

Those who create a personal mission have defined themselves and are on the way to find a deep purpose in life. Many of us feel we are not living the kind of life we wish we could, the kind we dreamed about when we were young. But we all have the potential to achieve and excel. Every one of us has latent, underutilized talents, strengths, skills and abilities. We all have within us the seeds of success and fulfillment. If you feel that you're not yet where you'd like to be, that you haven't accomplished many of your goals and aims, and that you have yet to find satisfaction and fulfillment, you must begin to create your personal mission now. It is imperative as you leave college that you learn to define yourself and your goals clearly, and start to move forward in pursuit. This will be your mission.

To get started on your personal mission statement, ask yourself the following questions:

- *How do you want to be remembered?*
- *How do you want people to describe you?*
- *Who do you want to be?*
- *Who or what matters most to you?*
- *What are your deepest values?*
- *How would you define success in your life?*
- *What makes your life really worth living?*

I would like you believe that leaving college is the beginning of your transformation. Think of the caterpillar in a cocoon. For every caterpillar, there comes a moment when it begins to feel an odd sense of discomfort, a tight feeling, an unbearable itch. It can longer stay the way it is; it must either shed that tight, dry covering or die. This trans-formation occurs when the cocoon splits and the caterpillar emerges as a butterfly. The butterfly is free and fluid, gliding through the air. The butterfly can be florid in color because it does not fear being caught or harmed. The butterfly is authentic in its new being

But becoming a butterfly means that many things must be left be-hind. The butterfly glides through the air, but no longer has the ability to walk upon the earth. Finding and living your personal mission is much like this process – it means giving up the old ways of reacting to life and adopting new ones. But while the old ways may have been good for the caterpillar, they will only hold the butterfly back. Adopting a mission in life and undergoing a personal transformation means we must dare to fly where once we walked. Good luck on this endeavor, God bless you, and thank you all for giving me this opportunity to address this wonderful audience.

The speech was well received. His parents were proud of him. They could see how he had grown from that little kid in the play-ground to this adult who is able to speak to the entire graduating class and keep his audience so attentive. His entire stay at Iona was one wonderful adventure to him. He felt that he really matured and now he firmly knew where he had to be going and realized the challenges that lay ahead for him, but he understood that he had to weather the possible storms that he could encounter. "No," he said to himself, "this is not going to be easy but I believe I have the stuff inside me to see it through." Then he felt how wonderful and excit-ing the world he was entering could be and "at least I am the only guy here who is getting paid." With that he and three of his friends talked into the wee small hours of the morning.

CHAPTER FIVE

First Job: Assistant

Initial Triumph

Larry at 22 was a wide-eyed hopeful young adult who felt that the world was just one big celebration and he was invited to the party. He could hear the ringing voice in his head, "Come and get it." He just needed the right luck to come his way. There was that pull of his adolescence, the idea that hip guys don't wear ties and go to a 9-to-5 job or come home at night and spend it with a woman, his wife, or family. He didn't see the fun in that and it was fun that was at the bottom of it for him. He loved hanging around with the guys, especially his two friends from high school, but he hadn't seen them for a while. One was graduating from Middlebury and the other from Boston University. Of course he had a testosterone level that pushed him toward women, but remembering his history, he would stay away from any commitments. And there were women who felt the same way, so that worked out for the best.

But he did worry about himself. He remembered seeing two movies, *High Fidelity* and *Diner,* and almost saw parts of himself in these renditions of life, even though they were a bit exaggerated. But he never ran out of stories and thoughts he would relate to his friends. They could talk all night about movies, politics, history, and of course, basketball. He could be really honest with these guys and one night he almost broke down when he told them that he thought his playing days were coming to an end. He felt as if it was becoming too hard to compete with guys inches and pounds bigger than he. "Screw it," he admitted, "at times you just want to have the stuff to go above the other guys, to slam the ball into the basket or to post up with the opposition. I don't feel I can really do that and I am always playing from a lesser position. It almost starts out that way when I begin the game–whom will I have to guard or who is guarding me? And if it isn't their height advantage, then there are the extra pounds they have over me. I just don't like it anymore. I know I can't make the NBA and I have little interest in competing in Europe."

Finally, Cluess, the coach, called him in to his office. He talked to him about his future and congratulated him on his graduation speech. "Good talk, you really inspired them. But now let's get to the point. You know there is a loose association of Catholic colleges that form the nucleus of Jesuit and other representative religious associations. We try to stay in touch with one another, which is never easy, but it's a social thing. Well I heard through the grapevine that there is an opening for an assistant at Scranton University, I think I mentioned it to you before but now it sounds like a reality. Sounds ideal for you if you could get it."

Larry pondered this idea for a few moments. "Scranton is Division Three, I believe, and I don't think they are really interested in building a good basketball program. You know I study most of the schools in the East and I believe that Scranton, while they may be good in their particular area, will never really amount to very much. Secondly, how do you recruit for a Division Three team?"

"Yes, in looking at it that way you are right, but as I once told you, moving up in this field is often a matter of luck as to what is open at the time. The guy you look up to, Roy Williams, had this great spot at Kansas but then North Carolina just opened up and that is the way it is every year. The problem is that this is not one of the banner years for assistants or coaches, maybe unless you are Pitino's son or a Larry Brown who moves around a great deal."

"Well, I certainly would be interested if you thought I had the chance for it."

Cluess looked him dead in the eye, "If you want it, you got it."

Larry was dumbstruck; he hadn't known that Cluess would go that far out of his way to actively pursue the shot for him and he was touched by the effort that he was making on his behalf. "You have no idea of what this means to me and how I love you for your interest in my future."

Now Cluess went on, as there were other things he wanted to say to Larry. He then started: "From childhood to adulthood your life was consumed by basketball. Nothing else in the world distracted you, that is, you never took your eye off the ball. You never faltered and you rarely had doubts about your interest in the game. You never cry, but do you ever love. These are the integral elements of human experience and I am worried that your total commitment to the game has limited other parts of your life, the things that make for a more rounded person. In short, is basketball absorbing all your interest so that you move away from other important aspects of the living process?"

Larry thought for a moment, trying to take in and absorb what the coach was saying. "You think that I am too strongly concentrated on the game and therefore the rest of my life is paying the price for it?"

"Something like that. I know you have friends and I know you like women, but do you think that your more personal relationships will suffer because of this consuming interest of yours?"

"I thought of this from time to time, but I think that eventually my life will work itself out differently. I feel now that I must put in the effort in order to get me where I want to go. But isn't it the same for people who are studying law or medicine? They work around the clock."

"Yes, you are right, but not really the way you are setting it up. But hey, I just felt that I had to call it to your attention, but not as a criticism."

Larry nodded his head in agreement and then replied: "Thank you and I certainly will keep this in mind. However, I thought about this also. It isn't so much that basketball consumes me as it is that it has changed my life in a very positive way. It has given me character and promoted a serious commitment to life. As I think about it, I feel that the game has paved a way for me to live out my life. But isn't this the way it is for others who have found a serious place for themselves at a young age? I remember in elementary school there was a kid who simply had a real gift for the piano. Finally his parents put him in a special school where he could be on the path to developing into a classical pianist. I sometimes see his name when he plays in particular concerts. His whole life became geared toward the piano, and he was changed into this really serious dude. You know, it isn't the same thing when it relates to baseball or football, because you need a whole team to be able to compete; but in basketball you can play with four guys or six or just shoot the ball yourself. It certainly is an advantage. I am not a concert pianist or violinist, so let's call me a concert shooter."

With that they both laughed, and then Cluess shook his head, "Now get out of here, I've got things to do but I will call you later when I know better about Scranton – that's for sure."

Larry walked out of his office in a kind of daze. "Yes it is Division Three but Scranton has a good reputation and it is a fine school with high academics, which could be good or bad. My high-school coach and now my college coach have smoothed the way for me. I think I inherited this social gene which will prove to be very beneficial in the future. And they were right, a lot of this has to do with luck, but also with people who are willing to go to bat for you and this may be a very good beginning for me."

The next thing he did was to call his parents with the news. But they had barely heard of Scranton. Then he called his high-school coach who was very enthusiastic. Finally, he made a call to two of his old friends, who rejoiced at the news. In two hours Cluess called him and told him that they wanted to meet with him very soon and gave Larry the number of the athletic director. Larry called and made an appointment for the end of the week. Now he thought seriously, "Where the hell is Scranton?"

That evening he got together with Phil and Paul. He asked Sherman to join them, but he wasn't sure he could make it. They couldn't wait to get together.

"Well," Phil said, 'I just got accepted to Columbia for my MBA and I am just so happy to be going there. My work really paid off and now I am off and running."

Paul then entered into the mix, "Well, I am going to law school at St. John's and I am tickled pink. So Larry I will join the ranks of your father and become a lawyer, I don't know where, nor do I know what kind of law I want to practice, but I will have three years to decide that."

Now it came to Larry's turn. "I have been offered an assistant's coach at Scranton and I am off and flying."

"Where the hell is Scranton," piped up Paul. "I don't think I am aware of that school."

Larry then went on to explain, "It's about two hours from New York over the New Jersey border and though it is only Division Three, I feel it is such a great move on my part." He then laughed out loud, "My future is right there before me and at least I am the only guy here who is getting paid." With that the three friends talked into the wee small hours of the morning.

But Larry was concerned about Sherman, who never called back and never said what he was going to do. He had some pretty good years at Providence but that does not always translate into a job at the end.

When Friday rolled around he decided to rent a car and drive out to Scranton, which he was told could be as many as three hours from Iona. Yet he thought it would give him time to look at the area; and then he could spend time driving and contemplating what this move would feel like if he even got the job. The drive along Route 84 in Pennsylvania was picturesque and it took about three hours, which wasn't too bad, especially with Sirius radio playing such cool music. The directions were good and he found the building quickly. Scranton had a very warm campus and the buildings were quite stately. The rest of the town looked pretty run down, as he had read that it once was a coal mining region that fell on hard times. His appointment was for 3:00 p.m., which gave him a half hour to gain whatever composure he needed. And then he made his way to the room for his appointment. A slight knock and a voice that yelled "enter," and he walked in and met the director with a few other people. The director was a friendly-looking guy with a warm personality.

Then Larry found himself at the end of a barrage of questions that were quite easy for him to handle. The director, Fred, already had a whole bunch of recommendations from high school to college, so the questioning was more of a formality.

"Do you really want the job?" Fred asked.

"Yes, it would be a major move on my part and you know I grew up not far from here [in the Bronx???] and I think the way it looks, I will become part of the Jesuit system, which ain't bad."

Fred extended his hand, "Glad to have you aboard, do you think you could start at the beginning of June so we can get our recruitment in order and straighten out the salary and housing? I believe you will be happy with the arrangements."

"No problem, I am a free man as of yesterday, so I would like to get started as soon as possible."

Fred told him that he would have someone come up immediately to help him with the faculty accommodations, which he assured him were quite comfortable. "We treat our faculty with kid gloves around here, and anyway it will give a chance for you and Jack our coach, who was asking you all the hard questions, to get to know each other. How does that sound?"

Larry grinned, "Terrific!"

On the way out, Jack turned to him and welcomed him into the fold. Then he added, "I can see how you can be quite a salesman, but I guess that is the ballgame."

So now he was employed and on his way.

The drive home was very easy and enjoyable for him. Now his future was laid out for the next number of years. He really couldn't get the idea of what Division Three ball would be like and how difficult would it be to recruit for that division. On the other hand, there are many Division Three schools that field a team every year, so it must not be magic.

And then he skimmed through his life, remembering highlights of his playing days and the times when he scored a high of 35 points. That was a game where he couldn't miss anything that he threw up; and then he went through other games throughout his four years. Iona, after all, had not been a bad place for him and his high school coach had it all figured out. He wondered what it would have been like if he could have made Kentucky. Probably just the way Tim, his high school coach, would have predicted. I would be warming the bench rooting for the starting team, but here I was *on* the starting team. So is it better to be a starting player at a second rate school or a bench warmer at a first rate school? I'll take the first, he said to himself. There is nothing like playing and being the guy for whom the crowd yells: the guy they write about in the school newspaper and the one who is recognized everywhere he goes. He wondered how the players who rarely get into a game react when their team wins or loses. All you are really doing is watching your team competing as well as they can but without you. And then that last game against North Carolina. Wow! That was big time for us, but we really never had a chance against them. They all looked like Tarzan in Carolina uniforms. And Williams walking up the line to greet us and me shaking his hand; but they lost two games later. Could he imagine that he would ever play the likes of a North Carolina, obviously not where he is going but somewhere in the distant future – are his stars looking out for him?

He remembered talking about this idea of a soul and on some level he would have liked to believe this. Then his thoughts raced through his mind that this soul motivates, protects and loves us. When he got back to Iona, he went up to his room and started collecting his stuff that he had accumulated over the last four years. Then he took a break and sat down on this an easy chair to spend a quiet moment with himself. He let his mind drift off and connect to one of the speeches he would give himself: "And maybe this soul has to do with feelings of uniqueness, or grandeur and with the restlessness of the heart, its impatience and its yearning. Maybe there is this motivating force that is calling me to a destiny, and acts as a guide who remembers that I have a personal calling in life that must be pursued."

Then he went on giving himself one of his speeches. He knew he needed to tell himself these things so that other doubts would vanish out of his mind.

"These sports figures help me because I do believe that we all need extraordinary people in life who excite us and give our lives an imaginary dimension. They make us face up to certain realities, questions we ask ourselves: this is what I must do, this what I've got to have. This is who I am. Maybe there is a sense of fate in this, a personal calling."

In the few weeks that lay ahead of him before he moved to Scranton, he was absorbed by an intense feeling of accomplishment. He made sure his thoughts of grandeur didn't become too manic, but rather felt life was moving like an arrow shot into space; that he was pointed in the right direction and what the hell, the sky's the limit. His parents were very excited with the news, as if they had caught the whiff of success from him.

At his dinner with his parents, they couldn't ask him enough questions and what did they know about Division Three? They had barely heard of Scranton but seemed more familiar with a town near it, Wilkes-Barre, which had the reputation of being a bit more upscale. However, they remembered somewhere in the past a distant uncle had worked there, but it was some time during the Depression when jobs were hard to find in New York. But the mere fact that they had an impression of Scranton was excitement enough. Larry mentioned that the salary would be a modest one, but this was just the bottom rung of his upward mobility.

"Believe me," he assured them, "I'm going to climb up that ladder, but I had better be patient along the way, unless of course I see a clear path to move."

He then went on to explain what his job called for. "It certainly would involve an intense concentration on recruitment. This is the backbone of any team, without good players you're not going anywhere." And he found that he couldn't stop talking about his anticipation, and what this really meant for him. He told them how both the coaches from Roosevelt High School and Iona went to bat for him and gave him such glowing recommendations. This was so important for someone in his shoes to gain the appreciation of respect of the coaches he played for. And then he thanked his parents profusely for their support.

"You have really given me the stuff I need to make something of myself. It is this ability to get along with people, to gain their admiration, that I have gotten from you."

Of course, they felt so complimented by this, even though they didn't totally believe him. For some time, they had detected that their son was a kind of salesman who had the ability to hype himself to believe anything he needed to, in order to convince himself as well as others that he was on the proven path of success. Whatever Larry had ventured into, it was sure to be the best thing possible from Larry's mouth. After he left, they talked among themselves.

The point the father was making was that Larry didn't seem to possess what one would call a critical gene. If he did it or decided to do it then this would be the best path possible. Now they knew that down deep he couldn't believe all of this, otherwise he would be too naïve to be successful; so they figured this is just the way he had taught himself to talk. But then they agreed that there was nothing wrong with this; it could actually be of big help in life where there are so many doubts about one's motives and so many challenges to overcome. And it probably is all for the best when you are able to rationalize your actions and construct them as if they were God's gift to you.

But when Larry walked out of their apartment he didn't just feel as if he sold them a bill of goods about his new job. No, he believed it with all of his heart in order to make sense out of his life. The next day he arranged to meet his two friends from grade school. Paul's parents had already moved to the West Side of Manhattan years before, but Phil's parents had stayed in the Bronx. They both knew what they were going to do: they would be going to graduate school. As he remembered, Paul had gotten into St. John's law school and Phil had got accepted at Columbia for an MBA, so they had so much to share with one another. Actually, Larry was the only one with a real job, and they seemed a bit envious but they also expressed an expectation of their own attainments. They wanted to know so much about the new job at Scranton. In fact, over beers they talked into the early hours of the morning, calling their parents to inform them not to worry about their coming home late. Larry was going back to sleep at Iona so he seemed to be the free one: he was the one that had moved on while the other two would just have to wait.

Cluess, Larry's coach from Iona, was as elated with his success as if he were his parent and he was able to bask in his achievement. They talked for hours about the advice that he could lay on him, and about the kinds of difficulties he would face and what he remembered were the things that had helped him the most. Larry took it all in and shot him one question after another. Finally, he saved one question for the end that made him feel a bit uncomfortable asking Cluess.

He prefaced the question. "Look, I feel funny asking you this but I will anyway. Where do you think I could go after this? I mean, do you see a trajectory for me to follow? It is Division Three but I figure it is such a good break and of course I thank you for it. But how can you recruit for Division Three, or are the players just walk-ons?"

Tim thought a minute and then told him, "Believe me, it's not a bad beginning for you. Recruiting won't be easy and most of the team will not have been recruited, but you will pick this up. You really have given so much to our team, worked hard, focused on the plays, were a hawk on defense, and now you are being rewarded for your hard work. People like me will look out for you, because we believe that eventually when you get your own team to coach you will be just great. But as I once told you, a lot of this is luck – that is, who knows which positions are open at any given time when you are ready, and, of course, the contacts you are building up will be immensely helpful. Now, I can't tell you exactly in what direction this all will take you, but I will tell you that you should be prepared to move anywhere – that's the way this thing goes."

When Larry left he went back to his dormitory room and decided to look at Scranton's basketball schedule once more. It wasn't easy for him to decipher the teams they were playing because he barely had heard of many of them. He skimmed down the schedule: Moravian, Drew, Ithaca, Merchant Marine, Muhlenberg or Wilkes. Who are these teams and what kind of game do you play against them? But they did win most of their encounters, yet they lost in the NCAA Division Three playoff to Hobart. He had barely even heard of that school. Their schedule looked odd to him, but then again, he said they did manage to win most of their games. "That's good for a start," he thought, "and "I'd better stop looking over their schedule, it doesn't change."

Scranton proved to be a bit lonely for Larry. The other assistants were married with a family as well as most of the other teachers. And there were a few who seemed to be gay. The female teachers were not really approachable and the religion thing may have been an issue. However, he spent most of his time on the road, recruiting the best players that he could, and he was quite successful at it. He worked out a perfect pitch that he could give to the high-school stars whom he approached. And then he found a cute town about 40 minutes away called Milford that was also in Pennsylvania. On Fridays or Saturdays, one restaurant there had a most gifted cabaret pianist who really enhanced his weekend, and he would try to get over to hear him at least once a week.

The season was a lot of fun and, as he expected, Scranton could beat most of the teams they played. However, most of the games proved to be a bit sloppy. The passes weren't so accurate and some of the shots the teams took were really ill-advised. But he found that the team took direction and managed to remember most of the plays that were programmed for them. He also befriended a number of the players and they would spend a few nights together with just the guys. But he really did not find that any of these guys could take the place of the friends he had back in college or high school. The coach and he became quite close and they would talk about hoops sometimes late into the night. The one trait that Larry had - getting close to people– seem to follow him everywhere.

Scranton ended the season on top of their conference and then went to the smaller NCAA tournament. However, as had happened once before, they were defeated in their first game by the very team they had demolished earlier in the season. The coach and he made every attempt to cheer up the team in spite of their loss. And now he had some time off and didn't know what to do with himself. He thought of traveling but he had no one to travel with. He had tried dating a few women but they seemed too different from him. He didn't feel *simpatico* with any of them and started looking for groups that traveled together. He found one and then went to Greece and

Italy. On the trip he met a lovely woman and they hit it off quite well except that she lived in the Midwest and he really had no intention of carrying on a long-distance relationship. However, he felt as if he was in the early phases of his career and preferred to spend the major part of his week immersing himself in the intricacies of basketball.

In his second season, his team became even stronger, with some very good players whom Larry had recruited. They were taller and stronger than the previous team, but a number of the varsity had graduated. Toward the end of the season, the coach brought Larry into his office.

"I want to talk to you about something quite important in your career. Two assistants at Villanova resigned and I think I could get the coach interested in you if you want it."

Larry was dumbstruck. Villanova was a Division One team that played at a highly competitive level and already had won an NCAA tournament. This was big-time and the opportunity was amazing to him. "Of course, I would be interested if I have a chance at it."

"I think you have a very good chance," he replied, "I've already talked to the coach, who knew about you and had high praise for you. In addition, your coach at Iona threw in some great words. We both think you bring a lot to the team, and your work ethic is sometimes amazing. With that I will give him a call and see about an interview."

Larry couldn't believe this opportunity. In two years he would find himself in a Division One team where he would have the chance to really prove himself. He knew that this could eventually lead to a coaching position for himself. This could open so many doors for him. He felt so appreciated at this moment. We often have a sensation when opportunities befall us that the gods have paid us special attention– that we may be the chosen people of the earth. A break like this seems to be a message from the angels that we are so deserving and special. How could it be otherwise? In fewer than two years, he could attain an interview with a top team from a backwater program and continue to one of the major teams in the country. So when Larry received an email about an interview, he answered it immediately and they settled on a time. He then made plans to drive down to Philadelphia for the interview that could eventually change his life.

The interview went especially well. He found himself on a roll and just expressed some of the most insightful slants on basketball that he never even realized that he had tucked away in his unconscious. The coach, Jay Wright, was deeply impressed and quite taken with him. His love for basketball gushed out and it was clear that none of this was a put-on – no, these were deep feelings that had been nurtured since childhood. Jay then asked him about what he had found most successful at Scranton.

Larry thought for a moment and then went on: "Well I would chart the games. I found the list of stats very important. I tracked five categories that I thought most important. Blocked shots, loose ball recoveries, steals, tips from behind, and ball pressure deflections. I also tracked every offensive possession – who scored on what play, who missed, who rebounded; and I tacked every defensive possession. We would watch on video and analyze who ran plays correctly, who was out of possession, who took shots out of their range and who passed out of double teams."

Larry felt so good being able to express all of this from memory. He had never been put in the position of having a chance to express his main thesis of what needs to be engendered in every team if they are to be victorious. He was on a roll, and Jay knew it and was so taken with it that Larry was hired on the spot. He looked at Larry when there was a long enough pause and blurted out, "You're hired! You are an ace salesman, when can you start?"

On the drive back to Scranton, Larry felt a bit uncomfortable about having to tell the people at Scranton that he was leaving. Even though everyone knew that he had a good chance at Villanova, Larry still felt a bit funny. And then he realized how often this must happen to coaches. He knew it happened often at law offices, but often the lawyers never got so close to other people as they do on a basketball team. But he knew it happened in the NBA when players get traded or decide to go for a better deal. Still, he just was not that comfortable. Yet in a few days he packed and drove to Villanova.

Now he studied their schedule. They won most of their games; however, they never seem to do that well when it came time to play in the NCAA tournament. Getting to the tournament didn't seem to be the problem; yet their schedule was filled with playing a lot of weak teams– but that is certainly one way to stay on top of things. Now he was to go on some high-level recruiting around a huge geographical area. The coach and his two assistants felt as if they could compete with the best of schools, so they needed someone who could sell the team to the best players. They sat around evaluating all the players that came to their attention, especially from the McDonald's All-Americans, the ones who came to compete at the various summer camps; the best of the high school players. They carefully went over the stats of each player, their shooting percentages, assists, rebounds, and most of all whether they made the team better. Do they add to the chemistry and strength of the team? This is a difficult assessment to make but it is crucial for a winning team. You want players that add an important dimension to their team. And that's what Jay and his three assistants worked on and then it was Larry's job to bring them in.

And bring them in is what Larry could do best of all. He had developed into such a likeable guy that within a short time of talking to you, he had you in his confidence. This is a guy you would trust, look up, and follow; and he was just an assistant. And when recruiting he was very sensitive to how each person might affect the group cohesion. He just didn't watch them play, he watched how they responded to coaching, and how they responded to their teammates when they were out of the game. Is he listening when the coaches offer feedback, or is he staring in space? Is he cheering for his teammates, or has he checked out emotionally because his stats can't get any better on the bench? Larry knew that most high-school stars will not be as successful in college– that's just the nature of the beast as the level of play increases. Those whom he saw averaging 25 points per game become role-players, earning only a fraction of the playing time and adulation they were accustomed to at a lower level. He told them that a guy who averages two points per game can still make a big impact in the locker room. Each player must bring some value to the team. He also loved talking to the families of the players and felt so good in praising the school and the opportunities that their sons would have.

Larry continued to look for players with a natural proclivity for unselfishness: those who cared about their teammates and who get excited when they see their co-players succeed, and feel awful when they watch them fail. He knew it was up to the coach to shape this attitude, the chemistry that instills strength in winners. A coach shapes it with love and discipline in the right doses, with positive and negative reinforcement and of course, by example. Finding the right formula, with the right ingredients and elements, is the key.

The position at Villanova was just perfect for him. The recruiting and travel became quite heavy at times; he went from the West Coast to the East Coast as if it were traveling from Scranton to Manhattan, but he never minded it because he was so totally focused on keeping stats. The assistants had draft information on the basketball strengths and weaknesses of every player, plus analysis of how they would fit into their system. They compiled dossiers on every potential draft pick's life, right down to speeding tickets and parking tickets. Anything there was to find out about a young man, they found out. It resembled a private investigation into every player's background.

He was able to make some friends there, as it was a much larger school than Scranton and it was less parochial, so that he found it easier to date. His accommodations were more spacious and grand

and many evenings he just sat in his room and read or would meet some of the other assistants and go over some of the stats of the game. In addition, he got to like Philadelphia where there was so much to do and in addition there were many other colleges where he could socialize. Yes, he felt his life was just coming together. And of course some weekends he traveled back to New York.

Both Phil and Paul were doing well in their studies and they were almost through with the school year, but he was concerned about Sherman. They didn't speak that often anymore, but he knew that Sherman had taken a position coaching a high-school basketball team in New York. While he wasn't that happy, at least the position gave him security.

In one encounter with him they got into a rather unfriendly give-and-take.

Sherman had a need to defend himself: "The high-school job gives me a chance to lead a team and at the same time I can make a solid living. I mean, in about ten years I will be making close to a $100,000 a year and that comes with tenure so I don't face being fired."

As he talked he could hear the sentiments of his father, who had latched on to the Board of Education and in a sense they were both right in their thinking. This had been the right path for his father, yet he felt that it shouldn't be the way that Sherman should be going.

"Would you please tell me what happened at Providence?" Sherman shrugged his shoulder and answered in an annoyance. "I started to get into some mess with the coach because I felt he did not play me enough. I should have kept my mouth shut, but I was on some destructive path to undermine myself. I see it now, but I didn't see it then. Maybe it was just too damn good for me."

Larry was not sure how he could mend Sherman's feelings nor did he know what he could do for him.

"Look, the best thing we can do is stay in touch and I am sure we can find a way for you to get out of this—that is, if you really want to." They changed the subject and then went to dinner discussing a million other things. Larry knew that Sherman was just too good to be where he was even though he was not in that bad a situation.

In the summer Larry together with the other assistants went to sports camp, especially McDonald's, where they could observe each player in a game. Again they watched everything about a player, his moves, skills at handling the ball, his shot selection as well as his defensive capabilities. Of course, the biggest part of the job involved how they were going to actually recruit the best of the players: letter-writing, telephone calls, and making contact with those people who had an influence with players. By this time, Larry was getting a reputation as being one savvy guy: someone who was relentless, driven, and certainly determined to assemble winning teams, and in his second year, Villanova certainly shone. The team had height, brawn, and talented shooters who could win most of the time. However, they tended to freeze in the big games. This is when you can really gauge the talent of your team. As games get more important, some teams start to miss more of their foul shots, and this easily could be the difference between winning and losing. It was incredible the games Larry witnessed when the teams just couldn't make their foul shots. Now, we are talking about a two-to-three point difference. Larry also was very careful to assess assists and rebounds, the number of points scored speaking for itself.

And then Jay called him into his office for a serious discussion. "You know, Larry, when I hire assistants I am also hiring future coaches. It gives me immense pleasure to see one of my assistants get a coaching position. One of the most rewarding parts of my job is seeing the people I have tutored move on to have success of their own in our chosen profession. And I have come to realize that you can't be afraid to hire assistants who will leave you. If you are hiring people nobody else wants, how much good are they doing for your team? You have to risk turnover if it means you're bringing in quality workers. You are probably wondering what I am getting to, am I correct?"

Larry was sitting listening to this grand speech and at the same time was quite puzzled by what was underneath it. He certainly was not going to interrupt him, so he just kept quiet.

Jay went on. "I have watched these past two years and I have become very impressed with your work habits and the intensity you bring to the job. I think you have all the ingredients of a winner and you certainly are headed in that direction. Well, something important has come up, and I want you to consider it. The head coaching position at Fordham is open, and I think you would be perfect for the position. I know you come from the Bronx and you know your way around New York, because the job is certainly going to entail major recruiting if Fordham has any dreams of increasing their stature. Well, what do you think?"

Larry was almost in a state of shock; this opportunity seemed outrageous to him – this was the beginning of a dream future. He wasn't even 30 years old and already he had moved like a torpedo through the ranks of college coaching. He tried to shake off his sensation of too much elation, but he couldn't when he replied.

"I have only been here for two years–do you really think I have a chance for the position?" He never would have asked if Jay thought he wasn't ready for it; that has to go without saying.

"More than a chance, there has been much discussion about it. I will have to tell you that a number of people have been approached but turned it down. And then we went over your experience and it is all good, everyone has high praise for the job you did going back to high school. Others have turned down the job, but all the better, because now you could become the prime person for the position. Well, what do you think?"

"I am so overwhelmed and almost stunned by this offer that I will just say well, of course I would be interested. This would mean that a lifetime of hard work really pays off the in the end and who would argue with that?"

Jay ended the talk with these words: "Look, you sold Scranton, you sold me and I think you can sell Fordham. That's what this job is all about – selling."

The interview at Fordham went exactly as he had hoped. He was prepared for every question and then went into some points they hadn't even considered. He showed them by illustration his strategies for building a winning team and they seemed impressed. But they already had most of this information from the coaches at Villanova and Scranton. Toward the end of the interview, the athletic director told him that they were impressed with the commencement speech he gave at Iona. They asked him about it. Larry explained that while he was not religious he was spiritual, and then expounded on what he meant by spiritual. This impressed them and they told him to wait outside so they could discuss him for the position.

CHAPTER SIX

Coaching Position

Quest for Prominence

When Fordham called Larry back, they told him that the job was his and that they were eager to have him come aboard. He knew it had to be more than just luck, that it consisted of his hard work; and yet he had a sense that it was even more than that. He felt again that the gods above were looking out for him and somewhere he just had the belief that someone somewhere in the world was guiding him along a very successful path. He told himself that his soul must be looking out for him, directing him and keeping him on the right track. He was obviously being cared for and encouraged to continue on this course. He reasoned that it had to be more than luck, but he stopped himself before he became too carried away.

What Larry had overlooked was that he was more than just a nice guy; that people wanted to do good things for him; they wanted to advance his career. This is certainly an attribute that leads to being a winner. There must be something embedded in our character that gets expressed to others, yet it is hard to put one's finger on it. It's more than just that people like you, but a quality that would prompt them to want to do things for you, furthering your career, advancing your future. It acts like a confidence gene, positive and almost addictive, that has a strong influence on people who affirm, "I really like this guy and I want to help this guy." Many coaches have this quality. Just look at the life of Rick Pitino; at crucial times in his career someone stepped in and gave him new life. He moves from one college to another and people bid for his services. With Pitino as the head coach, recruiting becomes so much easier. Star players want to be on his team, they believe in him, they trust him, and they certainly feel that he can improve their game. This is the ingredient of all great successes yet it is not discussed too often because it is not an easy aspect of character to understand. Let's just say it is an irresistible part of oneself that gets projected to others, and in addition it becomes contagious.

Larry thanked them and then asked whether he could hire a few assistants. The athletic director smiled at the question. "Well of course you can, let's say up to two who you feel could help you in the game. That makes sense, if it is okay with you?" Larry thanked them, shook their hands, and walked out in a daze. This almost too much to absorb in just a few years.

Of course, Larry's parents were thrilled and proud of their son's new position. And this carried over to his coach at Roosevelt High School, as well as Scranton and Villanova. Everyone wanted to cheer him on – he had finally graduated to the top ranks of basketball, a head coach–and that was before he was thirty. He got together with his two close friends and that is all they wanted to talk about that evening, what he was planning for Fordham and how he would build that team into winners. As Larry told them, one of the drawbacks was moving back to the Bronx. He had hoped he would finally move far away from there but he reasoned, as he told his friends, "This was not in my karma, I guess that I am a Bronx boy down to my underwear."

On the first day up there in the north Bronx, Larry walked around the campus. It was certainly gorgeous, even though it seemed a bit isolated, but it was near everything he had known growing up.

"He thought to himself: "Iona, and now Fordham—I guess the idea of a Big Ten team is never going to be part of my karma." He knew he had one more important piece to work out, a piece that could make it all become one beautiful pie.

He called Sherman to get together, but as yet did not tell him about this new position. That evening they had some beers and he asked Sherman how everything was going.

"Well we had a pretty good year, and we won about half the games, but I feel that the players are not driven enough—they don't seem to have that will to win that I think we had. They are not hungry enough. But this coming year may be better: you can't believe I recruited this 6'7" monster of a guy who could really control the boards, so we'll see."

Larry then broke into Sherman's conversation. 'Look, I have not told you about me as yet. So here it is: "I was hired as the next coach of Fordham's basketball team. I was shocked when it was first presented to me but I am finally getting used to it."

Sherman reacted as if he had been struck by lightning. "Oh Lord, I am so happy for you, and you certainly earned it and now you are on your way up to the top."

"Larry made light of it: "Yes, it was one great break and I am slowly getting used to it, but it is going to be a challenge. Yet this is only one part of what I want to tell you. I can hire assistant coaches and I want you to come aboard, in fact, when it comes down to it, I need you."

Sherman sat back; he had difficulty finding the right words. "Thanks for thinking of me, but truthfully I am OK where I am now. It's really a good position but I am so overjoyed for you, I can't tell you how happy I am for what lies ahead for you."

Larry shook this off: "You may think what I am trying to do is for you but really I want you to do it for me. Yes, I told you about all the good things that have gone on in my life, but I've never told you about the loneliness I felt a lot of the times. The people I work with are usually good guys but I don't relate to them. In fact, at times I don't know where they are coming from. But I feel so close to you, ever since we faced off at that school yard over ten years ago. It would mean so much to me to have you come and help me. It's really been a dream of mine and now it can happen. How can you turn it down?"

The ball was in Sherman's court. "I don't know, you just come from out of nowhere and I really have to think about it."

Larry was not to be put off: "No you don't have to think about it, damn it. We can have a ball together, in fact, I started to like your music even though it's not easy, but that does not mean I am giving up on Sinatra." With that they both laughed. "No it would mean so much to me to be together with you, we need each other now, and I can't let you turn down this opportunity. For me, please come aboard."

What Larry did not realize was how touched Sherman was at the offer—so touched that he squashed an impulse to cry. He felt that other than his family, he had never known anyone who was so concerned about him, and here he was, a white guy.

"Come on Sherm, let's seal the deal and become masters of our souls." Larry kept on talking in an attempt to wear him down, telling him how well they got along and how their interests overlapped and that they wanted the best for each other.

Finally, Sherman interrupted, "All right already, how much longer are you going to go on? I'll take the job, though I may be crazy, and I'll see about a leave of absence. You can really wear someone down, but I know you want the best things for me." With that Larry moved across the table and wound his arms around Sherm, then moved back and said to him: "You have just fit the last piece to the puzzle and I am damned happy. Let's see, it's Thursday, let me meet you at Fordham so I can show you around. How is Saturday at 10:00?" Sherman moved his head up and down as if he were giving in to this powerful guy opposite him, but he knew this guy really wanted, if not needed, him and that was okay.

Larry sat in his room and had some papers in front of him and then started thinking as clearly as he could. He said to himself: "All one has to do is to look at the Atlantic 10 Conference to see how bad Fordham was, in fact they were in last place–and over the years have had one impressive statistic, and that had to do with their long losing streaks, not something to be proud of. Their last good teams were under the guidance of Digger Phelps who then left and went on to Notre Dame. They really have not been too effective since then." Larry knew that he had quite an uphill battle. He then had continual meetings with the three assistants, who accepted Sherman very positively; and they told him that the team lacked a spine, they didn't really compete, and possibly they were demoralized by the countless losses. Together they went over each player's stats, which didn't look so great. In addition, the assistants told him how difficult it was to recruit while the best players showed little interest in attending and in playing for Fordham. In addition to all of this, the academic standards at Fordham were pretty high, so that future players needed decent grades and SAT scores. There were scholarships available, which certainly was an advantage over Ivy League schools that did not dish out scholarships; and rarely does one of their teams ever emerge out of the pack of losers.

Larry got right to work. He realized that he was stepping into a program that hadn't had a winning season in years. He knew that if he didn't find a way to get the players to work as a team and become appreciably better in a very short time, then his dream of coaching was going to end up in a small college gym somewhere in the boondocks. From all that he had read, he knew that the great coaches motivated players to achieve victory. His goal was to help the players realize their strengths and weaknesses so that they could figure out how they were going to improve.

Basically, he had no illusions about himself, that he actually knew so much more about basketball than other coaches, or that he had a better strategy. All coaches work hard, put in as many long hours, and are just as dedicated. His one talent was in selling, that in the past he was able to get people to do things they didn't think they were capable of doing. Another talent was to get the teams to think of themselves as if they were a family. He knew that the road to success was to make twelve individuals into a cohesive unit. The way to get Fordham on a winning path was to engender hard work and togetherness.

And Larry was very good at lecturing the team on what he would call the basic victory plan. He tried to get his point across that success is truly a choice for the team to make. Each player must develop a certain discipline, establish a work ethic, create a sense of self-esteem. The team lacked an essential discipline; they had no plan, no vision of what's necessary to get from the starting point to the finish line. And it was discipline that Larry drilled into his team. He got each player to become aware of what he needed to do in order to get his game to a higher level. Each player needed a plan; there's more to it than simply making the effort. The effort must be one with a purpose, a sense of direction. He told them that the purpose they will develop is called motive. Once you have a strategy and are dedicated to fulfilling it, then hopefully success will smack you the face. And in practice he drilled shot blocking every day. Blocking shots with your left hand, with your right hand. They practiced boxing out on free throws and calling out their assignments. They did full-court ball handing drills, full-court shooting drills, three-point shooting, one-one-one moves: basically, every offensive drill he could think of.

The hardest part for him was in recruiting. He began to leave a lot of this to Sherman, who was fitting in so perfectly. Yes, he knew all the high schools throughout New York and who were their star players; but trying to get them to come to Fordham could be a tortured route. He knew he must improve the team in his second year and this could take just a few big guys. The rest would be up to him, to improve the team's chemistry and inject some important basic principles such as defensive alignments, picks and screens, and taking the best shots you can. But more than that, for each it was making his fellow teammates better and more effective players.

As difficult as this whole process became for Larry, it never detracted from his sense of achievement. He could refer to himself as a head coach; he would go to coaching conferences and present himself with the self-esteem that he had built up. And he had the facility for kidding himself in front of others, especially those who said they felt sorry for him because the bar to success was so high.

He would reply to questions about the problems that lay before him with some funny remarks: "You know, it's better to start at the bottom because it is only uphill after that." And he would go on: "The title of one of my favorite songs is 'I've been down for so damn long that it looks like up to me.'" And of course this was all said with a smile.

From the beginning of his second year, it was clear that the team was getting better. The practices that he put the team through started to pay off. He organized training time with a clear vision of what each player had to work on. There were specific shooting drills from different spots on the floor, with one of the assistants charting the results and the other assistant on hand to observe and critique. At the end of the workout, each player needed to accomplish a specific goal and have a clear picture of what he had to do in order to reach a higher level in his game. All workouts were charted so as to plot the level of improvement. And the wonderful part of it all was that he could go over the stats with Sherman, who was really becoming serious about this.

In the heat of a close game, thorough preparation is vital when performing under stress. Pressure usually brings out the best in a person. The coach with a thorough knowledge of his opponent and his own players will know what weaknesses he can exploit, especially when drawing up a last-second play. But the basic way for Larry to improve his team was to inject a passion, hunger and a drive in their quest to win. It is hard for coaches to have strong aspirations if their team loses too often. While Larry was ambitious and single-minded, losing could wear him down. But his determination to win rubbed off on the team. Thus, Fordham began to emerge as a daunting competitor and other teams took notice. He was written up in all the sporting pages and magazines as one guy who had a voracious appetite to win. And now it looked as if he were able to turn in winning seasons. His life as a coach at Fordham was secure and only good things were predicted.

So now he had spent two years at Scranton, another two years at Villanova, and he was into his third year at Fordham. He was approaching his 33rd birthday and the angels were singing his song, so he thought. The phone rang while he was in his office and his father invited him to dinner with his Uncle Sol, who just flown in from Israel. Apparently, Uncle Sol had made a fortune in the semi-conductor industry but at this point in his life, he was more involved with charity work. Larry had a deep fondness for Sol and he remembered him as the person who had introduced him to basketball and had taken him to so many Knicks games. For some reason, Sol was a devoted basketball fan who loved the sport almost as much as Larry. Larry accepted the invitation and was even more proud of his parents because they had moved to the Upper West Side of Manhattan; in a sense they finally made it. He liked coming down to that neighborhood and buying stuff at Zabar's and Fairway grocery stores.

Larry's father told Larry how well his brother was doing. He had a big job at some tech company and all his studies and hard work really had paid off. Larry was so happy to hear this. In some ways he missed his brother and he knew in the years to come they would become better friends. Bill was now married and had two sons and Larry was so happy for him. His father told him that Bill also felt so proud of Larry's accomplishments and wanted to get together very soon.

Over dinner, Sol told Larry that he had become a big contributor to NYU as he had graduated from there, and he had become involved in alumni business. He also invited Larry to an important dinner that was being held at NYU.

"Why would I want to go there? I have nothing to do with the school–in fact, I am opposed to how they are expanding in Greenwich Village."

"So what?" Sol retorted, "You'll be my guest, come and keep me company if only as a favor for me."

Larry accepted against his better judgment, but it would take him out of the Bronx and he always wanted an excuse to travel somewhere else. When he came to the dinner he could see that he was in the company of some heavy hitters. More and more he grasped an understanding of how the real big successes carry on, what they talk about, and the way they conduct business. He had first-hand knowledge of the way big-time, successful coaches presented themselves, so he figured it was similar to these very wealthy business men who knew the power they brought to the table. He saw immediately that these gentlemen got down to business and it all was a power play on their part. They knew they possessed he stuff needed to put their actions into play. The endowment at NYU was huge, graduate schools were expanding, hiring the best teachers was a reality, and the school appeared to him like one gigantic steamroller that was going to level out a gargantuan playing field. Who could stop this skyrocket from soaring to its goal? He thought in terms of basketball and wondered how the old NYU team could ever stack up against the University of Kentucky. They used to be winners and now look at them, just basketball midgets.

And then the discussion moved to athletics. An architect laid out the finished plans for the athletic field, capable of sitting upwards of 12,000 people, which impressed Larry. Then the athletic director stood up and gave a short report.

"What I am going to say, I want kept in this room." Larry had no trouble with that, because who would he be telling this to anyway? Then the athletic director went on: "We are in the process of moving to Division One basketball. A lot of us are not happy with the plight of NYU's basketball program. Although we had some good teams after the 40s, our major achievement was stalled back then. Some of us older guys remember Sid Tannenbaum, Dolph Schayes, Donny Forman, or Ray Lump, or even Satch Sanders, but what has happened to us since then? New York doesn't have a team that competes, maybe except for St. John's, but where are they going? No, if we are going to lay out all these big bucks, we want a team that we can be proud of, we want a team that captures the imagination of New Yorkers. I am tired of reading about UConn, or Kentucky, North Carolina, Duke, Kansas– and I can go on like this. When is New York going to enter into this mix? I know it is going to be an uphill battle but if we prepare for it we can do it. Nothing is going to stop NYU, that's a promise I am making to you."

At the end of the meeting, the athletic director came over to Larry. "We like the job you are doing at Fordham and your resume is quite impressive. You are going to get a winning team there and you should be proud of yourself. Now, how would you like to come to NYU as our next coach?" Larry was flabbergasted; why couldn't he have been told before by Uncle Sol so that he could prepare himself? He thought, "These guys are so filled with drama that they overlook some essential human behavior."

"Well this does come as a real shock to me and I would have to think it over. I have no idea what you have in mind."

"Of course we know, we just wanted to see if you were willing to throw your hat into the ring. We are interviewing a number of other people for the position and we will get in touch with you." Oddly enough, he never asked Larry whether he would be amenable to the position.

"Does big money really do this to some people?" thought Larry as he tried to put this in a reasonable context. Who could possibly entertain such an idea on such short notice?

The meeting broke up and Larry rushed to consult with Sol. "Did you know about this?" he asked him.

"Well, in a way I did and I was the one who promoted you and I thought you might get a kick out of how it was presented to you."

"A kick isn't quite the term, more like a collision of race cars." The director approached Larry again and proposed that they set up an interview, that there were a few people they were considering. Larry looked him in the eye. "Look, I am not sure I am even interested in the job, why should I rush into an interview?"

"It can't hurt, can it, and we would like that. I'll call you about an interview."

Larry felt overwhelmed by the whole tenor of the meeting – these guys stopped at nothing – they were born with a silver spoon and now they go through life gobbling up all that lay in front of them. But he did agree to an interview and of course told no one about it.

Larry was both excited and filled with fantasied hopes, yet he couldn't keep his doubts from surfacing. If he even got the position he would have to start from scratch, which would be a daunting proposition. But he remembered reading that NYU has built this huge athletic stadium on the west side of the village near the highway. And now he was told that it seated 12,000 people and it was a state-of-the-art operation. He thought further: "New York really doesn't have a class team. It was always a problem recruiting for Fordham with their campus in the North Bronx, and who else stood out? Columbia was low in the Ivy League, City College had given up Division One right after the scandals. St John's was a continual disappointment, which then left Hofstra, which struggled every year. And even in New Jersey, Rutgers was never able to do much. This could be a real challenge, but who even said that they would hire me, and why would I think I would even want the position?"

In a few days Larry received a call from NYU's athletic director, who introduced himself as *Robert Green*. "You know that now we are looking for a coach for our Division One basketball team, which you heard about at the dinner. Apparently, you have made a great impression from the number of colleges you have been involved with. We would like to meet with you and discuss how you think you would develop our team. That's if you are interested?"

"Well, I would certainly like the opportunity to discuss this with you and I would be more than willing to come down and talk with you." So a meeting was set up for the following Tuesday at 1:00 PM. Larry took the train down to Greenwich Village, got off and then looked around. He remembered the Village from his days of growing up in the Bronx. This used to be where all the action was and as he looked around it seemed as if the action were still there. There was just a bustle about the place, it always stood out as the *in* place in New York. And from all that he read, NYU seemed to planning to take over the Village. They were building everywhere, in empty spots or else ripping down buildings and then building their own high-rises. Because of this, they were facing real opposition from both the residents of the Village and even from their own faculty. But nothing seemed to stop them. They felt as if they had the right to do this. He looked around, "This is one power house," he smiled to himself, "Given the right chance it looks like they will own New York." Larry looked at the address again and found the street, then entered and took the elevator to the fourth floor and walked past the glass door where he was met by this Mr. Green. "Good meeting you, come on in."

Green asked him some *per forma* questions about his team at Fordham and then switched to discussing the issues surrounding their search for a coach. "Okay," Mr. Green inquired, "What makes you think you could do the job?"   Larry had prepared this presentation very well, going over in his head, point after point. He broke down the major issues in recruiting, how he would run the

offense and the defense but most Larry talked about the importance
of chemistry among the players and how he had created this at the
other schools. Green and his assistant listed attentively and broke in a
number of times to get Larry to expand his ideas. Larry realized that
they were quite savvy, probably from previous interviews. He was
very exact in his points, especially when it pertained to recruiting,
because he knew that's where the big obstacle would be. What class
player would be willing to come to a school that is in the infancy of
their its program? As he was talking he began to feel as if this were
not the right kind of position for him, and he was still young enough
to put in some very good years building a first-rate team at Fordham.
But what really grabbed Larry was his reading about the team in the
40s and the 50s. Sid Tannenbaum, Dolph Schayes, Donnie Forman
and Ray Lump. He was so impressed with New York City basketball
of the 40s that he had memorized their team as he had done with
CCNY, LIU, and St. Johns with Dick McGuire. He thought that
this was the stuff of legends. Could he really pull this off if he were
offered the opportunity?

After a few hours, the meeting was concluded. They thanked
him for coming and told him that they would get back to him – that
they would be interviewing a number of other people and would
come to a decision very shortly.

As he was getting up, one of the interviewers asked him what
he thought he would change if he came to NYU. Larry turned and
faced him with a smile that enveloped his face. He was waiting for
that kind of a question and thought that the answer he would give
would have to be impressive.

"Well," he began, "do you remember the movie *Shane*? Someone
asks Shane why he wears his gun high on his hip and he responds,
'Son, I've found my method is as good as any and better than most'."

"That's how I feel about my position as both an assistant and
the way I've coached. I feel my method is as good as any and better

than most. There's a lot of parts of that that I don't feel need to be changed, but other parts I am working on."

Larry left feeling quite good about the meeting. They were cordial and quite respectful. Maybe Larry's reputation was far greater than he was aware. Word does get around in this field and maybe he appeared better than he thought. He didn't really need the job and he could rationalize that if it weren't offered to him that it would be just as well, because NYU was starting at the bottom. At least Fordham was beginning to play competitive ball. And NYU had to get into a conference and have other teams willing to schedule it. When he came back to his apartment, he called his high-school coach and told him how the meeting went. They had a good discussion and then Larry asked him if he knew who else they were interviewing. His former coach told him about one major candidate they had seen, but that he was sure that the guy did not want the position. It was just too risky at that point in his life. The other two possibilities did seem to make sense, because the coaches involved were at the right time in their lives to move on. Larry then felt that it would be better to keep this from everyone, especially Sherman.

About two weeks later, Larry received another call from Green, who asked him to come down for another interview. He immediately thought that this was a positive sign, so now he had to come to terms with making the decision. He decided that he needed to meet with Tim, his coach at Iona, and go over the pitfalls of the job if he were offered it. Tim thought that this would be a major step for Larry, because NYU was such a dominating college, was loaded with money, and had built this beautiful facility. It held about 12,000 people and this could be a mecca of activity. In addition, if the team ever took off, they could play in Madison Square Garden or even Barclay Center, so all possibilities were covered. They then discussed the importance of this move at this time; and what if NYU never were able to field a winning team—then where would Larry be? Tim looked Larry squarely in the eye: "A lot of your decision will depend on your level of self confidence, how much you really believe in yourself and what is the quotient of your risk factor. It really gets down to that, so that it becomes a very personal decision for you. Are you ready to take on the big guys?" Larry thanked him, then hugged him and left.

He arrived at the meeting and this time there were three other men in addition to the two he had met with before. Now the questioning became something more of an assault. This was the moment of truth, and he knew he had better reply to their questioning and bring it right back to them. And he was proud of himself, the way he was able to recall statistics, the way he could break down plays, the manner in which he could show them how he recruited and his strategy for getting the players to feel part of a team. He showed them how he improved every team's performance when he came aboard, and that his trajectory was straight as an arrow. After a few hours, they suggested that he go out and grab some lunch and they would call him on his cell phone to tell him when he should come back. He walked out with his posture resembling that of someone who was going places. And this was not wasted on the people in the room. And then they started discussing him in detail. Could he really bring this program up to scratch in the least number of years— especially after the student body was informed that they were moving to Division one? There would be so much riding on this. Among the five in the room they took a vote and it came down to three for and two against. So Green asked the three in favor to press their decision to the two against. They went over Larry's references from the time he had played high-school basketball. It seemed that everyone who had had any contact with him only had high praises for him. That in some ways he was a born leader who was fired up with energy. He also took praise and criticism very well and never defended himself with apologies and never gave excuses. He backed up this high expectation of himself with the hard facts of his success. They talked for quite some time, while Larry in the meantime began to squirm seating on a bench in Washington Square Park. So he got up and walked around the Village. There was every conceivable restaurant and the streets were packed with strolling people from different age groups. He liked that and the action that went with it. There was so much going on and yet what he missed was some part of a bucolic atmosphere. If he were to change now or in the near future, wouldn't a university with large patches of grass and trees be a place to coach, much like Fordham with their large campus? But so far he hadn't been offered anything, so this might just be wishful thinking. Finally he sat down in the park and his eyes fell upon the Washington Square Arch. What a beautiful sight, what history. He remembered Henry James' writing about Washington Square. Growing up in the Bronx, Greenwich Village always loomed as this exotic, almost foreign spot on the face of the earth. He felt as if he were talking himself right into the job. Something was pulling him back to the memories of childhood – to the lore of forgotten recollections when he used to ramble through the streets of the Village as an adolescent.

While he was deep within the recesses of his mind his cell phone rang. He picked it up and heard Green's voice on the other side beckoning him back to his office. As he walked toward the office, flashes of his life passed before him. Where he had come from, and the places he hoped to go to; his dreams and of course his limitations; but were there really limitations once he stopped playing basketball? No, he thought he could get to wherever he wanted to go; he was primed for hard work and he knew he was driven to succeed. As he entered the room he saw the same five guys sitting in a semi-circle staring at him. He sat down in his previous seat and waited. Green paused and then spoke straight at him. "Are there any last thoughts you want to share with us?"

Larry paused a moment and then spoke: "I have no illusions about myself as a basketball coach. I wouldn't say that I know more about basketball than other coaches or that I have a better strategy.

I know that many other coaches work just as hard as I do, put in as many long hours, are just as dedicated. I learned long ago that coaches can be successful using many different philosophies and that there is no sure-fire method to success. I have been successful as a coach because I've been able to get people to do things they didn't think they were capable of doing. I've found that hard work and togetherness helped me soar to the next level. We can't win on the basketball court unless we have the right chemistry, and I feel that this is what I stress."

Green was impressed. This was the kind of guy he wanted, the kind of language that he admired, with the force that loomed behind his words. "Larry, we've decided to offer you the position as head coach. We hope you accept it and begin very soon. We will work out the salary at a later time, but we want you to know that the position comes with NYU housing, and, of course, all the benefits. So what is your reaction?" Larry moved up in his chair and as he shook his head he asserted, "I would be honored to accept the position and, as I said before, but I need a few days to give it my final thought. I just need to consult with some people."

Green accepted this, gave Larry a private number, and they arranged to talk by the week's end.

And then as Larry was walking away from the office, he did something crazy; he put in a call to Iona University and got the athletic department. When someone picked up, he asked if he could talk to Rick Pitino who recently became the head coach.

"Who is calling?"

"Tell him, Larry Evans, the coach of Fordham University's basketball team."

Within a few moments, Pitino picked up the phone and asked what Larry wanted.

"We met at a coaches' conference last year and you were very encouraging. I wonder Mr. Pitino, if I could have 30 to 40 minutes of your time. It is something important."

"You know how busy I am, but certainly I could do that. What's the question?

"Well I would like to come to see you for the 30 minutes, if that is possible."

Pitino shot back at Larry: "You used to play for this team, as I remember." Larry smiled to himself, "Yes I did; and I have fond memories of Iona and I hope you are successful there."

"Well thank you, and of course I am trying."

When Larry got up to Iona he looked around and felt quite nostalgic. He would always have a soft spot for the school and the surroundings.

At 3:00 PM he asked the secretary to tell Mr. Pitino that he was here. She called him on the phone and then told Larry to go down the hall and enter Pitino's office. He knocked on the door and then entered. Rick got up to greet him and then asked how he was doing and told him that he seemed to be doing wonders at Fordham.

Larry gave him all the details of his life, from Iona College, to Scranton, to Villanova and now Fordham. And then he told him about NYU and its upgrading to Division One basketball and that they had made an offer to him for the position of head coach.

Pitino grimaced for a moment. "Do you have any idea what the risk would be?" It could take years to get that program up to snuff. Why would you want it?"

"Well I've grown up in New York as you have, and NYU could be the biggest thing in the city to have a major presence in the country. No other team, including the one I coach, would come near it, but the doubt I have is whether this would be the right move for me at this time? And I've really come to ask you what you would do. You know they've built a state-of-the-art athletic field with seating for 12,000."

"I could see why it would be tempting. If you are successful you would be the biggest guy on the block; if you fail, then there could be excuses, but you have to consider how long it would take you to put a first-class team together. It would take a monumental effort to get that team up and running. Recruiting would be close to impossible at this point. And here you are the coach of Fordham with a team that has a history."

Larry looked toward the window, "Well, what would you do? This is really why I came out here, even knowing it is a bit preposterous for me to ask you."

Rick paused again, then got up and walked over to the window. He wet his lips and then continued. "I think if it were me at your point in life I probably would go for it. It has great possibilities, and from what I have read they have a big presence that could bring national fame. But that's me, and not you."

"I thought you would say that, especially seeing how you have moved around and changed teams but always seem to be going upward. I just questioned whether this move is part of my character, or whether I should just stick it out at Fordham and see what transpires. Thank you for your time, I appreciate it. I feel that you have answered my question."

On the train ride back to New York, Larry felt a huge sigh of relief. He had known in his heart that Pitino would say exactly that, and yet he had wanted, if not needed, to have it come personally from him in a face-to- face encounter and he had pulled it off. That was the last chapter in this decision.

When he came back to New York, he called NYU with his decision, and then went to the athletic director at Fordham to tell him about his future plans. Of course, he was sorry to see Larry go and they talked for quite a while about replacements. Then he called his parents and told them the big news. They were bowled over by it and why not? Then he called Uncle Sol in Israel and oddly got right through to him. Sol was ecstatic with the news, and he told him he was coming in soon to celebrate: "And it's going to be a big deal, I promise you."

Now it was time to tell Sherm about it and how he would replace one of his assistants with him. Sherman was a bit startled. "I've just become settled in this place and now we are leaving."

"Yes," Larry said emphatically, "We are leaving for greener pastures and we are going to make our presence felt in New York, that is, Manhattan. And the best part of it is that I am going to have you by my side and I am going to be by your side, so we are even. Please don't start thinking about it, it really is a great opportunity for us to move on. We'll have a ball in Greenwich Village, but you know something else? Apart from changing colleges, I've always felt some heavy cloud over me while I was in the Bronx. I want to get away from my childhood and witness other parts of the world; even though I may have had them in Scranton and Philadelphia, it won't be the same. "Okay," shot back Sherman, "when do we start?"

Larry signed the contract for three years and then moved into his new apartment. It looked great and Sherman's looked terrific also, so they both were satisfied. He walked around the Village with Sherman, feeling a bit embarrassed by what he felt were the riches of his new life. He remembered being told that Greenwich Village was one of the most expensive places to live in New York. And here he was in the center of all this activity. The athletic department was very friendly and he usually had dinner companions every night who were bright and sophisticated. He felt as if he had been elevated to a higher plateau in life. Most of the time he wanted to be alone so he could absorb the success of his new existence. He so wanted to prove himself and to be thought of as a leading coach. But he knew the importance of patience and how he must become almost obsessive in the quest to get good players.

The real excitement erupted when the school found out that their team was going for Division One status. Half the school hadn't come to NYU for their athletics nor were they interested in that sector; they had come for the intellectual stimulation and sports were seen as beneath them. College basketball was relegated to the Big Ten and the large state universities, but not NYU. This was the school for the intellectually privileged, the undergraduates who went in for the study of theatre and films, but not athletic contests. However, this soon gave way to the thrill and enthusiasm that sports brings to a school. In fact at the tryouts for cheer- leaders and the band, there was an overflow of students turning out.

Larry would often talk to Sam, the athletic director, about this. Sam told him that they were lucky to draw a few hundred at a game. And who knew what would happen?

Larry was annoyed at this thought and he fought within himself to cast it aside. He wanted to change the focus of the school, but it held the idea that sports were irrelevant. He used Sam as a sounding board. He needed to express his philosophy and impart to Sam the things that swirled around his mind. He looked straight at Sam and then took off upon one of the themes of his life. He had to unburden himself by launching into one of his pious sermons.

"I realize that some feel that sports are childish, or at best adolescent. When one grows up, then he ought to put aside the things of childhood, but what if participation in sports is the mark of a civilized person? What if it has an impact on our psyche? The serious ones say that sports are an escape; but I think work can be seen as the escape. History is an escape and there are many escapes, but the heart of human reality is courage, honesty, freedom and excellence: the heart of sports."

Larry paused in his overblown expression of faith in sports and looked at Sam to see if he had made any impact. Then Larry got up and walked around the room.

"Of course," Larry went on once he felt that he was in his element, "sports are not all of life. But sports celebrate many qualities in order to hold them clearly before the aspiring heart. What I have learned from sports is respect for authenticity and individuality. Each player must come to terms with his own true instincts and style.

"The mind at play, the body at play – these furnish our imaginations with the highest achievements of beauty the human race attains. Those who have contempt for sports, our serious citizens or students, are a danger to the human race, ants among men."

Larry started walking around the room totally absorbed in expressing this intense viewpoint. He almost forgot that Sam was in the room and then continued to take off on this thesis.

"I don't think that I ever met a person who disliked sports, or who absented himself or herself entirely from them, who did not at the same time seem to me deficient in humanity. What I mean is that a quality of sensitivity, an organ of perception, an access to certain significant truths all appear to be missing. I find myself on guard against them, and I expect them to have a view of the world that is far too rational and mechanical."

Sam interrupted him, almost laughing in the process, "Don't you think you are overstating your case and being a bit too flowery? Your thesis does border on an almost fascist mentality."

"Oh well, I told you how I feel about this and I used to stand up in class and bang away and the guys would go crazy, but the girls found it boring. Well, many women have had less access to sports and have been denied heroic modes of behavior. They would diagnose sports as a source of *machismo*, but isn't that like diagnosing love as the source of selfishness? Certainly without it the race would be much poorer, and those who attack it must weigh how much its loss to humanity would cost. I would hope that more women would learn to share in it, as many already do, especially with the prominence of women's tennis and basketball."

A slight sadness enveloped Larry as what he was saying slowly caught up with his emotions. He seemed to wonder whether he was fighting an uphill battle and possibly for the first time he would find himself in a losing position. Yet, he knew that the school would embrace his basketball team as much as he did.

CHAPTER SEVEN

First Game: Test Of Time

The basketball year started in a very precarious fashion. The team consisted mainly of hold overs from their Division Three category with a few high- school players who were walk-ons, but yet who were pretty good even though they were never recruited, but had decided to come to NYU and try out for the team. Larry was in constant touch with his two assistants, with Sherman taking the lead and Mike, the other one, who was a bulldog. They were planning plays, watching tapes, and meeting with the players. But underneath it all the team just didn't have it, there was no cohesion, no real regard for winning. In short, he looked at them as if they were a bunch of hicks who had to reach a higher level of sophistication or gain a deeper sense of who they were in the scheme of things. In short, the team was a wreck. Talent was in short supply and the players' conditioning was awful. The athletic department had warned Larry about the players. They were out of shape, lazy, and underachievers.

Larry knew that he was not expected to produce a winning team and the school knew that it would take some time to build these guys into a winning unit. But he hated to lose and that's why leaving Fordham wasn't such a hardship. As time went by, Larry began to feel as if he had made a mistake, that this job was going to be a bigger deal than he had originally imagined. He started going to high- school basketball games with Sherman, but many of the good players really wanted to get the hell out of New York, not hang around where they grew up. So he had to develop a more effective presentation, which was a real challenge. He needed to sell New York as the mecca of basketball, even though he knew Kentucky, Indiana, or even North Carolina would better qualify for that distinction. Then he thought back to that old conversation he had with the psych professor at Iona about the achievement motive; and he reverted to the sense that this was just another challenge to prove oneself and decided to leave it at that—besides, no one was complaining. NYU won two games that first year, and one was on pure luck. But then again, their conference wasn't that bad, certainly a better one than before with tougher competitors. Larry managed to get a few recruits for the next season so things could get better. But his first season proved to be a disaster; the team won only two games. He couldn't see how the next season would be any better, but determination and the inner speeches he made to himself saw him through the rough times. He was so thankful that he had Sherman, whom he used as a sounding board; but oddly, Sherman was not that negative–he saw the possibility of really capturing the vitality of the city.

Along about the end of his first season, his father called and invited him to come to dinner because Uncle Sol was in town from Israel and he wanted to celebrate. So they met at this very nice restaurant near his parents' apartment and he remarked to himself how much better it was now that he could visit them living on West End Avenue. When he came to the restaurant, there were his mother, father and Uncle Sol locked in deep conversation. Sol was so happy to see Larry and praised him on his new position. Then Larry during dinner related to him the difficulties he was having and how he was trying to remedy these problems.

Sol listened attentively, shook his head, then faced him and told him, "I wanted to talk with you for some time when I heard you had taken this assignment." Larry's father was very much interested in the conversation as was his mother. And Sol went on:

"You know I love the game almost as much as you do, but I could never play that well so I gave it up for a business career. But let me get to the point. There is a fellow in Israel who is a really dynamite player. He is 6'10" and he burns up the court. Now he is not a forgotten item–he is being recruited up and down the line. But I know that he could really get a team going: he plays a dominating role as center, can score, play defense, is fast up and down the court; and I think he could become a real presence for your team."

Larry had to smile at this description. Sol was so earnest in his belief. "Well," Larry inquired, "why would he want to play at NYU when bigger and stronger teams could make a better pitch for him?"

"Of course they could make a better pitch for him; but I know the kid and I have been helping the family for some time. Now that doesn't mean he is going to feel that he has to do this for me like it was some obligation, but I think I have this edge over the others–but first I needed to get your interest."

Larry shot back, "I have not seen a Jewish kid that tall, I think way before my time there was this guy who played for St. John's – his name was Harry Boykoff, who was 6'10"– but that was then and now is now. And I know you are going to bring up Dolph Schayes; but I think he went up to 6'8, and Barry Kramer was only 6'4". If I have to hear about these guys one more time…"

Sol interrupted, "Look, Larry, I don't know whom this kid is related to, but his measurements aren't supposition but fact. That's how tall he is and I wanted to bring this to your attention. So are you interested or not?"

"Well, of course I am interested, I mean who wouldn't be?– and he is still in high school, that is hard to believe."

"Come on Larry, Lew Alcindor was that tall in high school, why do you make it sound impossible? They want him for the Maccabi Tel Aviv basketball team afterward, but he has to pick a college."

Sol questioned Larry about genetics and then he launched into an explanation about what we inherit at birth. This also sounded like a talk that Sol had committed to memory. This was Sol, the failed academic, who in his own way could be referred to as a "know-it-all."

"I want you to listen as I tell you about the phenomenon called *emergenesis*. This has to do with what stuff you inherit from your parents. Think of our inheritance as a poker game. You might receive the 10 and King of Spades from Dad, and the Jack, Queen, and Ace of Spades from Mom, cards that had never counted for much in either family tree but with whose combination you might produce a new Olympic record. It is not just a pile of genetic stuff that makes for uniqueness, but the way your hand of cards fills out and forms a particular configuration. Who knows how you draw a winning hand? So that this kid in Israel must have drawn a full house or something like that, for all we know. But every big guy does not necessarily come from very tall parents. Now you may have drawn a good hand when it comes to coaching, but you certainly didn't draw an outstanding hand when it comes to measuring up in basketball. Do you get it? And to further the analysis, take a look at the horse, Secretariat, who won the Triple Crown and who sired as many as 600 foals, but none came close to his achievements. He must have drawn four aces, which is very unusual with one of the biggest heart measurements of all time."

Larry shook his head in agreement. "I think I once heard about this theory and it is a good one and I get it, so when do I get to see him?"

"When are you free to come to Israel? and it better be sooner rather than later. Otherwise he is going to be grabbed up." Larry thought for a while; this seemed almost too good to be true, and yet Sol was never known to exaggerate, and he always wanted to do the best he could for Larry.

"When are you going back," he asked.

"I'm leaving on Saturday."

"Okay," Larry shot back in this forceful manner, "I'll go back with you, I have a few days' break, and, to make matters better, I am bringing Sherman along so we can make a better decision."

They decided to fly back on Saturday and have Larry and Sherman watch the boy in action. Larry did not relish the long trip to Israel but he knew that people did it all the time, so what was the big deal? When Sam heard about it he thought that Larry was crazy going to Israel to recruit a player but he didn't balk at it.

They flew into Tel Aviv where Sol had made a reservation for the two guys at one of the leading hotels. They arranged to meet tomorrow at the gym's office in downtown Tel Aviv, walking distance to the hotel. The next day Larry got up fully rested, discussed the decision with Sherman, and then they had breakfast and afterward followed the directions to the office. When they got there, they saw Sol sitting behind a desk talking with the kid and when he[who? Make clear] saw both of them he got up to shake their hands. Larry looked up: he was impressed with the looks of this kid. He thought he could have played Gulliver, considering his size. Sol wasn't kidding, this was a monster of a boy. Larry introduced himself and then brought Sherman into the picture, but the kid shot back, "I already know who you are, and I guess you know who I am. So maybe we ought to get to the point."

Larry immediately sensed an arrogance about him, sort of a wise-guy attitude. This wasn't much different from the other Israelis that he had met, but this guy he could see could play it up.

So Larry went on, "I take it you are Yossi Bernstein."

"Correct, and I take it, you want to know how I am reacting to your coming here. This was all your uncle's idea, not mine."

"Well then let's get to the point of all of this, would you have any interest in coming to play for NYU?"

The kid smiled but the smile seemed to conceal a smirk, almost a profound disgust at being asked the question. "You have an expression that when one team leads by a lot of points, they empty their bench after taking out their starters. I think you refer to this as 'garbage time' or, with the accent on the first syllable, 'ga' bage time.' But this is how your team plays from the beginning of the game. Last year you were awful. You just got Division One status and I believe recruiting is one mess for you. Who wants to be on a team that is just starting out that could take years to get it right, that's if they ever get it right? I don't know if your uncle told you that there have been some recruiters who have come here to talk to me. I can't tell you who they are, but I can tell you that they have powerful programs and have been to the March Madness many times over.

"That's true," said Larry, "but you know NYU has a tradition from way before this. We used to be a class outfit and we are going to get there again."

"A class outfit? You haven't had a class team in many a year. Oh, you are talking about the likes of Sid Tannenbaum or Dolph Schayes. Yeah, I have looked them up, but they are like a Spanish Galleon that has sunk and no one has an idea how to bring it back to the surface. Old times won't work in this game and you know it."

"So what would you plan to do, go to Indiana or Kentucky or even North Carolina? A Jew doesn't fare too well in those places."

"Oh no? Lenny Rosenbluth, a Jew, was a leading scorer for North Carolina."

"Yeah, but that was years ago and after that the Jews went down like that Spanish galleon you talked about. But look, we are talking about New York, the capital of the world. You would be a celebrity there. There is no other team that would warrant the attention that you could bring. I haven't even seen you play and I am making this pitch."

"Wait," Jossi interrupts him, "Have you ever sent a player to the pros, have you ever won anything besides some minor tournament? Why the hell are you even talking to me?—because that sweet uncle of yours thought I would be a good fit?"

Sol was sitting quietly and seemed to be enjoying himself. It was as if they were rehearsing for a play and Sol was called in to assess its development. But it was clear he was not going to say anything. Why shouldn't they just work it out themselves?

"Have you ever been to Israel before?" asked Yossi.

"No, this is my first time."

"This is your first time and you are supposedly a Jew and you only came because Sol asked you to meet me. What does that say about you? You probably don't care anymore about Israel than you do about Ireland. For us living here this is sacred land and chosen people and we have to respect this. I think I am just another body to you, nothing more, nothing less, and you think that I am supposed to appreciate your interest in me. What interest, may I ask? I am tall and athletic, but that is your main interest as it is with the other recruiters; so I put you all in the same mix and that tells me that I should chose the one team that would do the most for me. And when I look closely at this mix, it surely doesn't come out to be you. I think you get my point."

"Yes, I get your point, but I want to tell you that there are more Jews in New York than Israel and that your presence could mean a lot."

"A lot to whom? The Jews are doing well in New York; they don't need a losing basketball team. To put it bluntly, I don't want to be a loser, I don't want to end up a loser, and I am carrying too heavy a load on my back. Why don't we just leave it at that?"

Odd that Sol sat quietly behind his desk sporting a slight grin on his face. Larry looked over at Sherman, who hadn't said a word but seemed to be enjoying the way the kid was talking. Larry wondered when Sol would jump in and take some part in this conversation that was not going too well, but it didn't seem too likely for this to happen. And then Larry began to feel that he was sliding off the board of reason – that he really didn't have much more to say but he knew that he had to push his vision of NYU's future onto this kid. All his strengths at being a first rate salesman eluded him. This began to loom as one of the worst recruiting positions he had undertaken and the other problem is that he has never seen the kid play. He was taking this on face value, both from Uncle Sol and some newspaper clippings about the kid's high-school activity.

The kid went on, "Look, I have to go now, and I am sorry that you had to make this trip for nothing, but many things about recruiting don't happen the way we want them to. I have a few good solid offers, so I think I will just play it safe and take one. Possibly I would like to discuss them with you so maybe after all you can help me—that's if you care to consider it, given how you have been treated here by me."

Larry had that sinking feeling that it was all over and this was painful every time he took a look at this guy who took on the role of some athletic monster. The size of him was awesome and if he were as good as Sol said than this would be a major coup. But the kid wouldn't budge, damn it. Just as all pleading broke down, Sol opened his mouth for the first time.

"Yossi, we have talked about how this arrangement could work out. I remember telling you about the advantages for you and your family and I don't think anyone in Kentucky, Indiana or North Carolina is going to have the same investment in you. Larry is a fine coach, he really knows how to sketch out plays both offensively and defensively, and he could really build the team around you. So let's say at the worst scenario, the team stinks to high heaven. But let's say that even with this rotten team you get to score big points and Larry would make sure of that. Don't you think you would be better off than playing some backup role for a good team from Kentucky? The press alone in New York would make you prominent. Big-time scorers from mediocre teams do better than mediocre scorers from top teams. This is fact, so let's talk about that."

For the first time, Yossi took a moment to take that in and, of course, all the things that Sol could promise him and his family. It seemed clear that the kid kind of leaned toward New York, but he needed to be talked into it; and Sol did it wonderfully. "Before we go further," said Yossi, "why don't you watch me play, otherwise we are talking to the wind."

"Great idea," said Larry and they then proceeded to go down to the gym floor where some of Yossi's team has been waiting for him while practicing. Larry was a bit puzzled that Yossi had planned this when he seemed to have no intention of going to New York. But what the hell, why look a gift horse in the mouth?

He looked at Sherman: "So what do you think? The guy could be one hell of a bombshell."

Sherman agreed but then said: "Yeah, maybe you are right, but the kind of aggression he seems to have would work better for the game. He is a real egotist who thinks the world of himself but then these guys are better players if they decide not to shoot all the time. Actually, I am enjoying this and the way he talked to you. I haven't seen this in some time." Larry shook his head and then walked to the sidelines to watch.

The teams took sides and began to play. Running up and down the court Larry began to see the power of this player as well as his vulnerabilities that would enable a somewhat-good player to heap on points against him. But he also saw the possibility of Yossi's taking charge of a team. His presence in the middle of the offense could strengthen his team's running their plays. And he was big and his body was solid. Well he was big against these players but how would he fare when he went up against players his same size? Larry thought about this; he wouldn't stand out so much, but then NYU's conference was not the strongest in the country. After 20 minutes, he pulled Sherman off to the corner and they both agreed that Yossi could be a real asset. Larry was ready to make a commitment to him. What he saw was enough to impress them and offer him a scholarship. So he signaled that he had seen enough. The four of them walked up to the office from which they had just come.

Larry started off, "I think you have the ability to really improve yourself and I feel that at this point we could really use you; and I am ready to offer you a full scholarship, that is, if you are ready to come aboard."

Yossi smiled; it filled up his face and it was clear that he felt appreciated. There was this glow that came over his body and it was infectious because Larry began to feel a similar sensation, as if they would enter this very wonderful enterprise together. But then Yossi asked for something else.

"I certainly appreciate the chance you are giving me considering that I can see that you have some doubts about my defense and my strength on the court. But I can work on these things. I want to ask you for a favor. I have a good friend that really no one knows much about." Now he turns to face Sol, and goes on, "The reason no one knows much about it is that he is a Palestinian and we have been close for many a year but have really kept it secret. We met when we played in Greece."

A look came over Sol's face as if someone just ran a dagger through his stomach.

Yossi went on. "You don't have to worry about him, he is 6'7" and can run as fast as anyone I have seen on the court. He jumps like a rabbit and he is a guy who is in constant motion on the floor. Unbelievable, but we needed to keep our relationship between us on the quiet side. We didn't want to upset our elders but I thought that I really would want him near me if I went to New York.

Then Yossi went on: "Omar is the only player of Arab heritage among players of Israeli Jews and Europeans. Basketball has not found a place in the Arab community as it does among the country's Jews. It's just not in their culture like soccer, in fact there are no courts in the Arab sector but for some reason, Omar loved the game from the time he was fifteen even though he couldn't find enough players to form a team. But he is damn good and I want you to see him."

Larry looked over to Sherman. "So what do you think?" Sherman countered. "What do we have to lose.?"

"So," said Yossi, "I could have him come over tomorrow and I promise you that we could play a game that would impress you."

Larry turned to Sol, who just twisted his shoulders and blurted out, "This is the first I have heard of this but I'm with Sherman, what do we have to lose, I have no beef with the Palestinians, it's only their leaders who are giving us all this trouble."

Yossi excused himself and went to the side of the office and called his friend's number. When he heard a voice come on he put his hand over his mouth and spoke slowly into his cell phone. After a moment or two into the conversation, he raised his voice, "Yes! Yes! Yes! You have to come here tomorrow. Do it for me." After a pause, a smile appeared on his face and he closed his phone. "Okay, Omar is coming at 11:00 tomorrow and we are going to play so you will see how we do. I think you will be impressed with him. See you then." And then he just left the office without saying any more.

Now Larry and Sherman were alone with Uncle Sol. "So what do you think of this glitch?"

"First things first," inquired Sol, "what did you think of him?"

"He has a number of good moves, he can really take up the middle and has the strength to power his way to the basket. He is a little lax on defense but we could work on this; but I want to say that as usual you have this keen sense of what makes a good basketball player. I hope you will be here tomorrow?"

"I wouldn't miss this for the world," shot back Sol.

Larry seemed pleased. "And now I am going on some tour of Tel Aviv with Sherman to see what Israel looks like. Yossi really insulted me when he asked if this were my first time I had been to Israel, not something I am proud of."

As they walked out of the office, Larry wanted to get more of how Sherman saw this guy play. Sherman told him immediately: "Look, he is big and tough, but every team has big and tough guys.

How he would stack up against a big black center is anybody's guess. They could eat him up alive, but then again they could provoke him to get better. I don't think this kid is the kind to back down so easily; and truthfully, I was impressed."

That afternoon they took one of those city tours of Tel Aviv and at the same time Larry knew he should really be seeing the whole country. He knew Israel was as small as New Jersey but he really didn't have the time and as he rode on the bus he began to feel a kinship with the people and the city. Ever since he knew he would be flying to Israel, he had started reading again all about its history and the wars that it fought with the Arabs. More and more he was proud of being Jewish, something he didn't feel too often. And those that said you must come to Israel were certainly right, this really brings you closer to the culture, the people, and the history of this miraculous country. And he felt a sadness to think that it all grew out of the ashes of the Holocaust, a country that rose to prominence out of the murder of so many of its people. He wondered, "What kind of justice is this?– and yet it may be the only kind of justice that one could contemplate. How else could Israel have become a nation? I need this Yossi more than I realize but I can't show him that; but let's see what this Omar has."

And Larry felt the need to engage Sherman in a more intimate conversation than they usually had. He asked him if he felt put off by being in Israel or whether he could feel the same way about United States as Larry felt about this place. They talked about it for some time, and Sherman was not sure where his family came from; he knew how they got here and that was tragic to begin with. He told Larry that he wished he had feelings for his heritage but it just didn't work and he thought that Larry never considered Israel with any special regard except now as an adult. "I don't think it works that way, we tend to forget our forefathers and I don't have to forget because I never had a memory, but I understand the need for an African heritage and why don't we leave it at that?"

Sherman told Larry that he would rather be alone that evening so Larry had dinner with his uncle Sol and they talked about their family and what brought Sol to Israel. He saw even more how different Sol was from the rest of the family: he was more politically minded and more thoughtful about life in general. He had always liked him, especially when he took such an interest in him and of course there were those Knicks games and now Sol might be bringing life to a team he had started to assemble. They parted warmly, and Larry walked back to his hotel thinking about the wonders of this newly found nation.

The next day the players, together with Larry, Sherman and Sol, assembled in the gym. The new guy Omar tended to be more quiet, possibly feeling a bit awkward with all these Jews around him, but then again maybe that was his character to begin with. This time their high-school coach was there and introduced himself to Larry and Sherman and they spoke while the players warmed up. Then he turned toward the players and chose up sides of 5 men apiece. He put Omar on the opposite team and brought the two players to mid-court, where he would have them jump ball. Omar faced Yossi, the ball was hoisted in the air, and Yossi knocked it to one of his men.

Larry watched the game intensely and saw what Yossi meant when he talked about Omar. The kid was in perpetual motion running back and forth, handling the ball well and always looking for the open man. He seemed to take on the role of the point guard, and that impressed Larry. His shot was just okay but he could leap much higher than a guy his size. In fact he was grabbing one rebound after another, but Larry could see that Yossi did not want to press him, so that he would look better than he was. But that was good enough for Larry, he had not seen many that he tried to recruit who could hold a candle to this kid. His athleticism was certainly better than what he had seen in the States. After half an hour, the coach called an end to the workout and now Larry pulled Sherman aside before approaching Omar.

"Okay, professor," he addressed Sherman, "Give me your take on his game."

Sherman replied immediately, "I can see this guy really motivating the game. He is fast and leaps high as hell. Reminds me a bit of Dennis Rodman, who wasn't afraid of being bashed in at times. And I could see that the kid thrives on competition and has strong athletic features, so I would go for him in a second."

Omar, Yossi, Larry, Sherman, and Sol retired to the upstairs room once again. When Sol closed the door, Larry began his speech.

"Okay Omar, I am not sure you want to come to the States, but Yossi feels that the both of you could work together and make quite a team. Sherman and I liked what we saw today, I think there are important skills that you are going to have to work on, but you really have the basics under wraps. Before I lay out the proposal to you, I'd better ask you what you think."

Omar talked with more of an accent than Larry would have imagined, but he was very serious-minded and insightful. "I want to get a good education and I know that NYU is one of the top schools in the country, if not the world. I would love to play with Yossi but I am worried that I am going to be lost in New York. I don't know my way around big cities, in fact I am not comfortable in Tel Aviv; but I think I could get over this."

Larry interrupted. "You would have a great deal of support in New York: there are Palestinian groups who would offer you much friendship, and there are 2,000 Muslims on the NYU campus who would reach out to you. I think that in no time you would find your way; and you will have Yossi, who feels so much love for you. We would need to start working on your game as soon as possible. I could offer you a full scholarship; and I truly believe that this is a once-in-a-lifetime opportunity. Now has anyone else come to you and offered you much the same?"

Omar shook his head and said that someone from Creighton

University had said they may be interested in him but he had no idea where the school was located.

Larry reacted, "It's a good school but it is isolated somewhere in Omaha, Nebraska. I don't think you would be comfortable there. It's almost like a foreign country." And then he broke out laughing, "I shouldn't talk, since I have never been there and it could be a lot better than that, but not anywhere near what New York is like."

They talked for some time. Omar had a lot of questions about life in New York, religion, and social relationships. He asked about the women, the drinking, and what he called the immorality of big city life. He thought that this could frighten him, but he wasn't sure. He respected Yossi and appreciated the fact that Yossi was like an older brother who always looked out for him even though they came from different and antagonistic cultures. The conversation went on for over an hour and then Larry laid out his plans and what he could offer Omar, who became quite impressed with the whole package deal. He looked at Yossi and kept nodding his head affirmatively, caught a very positive look in Sherman's eyes, then looked at Sol and then back to Larry and finally said, "I'll go!"

The room erupted into loud screams of joy and then Yossi grabbed Omar and twirled him around in a dance, hopping up and down. Larry cried out, "Yeah, yeah, let's go, Violets." Seeing that Omar had no idea about the reference, he spoke softly to him, "The violets are NYU's colors and sort of a nickname."

Omar responded "I get it."

When Omar left, Larry could now turn his full attention to Yossi. "How did you ever link up with Omar?–it seems as if it's an unlikely combination and yet you seem to be friends?"

Yossi began his explanation. "We met a few years ago when we both went to Greece to play in a tournament. There was something between us that seemed *simpatico* so we started talking together. I would meet him at a coffee shop and we could talk till 2 or 3 in the morning. We wondered why the Israeli-Palestinian peace talks always seem to go to the brink of collapse. We both had a deep understanding of the crisis. We knew the importance of a two-state solution. There had to be a Palestinian state in the West Bank and Gaza with borders on the 1967 line, and mutually agreed-upon land swaps that allow Israel to retain some settlements while compensating the Palestinians with land that is comparable in quantity and quality. The important thing is that Jerusalem will be the capital of the two states.

"We both felt that there would be no advantage for the Palestinians if Israel did not exist. They wouldn't make as much progress if that happened and for the Israelis, the Palestinians could represent a much-needed consumer population, and, in addition, they could be helped to advance themselves.

"But there is so much hatred and suspicion between them and this fuels the crisis. You can't have missiles flying into Israel from Gaza and not expect some kind of reaction. Omar and I agreed on almost everything and we found a kind of brotherhood between us. We realized that it would be hard to continue a relationship the way things stood, and we lived in different places, but we always kept in touch. And when Sol talked about my being recruited I knew that I could not agree to go anywhere that excluded Omar. We are a team and I am convinced that as a team we can do some good. Well that's the pitch. We just have a chemistry together; I know it's hard to understand, but I feel so close to him. I don't know if you get it or not."

Larry broke out in a huge smile and turned to Sherman: "I have the same feeling toward this guy over here and we have been friends and close for many a year, ever since, I think, we were fourteen... so I get it, and I hope Sherman gets it." Sherman replied immediately: "Oh I get it very well."

Larry nodded his head and then extended his hand to Yossi. "What can I say to this, you seem so vehement and I believe we'll work this out, I promise."

As Larry and Sherman left, Larry found it difficult to absorb what had just been thrown at him. How could he have figured that something like this would appear before him? This was really off the charts of any expectation that he could have imagined would happen. However, he did feel as if he had bonded with these two guys and that they respected him; that if he could get these guys to play together and integrate with the rest of the team, maybe he would have something.

So it was now June and he would have a good three months to get this team into a winning combination. For the first time since he was hired, he was able to conjure up in his mind some expansive thoughts that maybe this crazy idea of making winners out of a former Division Three team was not so crazy after all.

The one glitch in all of this was that some of the players who thought they had a lock on a starting position would be disappointed with Yossi and Omar coming aboard. But Omar would not start so that would leave explaining Yossi to the team. This would be a project waiting to be developed. He looked up and wondered whether it was a different sky up there. "I hope you are still looking out for me because I may need you more than I figure. Please guide me, I am going to need a lot of help," he prayed.

That remark by Yossi was unsettling: "I don't want to be a loser and I don't want to end up a loser." Someone who talks like this is so earnest in his pronouncements. "I have a job in front of me that will test every last part of my skills, my determination and my will to win. Well, buddy, you made a commitment to Yossi and this is your day of reckoning," said Larry to himself.

Larry and Sherman flew back on the following night's flight and straightened everything out with the athletic director. At first, Sam, the director, was a bit shocked at what he had accomplished but he did not feel that easy about the clash of two cultures and what this could do to the team or to any team. "Larry, it's as if we were treading on shaky waters; I hope you know what you are doing. If this kid Omar got a bid from Creighton maybe you should have let it go, they are not a bad team."

But Larry explained for the hundredth time that Yossi wanted him, that he felt as if he were a paternal guide to this kid, felt like taking him under his wing. "Besides," Larry persuaded, "What do we have to lose, it's one scholarship and one room with a bed. But I have seen him play and he has the potential to really drive the team."

"Yes, I realize that; but to have an Israeli and a Palestinian on the same team could create more problems that we are prepared for. It's a very volatile situation. It's not only the players, but how do you think the parts of the school that are Muslim and the ones that are Israeli are going to respond? They don't like each other and don't you think you are creating a rocky situation? But I realize that it is a *fait accompli*, so why don't you get out of here before you give me an ulcer, and good luck."

Later that week Yossi and Omar both arrived at Kennedy Airport and Larry was there with Sherman to greet them. He watched them walking out of the terminal. They were like little kids enmeshed in their glee, but their height made them stick out in the crowd. He looked again at the hugeness of Yossi and wondered how the hell he got to grow this way. And he wondered further whether he could really be a relative of Harry Boykoff, the St. John's center in the 1940s. But according to Uncle Sol who had seen Harry, he was one slow dude but few were as big as he.

Then Larry started to think of the big guys who roamed the court before his time. There was Bob Kurland, the first seven-footer who brought titles to Oklahoma A&M, and of course George Mikan, who everyone talked about in the books he read about the good old days. More and more guys got bigger, or was it that they may have always been big but they were hidden from view? But then there were Wilt Chamberlin and Abdul Jabbar. Funny, two white guys and two blacks.

And then he thought about himself, 'I'm a runt, but at least I can coach. Imagine if I were seven feet, although I am not sure I would want to be in that skin but hell, basketball isn't the only thing in life – or is it?" he questioned himself. And anyway, the average height in the NBA is 6'7" so another 5 inches wouldn't make a difference. Come on, you've got to make the most out of whatever you have, and the possibility is that this team might flourish and that would be the wonder of wonders."

At first there was a bit of tension when he introduced Omar and Yossi to the rest of the team. It was clear that one of the starters who thought he had a lock on starting would be replaced. So Larry called him into his office and had a long talk with him. He told them that he would have every chance to get into the game but that with the height of Yossi, it wouldn't make sense not to start him in the game.

"It also would be good for business to have these two foreigners as part of the team and would create a lot of hype." The meeting ended with smiles going all around. Larry had done some incredible work recruiting two particular players, Gilmartin and Johnson, both high-school standouts. He got them to see why going to NYU was in their best interest, whereas success in New York would be terrific for them. And they were two strong guards who knew how to distribute the ball. In fact they would be the real guts of the team. And Johnson was really working on his 3-point capability and was getting better and better.

So for the next month the team worked extensively on set plays and changing defenses. They studied films and dissected scouting reports, analyzing opponents' tendencies and foibles, their go-to moves in certain situations. Larry went over and over the kinds of strategies he wanted to employ, pointing out the difficulties and errors that he had witnessed. He stopped in the middle of one of his talks and said that he needed to point out something that was very important.

"Look, I have watched you guys very closely. There are some very outstanding deficiencies. You may not think this, but you must be able to dribble with either hand. You can't go for a layup on the left side and decide to lay it up with your right hand. That would be easily, so you must be just as proficient with your left hand as you are with your right one. You, of course, will find that putting up a shot usually involves one hand or the other, but not dribbling or laying the ball up. And I am going to have Sherman take this over... and he turned to Cliff, the other assistant, and told him to watch them on defense. Do I make myself clear?– this is what you need to practice."

He saw immediately that the chemistry among the team was not really jelling. "You guys just don't play together," he would repeat constantly.

This could spell trouble, because in a tight game his team could unravel. He wasn't really sure what was causing the problem, although he knew that he needed a sharp point guard to distribute the ball; but that could be said about any team in order to keep the tempo going smoothly. He realized that it must be something else–they really didn't like each other or rather were indifferent. They didn't seem to feel close to one another, or in short they hadn't bonded as a team. This may be the heart of the problem and this is one helluva situation to solve. Maybe if they all went out to dinner or hung out more, but that was unlikely, because down deep they really were very different in spirit.

There were an Israeli and Arab whose humor was so different from the rest of the guys. In fact, he wondered if they had any humor at all. He rarely saw them smiling. They were so damn serious all the time.

Then there were two guards, Gilmartin who was Irish and Johnson who was black from Harlem. But they seemed to enjoy each other and saw humor in many of the things that came up. The other player, Barnet was a black guy from Brooklyn and he and Johnson bonded well together – they shared so much in movies and music. Well music was another big issue, because they all had different tastes and it was a wonder that the three Americans could have come together from such different places. Obviously, Yossi and

Omar couldn't understand rap music or the kinds of sounds that came out of rock. Although they were drawn into it more and more, it was clear that this would always be a divide among them.

But then Larry thought about himself and how he seemed to incorporate the music of his parents, like Frank Sinatra, but none of them would waste any time listening to that old stuff. He thought way back when New York basketball was mostly a Jewish sport, there was much more harmony among the players, but that was before television and the expansiveness of the musical idiom. This issue of the cultural divide never had gotten to Larry before this, so it must have to do with the inclusion of the two guys from the Middle East. But many teams have players from Serbia or Africa and still bond together.

And of course the dating scene divided them entirely. It didn't seem as if Yossi and Omar had much interest in women, although Yossi was moving more aggressively in that direction, but Omar was a hopeless item. As time went along and July suddenly approached, Omar asked to speak with Larry alone. He entered his office and then closed the door behind him. Larry sat behind his desk and waited for him to speak.

"I'm unhappy and very lonely," he started. "I can't find my place here and I am homesick. Not that there isn't so much to do in this city but I find it so hard to get comfortable and I am beginning to have trouble falling asleep at night. I lie awake and think about my country and my family and the people I knew back there. In some ways I feel I abandoned them. My mother keeps writing that she misses me so and now she had gotten some education with the computer, so I get emails from her every day. First telling me what is going on and then telling me how everyone misses me. I can't stand this anymore, but what can I say to her to stop her from making me feel awful about what I did by coming here? I had to tell you this."

Larry listened very patiently and then spoke. "Do you have any idea what you could do to make it better for yourself? I hope you are not thinking about going back home, that would not be a good idea. We need you here, you are beginning to fit in so well and everyone likes you."

Omar waited and then spoke again. "Look, I am having troubling telling you this but now I have to mention what is on my mind. I certainly appreciate your bringing me to New York and putting me on your team. I'll always be grateful to you for this. But I feel so alone and I have to ask you this favor. I have a cousin back in the West Bank who I grew up with. Yossi doesn't really know him because my cousin Abdul was a kind of loner who never wanted to get close to the Jews. But he can really play basketball if he wants to. But now he's graduated from high school and he doesn't know what he desires to do. In short, he is a lost soul. But the one thing is that he is big like me. I think he is 6'6" at least, which is pretty big for an Arab, and it embarrassed him. I have tried to talk to him about his future and I think I am getting someplace with him but then he goes backwards. Basketball is the only thing he does that gives him any pleasure."

Larry listened attentively but at the same time wondered what was the point of this story. "So what do you think you could do, or how can you help him."

Omar waited for this opening and took it immediately. "Is there a chance you could recruit him for the team? I am telling you that he could be one good player. Maybe not at first, but if you give him a chance he would shine."

"Look Omar, I would have to see him play and then we would face the problem of whether he would fit in. Yes, we do have one opening for a scholarship but there are a number of problems. How do you know if he wants to come here? Also, you can't be sure that he could work well with this team. Have you even asked him about coming here?"

"Yes, we have been communicating often and I have finally convinced him that coming here would be a good thing for him; but I have been afraid to ask you, you have done so much for me already." A silence pervaded the room and the stillness between them evolved into a personal drama. Omar waited for Larry to speak, and it was clear that the tension had wrapped around him like a cloak. Larry breathed a quiet sigh and then got up and walked to the window before he answered Omar.

"Because he is tall doesn't necessarily mean that he can play well. One doesn't necessarily go with the other, but you have played with him."

"Oh yes, and I can tell you that he can leap higher than this ceiling and he runs as if he is in a race. I have seen him run so fast that he left the others way behind. For his height, there is something unusual about him, but of course you have to see this for yourself." And then Omar decided to push the point while he thought that he was ahead. "I could send for him: I think he would need a passport, and you could see for yourself. I would be so thankful if you would do this favor for me. It would mean so much for me and this may be a miracle for him. He is such a nice guy but so lost and down on himself."

Larry stared out the window, feeling a bit caught. If he said no then this could impact Omar and his game. On the other hand if he said yes and this guy couldn't make it, then it would loom as a major disappointment. And how would the other guys feel if I recruited him without ever seeing him play? They really would be annoyed at this. And if he were as good as Omar said and made the team, we would have three Middle Eastern players on the team. How would this appear when there are so many Americans around? This is not a black, white affair; this is the US and the Middle East. What would it look like? Fans would wonder what I was doing if I were to build a team with this kind of ethnicity. Larry felt caught and a bit annoyed that he was put into that place. Couldn't things just be easier? When Omar talked about this Abdul's quickness, Larry got turned on to the possibility that this guy could add some needed skills that they lacked. He felt as if he were a sucker for a tall, quick player and he knew he had traveled miles to see such players described to him, only to end up disappointed at their lack of skills.

But he contracted with Omar to tell the cousin to make plans to come here; and when the flight was decided he would be wired the money for the ticket. Omar was obviously so pleased he couldn't thank Larry enough, and told him he would call Abdul when he got back to his room. And Larry wondered – for a shy guy he certainly has no trouble asking for things.

Now Larry was worried at how he would approach Sherman. He didn't want to make it appear that he and only he would make all the decisions. Yes he was concerned about getting Sherman's approval; he was more than just an assistant, he was like an alter ego to whom he could express his doubts and concerns, and Sherman always responded in the most positive way. Now how is he going to feel when he pushed to recruit a couple of pretty good black players, a decision that Larry did not go along with? Okay for the showdown, he called Sherman into his office.

"Okay buddy," he started in friendly fashion. I think we are getting better and better, what do you think?"

Sherman looked a bit baffled: "We have gone over this a number of times and so why are you asking? Or do I suspect there is something a bit deeper than this?"

Larry started laughing out loud. "You really know me, don't you? Well, then I'd better come clean. Omar is miserable here and wants to go home." He knew he was lying but he went on anyway. "He asked for a favor and I want to play it off you. He has a cousin who he thinks is sensational and wants to have him come here. He thinks it would be a great fit."

Sherman took this in and then replied: "Another Arab on the team, how would this look?'

"Who cares," shot back Larry. "Winning is the only thing."

"Well," said Sherman, "If that's the case, we could have had these two players from that Long Island High School team but you nixed it."

"That's true, but we both really didn't think they had that work ethic. But this is different, it means keeping the team together; and you know that's our biggest concern."

'Okay, already, have him come in and we'll give him a tryout."

"That's what I wanted to hear, many thanks buddy, I'll get him here."

With that Sherman replied, "What's with this buddy routine?" He then smiled, got up, and walked out. And then came back a few moments later, "Oh by the way, I have a date tonight so don't call."

When Yossi heard about this he was annoyed. Yes, he was excited because he remembered watching this guy play; however, he didn't like the idea that two Palestinians would be on the team. He would have preferred another Israeli but that was unlikely at this moment in time, so he gave his blessings.

Two weeks later, the three of them drove out to Kennedy Airport to pick up Abdul. Larry waited behind the wheel with Yossi as Omar went to get his cousin.

"So what do you think?" Larry questioned Yossi.

"Now I have changed my mind about him and I want him to work out. We certainly could use his talents to build up our inside position. I remember his being very fast, but I don't have a memory of his playing ability, so I guess we have to rely on what Omar is telling us."

And then both of them caught sight of Omar walking together and laughing with his cousin. Larry looked closely and saw someone who looked almost identical to Omar except leaner, which was not necessarily a good thing. He could be blistered underneath the basket. But there was more to him: his gait was, and he walked with an assurance that impressed Larry. But who knows how he would react in a competitive game?

Larry got out of the car and approached Abdul and introduced himself. They shook hands and then proceeded to get back into the car and drive to New York. Along the way Abdul brought Omar up to date with what was going on in their neighborhood, leaving out any trouble between them and the Israelis.

After some time, Yossi came into the conversation and attempted to become friendly. But Larry could detect that there was an edge to their discourse, that Abdul seemed to be on the defensive. Clearly, he viewed Yossi as the superior one from the country that controls the destiny of the Palestinian people. How this would play out on a basketball court was the question that Larry was trying to figure out.

Larry handed Abdul to one of his assistants, Cliff, who would show him his living quarters, which were close to Omar's. And then Omar came into his room and they caught up on the missed time between them.

Larry gave them the next day off, but they were to meet the following day at 9:00A.M. When Larry got there the three guys were hanging out, chatting away. Larry proposed that Omar and Abdul go one-on-one. They started playing and Larry worried that Omar might let up on him to make him look better; but that wasn't the case–he played just as earnestly as he would in a real game. He watched Abdul jump high to shoot, drive toward the basket and try to block Omar's shots. There was certainly something impressive about him although he was a bit raw; his shots were not polished. He could see where he hadn't really practiced enough – he was just a bit too much of an amateurish player with so much confusion in the way he handled the ball. The question in Larry's mind was whether Abdul could shape up in the months to come. Larry called an end to the one-on-one and then decided to play a full court game and see how Abdul worked his way in.

The two opposing teams squared off with Yossi and Omar on one team and Abdul on the other. Actually, Abdul brought his game up to a higher level; his speed made up for a lax performance. In many ways Larry began to think seriously that this guy possibly could really improve his game with the right assistance. He thought of putting Sherman on him to get his game up to scratch. In fact, the more he watched him drive to the basket and leap for rebounds, the more he thought that maybe Omar was right all along. He would offer the kid a scholarship and a good place to live. Now the team began to coalesce and he figured that maybe by halfway through the season, he could look forward to winning some games, but that assessment came after his anticipation of another losing season. The three guys created an optimism and a hope for better things to come. Yes, this could be a possibility.

In the days that followed, they practiced with deep determination and intensity and the team, as well as Larry, began to see how their chemistry began to improve. They were looking for the open man and they were setting picks and screening for the outside shot. The two guards, Gilmartin and Johnson, were becoming sharp from the corners of the court behind the three-point arc. And Yossi was developing a strong presence in the pivot while Omar and Abdul were moving in sync from the outside corners. And the subs were coming around, especially Robinson, who was working out so well. Each player had a workout regimen in order to strengthen his body and firm his muscles. Larry was having them run the same drills over and over again so that they were etched in each player's mind He began to realize that maybe this was where he belonged all along, mapping out plays and devising effective strategies for winning.

Larry knew that he had to work with Yossi intensively because he was going to be the kingpin of the team. After one of their practices, he invited Yossi into his room and, sitting side-by-side, they watched a scrimmage. Larry turned to him and asserted, "Look at your feet, they are not in position." Then Larry got up and demonstrated the correct stance. They continued to watch the tapes and Larry again stopped the tapes and said, "Look at your hands, they are not ready." Yossi nodded in agreement.

Larry went on, "This is about precision and doing physical things to create better habits. This is how I coach the guys in the summer." After an hour he turned off the tapes. Yossi said that he was shocked that he looked so bad. Afterward the other players met him in the theater to screen some more of their plays. He demonstrated to Yossi multiple ways to maneuver without the ball into open spaces, encouraging him to let his instincts take over. "If you can learn to do this you will be very difficult to guard."

Later that afternoon Larry called a play that put Yossi in the high post. It was a test. Yossi caught the entry pass. He was immediately double-teamed, freeing up Johnson beyond the arc. Without hesitation, Yossi kicked the ball to Johnson who knocked down a three. "You see what I mean?"

One day, Abdul asked to speak to Larry alone, so they set up an appointment for later that day. Abdul entered his office and shyly opened up a discussion. "This is very hard for me to talk to you about this, but I don't know who else I could confide in." He then went on to express his problem "I have no experience with women and they are driving me crazy. Looking at them wearing their shorts and tight shirts, I can't think straight anymore. Back home none of this could have happened because the women wore their *saris* and you could barely see their faces. But here it is almost as if they are not wearing anything. And then there is this one girl who keeps coming up to me and asking whether I play on the team and about my history. I feel very awkward around her and I am not sure how I should respond to her."

Larry asked him some probing questions and of course he realized that he had never touched a woman, but had this high sexual drive that he couldn't satisfy. He faced Abdul and agreed with him that woman were quite liberated here and that men were put on the spot. "I think I'd better go over some of the basic moves with women, so listen carefully."

"When you get together with her, however casually, have some tea together. Then ask her out the next night for a light dinner. Not anything expensive." Abdul listened attentively, nodding his head. Larry went on, "After dinner, ask her up to your room and you have that couch where you both can sit down. Talk to her a while, tell her she is terrific and very attractive. Then after some time put your arms around her, show her that you are interested in her. If she is interested in you, the rest will take care of itself, you will see that yourself... and if what I have seen of you on the basketball court has any validity, then you will take control of the situation.

"I forgot to mention that if the situation between you becomes serious then beforehand you need to buy some condoms at the drugstore. You don't need expensive ones, just ones that will protect you from getting her pregnant."

Larry stopped at this point. "Has what I said become clear to you?" Abdul's reaction was on the money. Instead of responding with this sanctimonious seriousness, his face lit up with a smile; and then Larry knew that this guy is going to come around and become a real *mensch*. Abdul got up and extended his hand to Larry, thanking him for giving him the best words of advice. As he left, Larry wondered if much of the conquest were not on the woman's part. The man becomes a willing partner in the prelude of sexual strategies that made it look as if he were all-knowing, while all along it was the woman who was pulling the strings.

A few days later, Abdul approached him and asked to speak alone. Later that afternoon, he entered Larry's office and sat down. "I want to thank you for your instruction, it all went well except for a few things. She said that she takes protection so I didn't need any, but the problem was that after entering her it didn't take long for me to come. I tried to hold it off but I became so turned on that I couldn't contain myself. But she only smiled and told me that it was all right, that lying together was wonderful and she could tell that I was passionate." He smiled. "So you see it really turned out so well. As they say in the Jewish tradition, 'Today I am a man.'"

One late afternoon, Larry was leaving his office and as he turned toward the hallway he ran into a woman who immediately recognized him. "You are Larry Evans the basketball coach, aren't you?"

Larry smiled, "Yes, I am. I didn't know that I was so easily recognized, but it feels good." They started to talk and then they entered into a long drawn-out history of themselves. Larry had seen Ellen before but didn't know where she fit in at NYU. She was in the physical-education department and followed sports quite closely. She began to ask him some questions about the team; and Larry realized quickly that she was quite educated in this realm and then she told him that she had two older brothers who played the game and used to teach her about the foundations and elements. She then played a bit of basketball in high school, but an ankle injury had cut her playing days short. But then she focused on other parts of phys-ed. After almost 15 minutes of gabbing they parted and as she walked away Larry felt this surge of desire come over him. He turned quickly, yelled her name and then went up to her. "Why don't we have a drink some night so we can get to know each other better."

Her face beamed, "Great idea, what about Thursday at around this time and I will meet you right here. I have to be in this building also."

"Great," he replied.

As Ellen walked away, she felt a bit of remorse and elated at the same time. Almost three weeks before, she had been seeing this guy whom she had dated for almost two years. They had come back to her room and she felt a reserve, an almost withdrawn reaction in him. She had sensed this for the past number of weeks but found it hard to confront him about it.

But this time when they sat in her room he began the conversation. "I guess you have detected something that distances me from you. We have always been on the up-and-up with one another so I can't hold this back anymore. Last night I had a thing with another guy. I am not going to say I am sorry because I've had this urge for some time and he kept hanging around me until I just broke down and went to bed with him. In a nutshell, that's the story."

Ellen was obviously shocked to hear this. "Well, I would have been really hurt if it were another woman, but I don't know how to react if it's a man instead. Have you had men in the past?"

Joe went on, "Before I met you there were a few guys but then I felt that I wanted to go straight and that's when we met; but throughout our relationship I felt this pull towards men and I fought it. Now I realize that I really can't fight this urge, it is causing all kinds of stress, and hell, it isn't fair to you also, otherwise I would pick fights just to keep us apart–and you are really terrific, but Nature wins out in the end."

Ellen held her composure, it was clear that there wasn't much to be gained by further engaging in this conversation. She drew herself together. "Look, Joe, I am going to leave for about a half an hour, why don't you get together all of your stuff and leave so that when I get back you will have cleared out everything."

"Yes," he said in a rather dejected manner, "I guess that would be the best solution." And then she left.

As she walked outside she tried to put a better take on the episode. She thought she would feel worse than she did, but she realized that there would never have been any great future between them – this was never part of her fantasies toward him. Yes, he was a nice guy and very considerate but they really never had the connection that she wanted from a man. And then the last few months had been really draining. What will happen to him? she wondered… and then began to feel sorry for him and the life he would be leading. She had witnessed many gay guys who went through one guy after the other, and she hoped that this would not be his lot. But he could be different, however, and he might meet someone he would want to form a close attachment with. With all these thoughts, she knew that she didn't want to keep in touch with him. This whole chapter of her life had to be put behind her.

She looked at her watch and figured that this would have given him enough time to get his stuff and leave, so she walked back to her apartment. After entering she looked around, and saw that his photo was gone along with a few other items. Then she nestled into her easy chair and put her face in her hands and wept. She sobbed for him and for herself, and yet at the same time there was an experience of relief – this was a clean break, nothing was dragged out, so in the end she felt luckier than many women who went through tormented endings. "I guess I am one of the luckier ones," she said out loud. "Better luck next time."

When Larry met her at his office, she was certainly ready for another relationship but she didn't want to get ahead of herself. There was an ease between them, almost as if they were old friends. In their first meeting they told each other much of their histories. Ellen grew up in Long Island, her father was a businessman, mother a teacher, and she had two older brothers, one living in California and the other in the city. She felt close to them and would see them regularly at family occasions. She was going to major in history on the path to becoming a lawyer, but found that she loved sports, not only the playing but the study of it also. In high school, she coached volleyball and soccer and felt a kinship with the players. So she decided to come to NYU and major in phys-ed and then go on for a Master's degree. She wasn't sure what she wanted to do after this, although she felt that she did not want to teach in a small college in some remote part of the state. She loved living in Greenwich Village as well as going to the theatre, so that living here provided her with all the accoutrements of the good life.

While Larry was listening he felt drawn to her. There was something about her that was so attractive. He tried to put his finger on it but just couldn't get to the core. She had a particular stridency and talked with self-assurance. He could see how the years of sports had shaped her lovely body. And as she went on about herself he realized what was attracting him. There was a softness about her, not a weakness, but a tender manner—something yielding in her that would make it so easy to fall in love with her. He was a bit surprised that she was still single; but he realized that when all is said and done, many women carry a lot of baggage and who knows what lurks beneath that warm façade?

He almost told his story from memory: his disappointment at being limited in basketball so that he switched to being a coach and then finding such pleasure in it. Every game became a challenge and he found that he loved the stress of the competition and was a bit unhappy when the stress went away for too long a time, as it would in the summer. He told her that at first he had many doubts about coming to NYU because they had just moved up from Division Three ball, but he had decided to turn this into a real test for himself. As you can see, the first year was a disaster, he couldn't get his team to play together. Now this year could become one of the great turn-around stories of all time. Larry laughed when he said that, knowing he was being a bit dramatic but also feeling that it could be true. He couldn't believe that he was telling her so much about himself especially when this was their first date.

Often when couples meet initially they talk about a whole array of subjects. But Ellen became absorbed in Larry's plan to work things out for the team. He told her of some of his ideas and how these Middle Eastern players were going to dominate the play. It was just going to take some time to put the pieces together, but they'd already won two games and the pace was picking up. Ellen listened attentively, time was getting late, but she just felt as if she wed to hang on to his words a bit longer. He looked at his watch and realized that they'd better call it a night. She agreed and then he took her home.

At the door, he said that he really enjoyed himself and wanted to see her again. She agreed and instead of waiting for his call, they made plans to meet this coming Saturday. When she entered her apartment she felt that a whirlwind of excitement engulfed her. This made so much sense to her – what he stood for and what he was interested in, and how they could share their experiences.

On his walk home, Larry realized that he may have met the girl of his dreams. Her interest in basketball was for real, and yet at the same time it caused him some concern. Why is it, he asked himself that discussing sports with a guy is so very different from discussing it with a woman? Why doesn't it feel real enough? He knew that Ellen wasn't faking her interest in the game and that she loved sports to begin with. But it just didn't seem real to him and yet he knew this was just crazy; but he had to get to the bottom of it. If he discussed a movie with her, he would know that it was sincere and honest. So why not sports? Ah, he then said to himself, sports is masculine and women are feminine; and who leads the Connecticut women's team to the playoffs but a man, but who leads the Tennessee women to the finals, a woman. And could you imagine a woman coaching a men's college team?—hell, no– but it almost looks like most of the interviewers on TV are women these days, and they often ask more probing questions than the men.

He was having a good time with this so he went on in his mind about it. I can argue with a guy about teams or players and who is better, but with a woman I would feel annoyed if she picked out points that had escaped me. I think maybe one issue that women don't seem to care about is statistics, at least not in the way that men do. I think that maybe one of the differences is that they are not so concerned with a player's averages, or rebounds or assists. They seem to be more global, but do you really know this?– and he had to admit that he was not that sure. When he discussed old movies with some of his friends, some of them could remember things that would knock you out. Women would never get into a discussion like that, nor are they ever impressed with that kind of knowledge.

And then again, so what? Would you want to go up against Doris Kearns Goodwin in an argument about the Civil War? Hell, no. He hoped that he could lead Ellen into these deeper interests and have patience with how she grappled with them. He knew he did not want this relationship to go nowhere or, more positively, he wanted the relationship to blossom.

It didn't seem odd for them to see each other without any break. Neither of them wanted to bring this up to the other but neither of them wanted it any other way. They just enjoyed each other too much and then she started going to each of the games. Afterward they would talk about the game and he found that not only was she interested, but she was more than capable of helping him see things that he had overlooked. She became a real friend. Somewhere after the first month, they both realized that they had to bring sex into the mix. The last thing Larry wanted to do is to leave it to her to bring up the subject; and, secondly, it is not a subject you bring up for discussion, it is more an action-oriented thing, you just do it. Only older people talk about it first. And Larry made up his mind to go for it on this particular date. And Ellen was very receptive. The only concern that Larry had was bringing up birth control, but from all the lectures he attended he knew he had to. However, that went well, she was on the Pill. "So she has had sex with other guys, so what, doesn't this make it easier?" The big thing he found in the relationship was how well they shared things together. Forget about love, that's taken for granted, but sharing became the big issue for him. They talked on and on and were always interested in what the other person thought about. And the good thing is that she doesn't care for opera. He knew he could never make it through an evening of Wagner; one time was enough for him.

As we know, when matters go well between couples one of them is going to want to up the ante. It was never going to be Larry at this point; he could finesse change, but he didn't promote it. So Ellen brought it up after six months. And she was direct about it, but by this time she knew that Larry was hooked on her and possibly appreciated her as much as he could appreciate any woman. So she asked him point-blank, "Have you ever thought of living with a woman?"

He answered quickly, "Not really, I'm not sure it has ever come up."

Ellen pressed the point, "To put it bluntly, have you ever thought of living with me?"

"Yes, I have off and on."

Now she wondered, what the hell does "off and on" mean?—but let it go at that. "Well, would you want to?" she said more emphatically.

Larry was rarely at a loss for words, but this time he didn't know what to say. It loomed as one complicated piece of life that he wasn't sure if he was up to untangling. Wouldn't it be simpler just to let things go on the way they were instead of adding complexity to the mix? Yet he was smart enough to know that this was not to be, that it didn't make sense to have the relationship continue as it was without deepening it. Otherwise he would have still been an assistant at Scranton.

"Let me sleep on it, okay?—and we'll talk about it next week."

"Fine," she said, "no rush. This is just a thought and I don't want you to feel that I am pressuring you in any way."

"Actually, I don't feel that at all, you just happen to be more up front than me."

He knew he needed to talk with Sherman, who was becoming his father confessor. They met for dinner a few nights later and he launched into the subject of living with Ellen.

Sherman listened attentively and remarked, "So what's the big deal, you are in bed with her and this wouldn't be such a change. Besides you are old enough for it."

Larry felt a bit embarrassed by that remark. He had been feeling this way ever since Phil told him that he was getting engaged, and other people he knew were married. But he reasoned that this was the way they wanted to lead their lives. He reacted to Sherman, "Well, hell, you are still single–why haven't you lived with a woman?"

Sherman held his own: "You know, it never came up, but if it did I think I would go for it. Hell, being single can be a drag, it gets lonely at night. I have been wondering about this, but I want it for myself and now you are the lucky guy who has it placed in his lap. Besides, you seem like a horny guy."

Larry felt this sarcastic urge swell up inside him. "I am so lucky that I can always turn to you for your wisdom. I am not sure what the heck you are telling me but I know you mean well and I thank you for listening to me."

"Hold it a moment," shot back Sherman, "didn't you tell me that your friend Phil is getting engaged?– and I think Paul is seeing someone also."

"That's right, but I am not them!" With that they parted company until the next day when it was practice time.

That following week he made an appointment with the athletic director Sam, who told him that they were very pleased with his performance but it seemed as if there were something else on his mind.

"Look Sam, I have been going with this woman Ellen, whom you have met, for over six months. "Well she brought up the idea of living together and I wondered what you thought of it?"

"Well," answered Sam, "why would it matter what I thought of it?– this is your decision."

"Yeah, but how would it look, I mean the coach living with a woman?"

"So what, I don't think we get into morals around here unless you were sleeping with one of the coeds and then we wouldn't like it at all. But this is entirely different, so I think you ought to tell her your hesitancies because I think that is where it is, and you have become good enough friends, so tell her."

"I feel conflicted because I don't know how it would look to everyone. My team, fellow teachers, assistants, and even you? I mean I have never lived with someone before and it's not like we are getting married, but I wonder how you would view it?"

Sam stared him straight in the eye. "Don't you think you may

have a problem, some kind of conflict with this that you are project-
ing on to everyone else? That's what usually happens in these cases.
Maybe at Fordham I could see you being a bit queasy, but NYU is
in Greenwich Village, where you have every kind of sexuality going
on before your eyes. Do you really think that anyone would bat an
eye over this?"

Larry broke out with this wide grin, and he went on: "Yeah
you're right, I just couldn't get a handle on this, and it probably
comes down to my feeling guilty in the first place. I just hope it
doesn't screw up things between us?"

"I'll talk straight to you, I did minor in psych before I went all-
out for physical education. Guilt can really wreck things between
two people. You pick fights with the other person, you push them
away, or you find fault in what they do. So you'd better get a handle
on this or else put this living together in the future, otherwise you
may be in trouble."

Larry thanked Sam for his helpful replies and walked out in
something of a daze as if he didn't know what had hit him. "Maybe
I am not ready for living together at this time; but then Ellen would
be disappointed and I don't want to create that kind of situation.
Yet I don't want to walk around tense and all that – an idea struck
him that just seemed to solve the problem. This was to tell her that
it would be better when the season is over, because there are too
many issues on his mind and then who knows where NYU is going
to wind up at the end of the season. Yes, he thought, that would
take care of it and when Ellen heard the explanation she totally
agreed that there was too much on Larry's mind, so why add to it
with another burden? Of course, she knew nothing about the guilt
that Larry was feeling or the awkwardness that he could experience
once that happened.

The second season ended and NYU had won 15 games and
lost 10. What made Larry happy was that the wins came at the end
of the season when the team started jelling. It certainly was a vast

improvement from his first season and everyone congratulated him. He was so elated seeing how the chemistry of the team improved. They looked for the open man, set screens, and kept a quick motion. In fact, the players started caring for one another and would hang out together. This was certainly a decisive change, because it is hard to be a good team without a semblance of togetherness. And now Larry could feel that his hard work was paying off and he was excited about the next season.

He had noticed elements in Sherman's style that made him so happy. Sherman had this ability to make the players he was working with feel special. Rarely did he make any negative comments, but he dealt with the players' deficiencies in a calming, positive manner. And the players liked him a lot and usually went to him to ask him different kinds of questions. For a moment, Larry felt a bit envious, but then he snapped out of it and realized that the things he saw in Sherman were coming to fruition; and how astute he had been in seeing this in Sherman the first time they met. As he walked along the path in Washington Square Park he said to himself, "This guy has all the makings of a first-class coach and I am so thankful that we have him at NYU."

CHAPTER EIGHT

A Reflection Of Life

Larry was looking forward to the next season. He felt extremely positive but, more than that, he felt both lucky and appreciated, as if all the work that he had put in was paying big dividends. He started to put his life in perspective, a mental activity that he often engaged in. He thought about the right decisions he had made for himself, the paths that he had chosen, the people he had drawn around him, and the ethical and moral stance that he took when confronting the world. He was most proud of that last, and he wondered whether he could ever go off the beaten track and engage in behavior he would be ashamed of?

"No," he thought, "this could never be me. When I am recruiting some player, I would never begin to tell him all the wonderful things I could do for him if I thought any of these promises would border on illegal assurances. Yes," he said to himself, "I know that this happens all too often and has brought down some of the great coaches like Tarkanian of UNLV. And it all has to do with money, and I am so proud of myself that money has never motivated my life, not as much as success and winning. No, I don't think that winning at all costs is the proper prescription for life, but playing the game in a fair and honest way is the clear path you need to take."

He had been asked to address an alumni function at NYU and

he agreed to give a short talk. By now he was getting noticed around the campus and it felt good to have this recognition. He came to a large room where the alumni had assembled and was met by the president of the association. He gave some introduction and then Larry stood before the group.

"I appreciate your asking me here and I certainly am impressed by your loyalty, dedication and commitment to NYU. I know many of you attended the school quite a number of years ago and some of you were here when NYU had their great teams. I want to tell you that I hope to have you feel proud of our team once again."

Larry then went over some to the strategies and plans that he hoped to inject into a winning team. He spoke once again of the great era that the team once had, the neglect and now the renaissance. He spoke without notes and then sat on a desk and went on about himself and how he would want their devotion and enthusiasm once again, as he knew he would have winning teams. At the end of the talk, he fielded some questions and then the meeting was called to an end. As he waited off to the side, a man, somewhere in his eighties, came up to him surrounded by six other men.

"Let me introduce myself: my name is Jack Grossman and I was impressed by your speech, even though I have doubts about what you hope to do here."

Larry looked at him quizzically and reacted. "Could I ask you why you harbor such doubts?"

Grossman thought a minute and then replied: "I think when you have been a loser for this length of time, it would be too difficult to come back with a winning and successful team. I know you won more games this last season, but that won't get you into any tournaments. And we have been losers for many a year. I am of the age where I remember the winning teams of the forties, but even then we never won a championship."

Larry interjected: "Do you have any idea why not, when you had some of those premier players?"

Grossman went on: "Yes, we had great players, but we had a mediocre coach who didn't know how to organize a winning team—yet we did have winning seasons. But what I am going to say I am sure you already know. There are potentially great high-school players that are being recruited all over the place. But these players would have no interest in coming here, not when a Calipari can entice them to come to Kentucky. Players don't really want to come to a school with a losing record, nor do they want to come to a crowded place like New York. So you are going to have to compete both with a losing record as well as a campus that is grounded in this city. Believe me I wish it could be different, but whom are we fooling? Losing can cast a dark cloud over everything you would want to do. That's why I harbor no illusions about coming up with a winning team."

Larry could certainly see his point, because had once been his attitude and his thoughts about recruiting a winning team. He started feeling a kind of pity for what he wanted to do, a pessimism that he wanted to ward off immediately. He never could stand to sense this feeling coming over him and he knew immediately that he must turn it around before it grew inside him like an infection. So he reverted to his talk and instead of asking questions he turned it into one of his sermons. They had worked before and hopefully would work again.

As far as recruiting goes, I know what will bring good players here and we can match any school when it comes to TV and newspaper coverage. I will describe New York as being the mecca of basketball, l and NYU really will be the one team with a group of outstanding players who will emerge as national winners. We have the finest scholars here and we can match our departments against the best in all areas, including law, science and medicine, but you already know this. I have assembled the best assistants that will work alongside me and when we really get strong I will try to play in Madison Square Garden. I think some of these players will like that. Now as far as a campus goes, if that were so important why do we get so many applicants every year? Some of

these high- school players come from small towns and cities and I think
would welcome the opportunity to be heroes in the largest city in the
nation. I have already addressed your concerns and, believe me, they
will not deter us from getting a great team… and don't forget we had a
winning team this past season.

But now he wanted to change the subject so he asked these men
about their memories of the great teams from the past. Grossman
started talking immediately, as he was prone to being the big talker
for the group.

"Our greatest player was a good friend of mine and we grew up
together. His name was Dolph Schayes and we both came from the
Bronx and went to the same high school, DeWitt Clinton. It was
quite a school in those days with alumni such as Richard Rodgers,
Ralph Lauren, and even Burt Lancaster. And Dolph was our outstanding player and he was actually the center on the All-City high
school basketball team. And he was heavily recruited by college
coaches."

Larry saw a good opportunity to question him. "So why would
he want to go to a New York school?"

Jack, seeing the point related to something he had said earlier,
smiled at this and answered it. "Yes, he could have gone to West
Point or Purdue, but you may not have known this: at that time
NYU's main campus was in Greenwich Village, but it also had
an uptown Bronx campus called University Heights and the gym
was there as well as the aeronautical engineering program in which
Dolph was interested in majoring. This campus was in walking
distance of the family's apartment. And walking to school was a big
plus for him as well as anybody else. In addition, the Violets played
almost all of their games at Madison Square Garden and in 1945 the
Garden was the "mecca" of college basketball. I remember that they
drew 18,000 fans and NYU also had an academic reputation and
he won an academic scholarship. The big problem was that Howard
Cann did not have set plays and was not terribly interested in the

X's and O's of basketball. I remember it being called 'pure basketball 'where the players spread out with constant movement.

"I feel funny saying this, but there was a predominance of Jewish players on all the college teams. CCNY also had many Jewish players, but the scandals fixed that permanently. You may not know this, but in 1945 five Brooklyn College players were removed from their team for accepting a bribe to throw a game. And I think the coaches should have been more sensitive to the gambling that was going on, but it blew up in their face in 1950. You know I remember one game that had a crowd of over 18,000 screaming fans where Notre Dame beat us 66-60. After this game, writers began to see Schayes as being one of the future greats in the game. It is also funny that smoking was allowed and by half time the arena was so filled with this haze from the smoking. And then you know that Schayes played most of his professional career in Syracuse, which outbid the Knicks by a few thousand dollars. As I am talking, I am so glad to see you taking over and maybe you can bring us back the prominence we once had."

With that Larry thanked the guys for coming, extended his hand, and left. He actually liked the give-and-take and the reminder about how good NYU had once been. He had something to live up to but he also was hurt by this fellow's talking about the scandals that had disrupted New York basketball. How could a player possibly accept a bribe to throw a game that he must have loved in order to play it? But then he put it out of his mind and started thinking about the task that lay before him.

Accepting a bribe is such a cruel thing to do to a school, especially when the students are cheering you on and yet you are betraying all their confidences. "Thank God this just doesn't happen anymore in college basketball."

A few days later he had just gotten out of bed when he went into his small kitchen to make some coffee and read the newspaper. He picked up the *New York Times* and ran through the news of the week and then went to the sports page and toward the end of it he saw the obituaries. His eyes focused on one particular obit that stunned him. There in bold letters he read **Irwin Dambrot, 81, Dies; Caught in Gambling Scandal.**

He read on and saw that Dambrot helped lead City College to the 1950 N.I.T. and N.C.A.A. basketball championships, only to be engulfed in a national point-shaving scandal that tarnished an unprecedented feat and rocked the college game. He hadn't realized that the City College team all came from New York City. He knew that they were the only team to win the double championship and they defeated the same team in the final, Bradley University from Peoria, Ill. He saw that Dambrot hit the winning basket, blocking a shot and then throwing a long pass leading to another basket in the final minute of a 71-68 triumph over Bradley. Dambrot was 6 feet 4 inches tall, scored a team high 15 points in that game, and was named the tournament's most valuable player. In fact, Coach Nat Holman called Dambrot the greatest player he ever coached. He smiled to himself, "We could use this guy now; good players are always good in whatever era."

The whole city had gone crazy with those victories but in the winter of 1951 it all came crashing down when Dambrot and six teammates – his fellow starting players, Ed Warner, Ed Roman, Floyd Lane and Al Roth and the substitutes Norman Mager and Herb Cohen–were arrested in a point-shaving scandal. Other players around the country from Bradley, Kentucky, New York University, Manhattan and Long Island University were also implicated for agreeing to take bribes from gamblers to keep final scores within the established point spreads in order to win the bets. Then Larry noticed that Dambrot was born in the Bronx and attended Taft High School and he was the Knicks first-round selection in the April 1950 N.B.A. draft. Yet he passed it up in order to attend dental school at Columbia University.

The article also mentioned that his nephew Keith Dambrot coached the University of Akron and in an interview he said that his uncle had never really recovered from that totally. Sadly, in later life he developed Parkinson's disease. Dambrot was accused of agreeing to bribe offers in two 1949-50 regular-season games and receiving $1,000, according to prosecutors. He was never given any jail sentence.

Larry was both interested and yet repulsed by what he was reading. He saw a piece from an interview with Norm Mager, who had blocked a key shot at the end of the game. Mager said that for a long time he didn't talk about the scandals. And when people asked him if he were Norm Mager, he'd say no. He didn't tell his kids about it and needed to keep it private. Then his wife got a call from a newspaper saying they were going to run a story about the scandals. She threatened to sue them but when he got home and she asked him, he said it was true.

Mager talked further and said: "Eventually, I started to get over it. We were just dumb, naïve kids, 19, 20 years old. We didn't know of any law that said you shouldn't shave points – we weren't throwing games, after all. And we thought, hell, the money looked pretty good. Even if it wasn't a lot, it seemed like a lot to us since we had almost nothing. Sometimes," said Mager, "life doesn't go the way you want it to, or expect it to. As for the scandals, I think the time has come when people say 'They've paid their debt to society and it has been 46 years, for God's sake.'"

Two items really caught Larry's eye, that Dambrot and Roman went to Taft and that they beat Bradley from Peoria, IL. He remembered that his mother's grandparents lived in Peoria, which was about 100 miles south of Chicago. He decided to call his mother at that moment to ask her. She corroborated that they did in fact come from Peoria but she hadn't been there in quite some time. They talked a bit more about the city, a place that Larry had barely ever heard of. He knew his dad's grandparents settled in New York and then wondered why his mother's family went to live in Peoria.

After reading this, Larry decided to take a walk and reflect on what had happened in 1950. He thought about anyone's making a bad move in life, a decision that would cast a heavy pall over the years that followed. He didn't believe Mager's comment about how they were to know that shaving points were against the law. "That is nonsense," he reasoned to himself, "shaving points is almost like throwing the game. You are supposed to make every effort to win, not to play within the point spread. It's so disingenuous to talk that way. On the other hand, if they were poor, the money would look that much greater, but at what cost?

"These guys betrayed the very kids that trusted them, that looked up to them, that envisioned these players as shining examples of the all the blessed virtues in life."

Larry decided to call his grandfather, his mother's father, with whom he rarely spoke and only saw at family functions. Now he had to call his mother back to get the number and when he did, he put in a call to his grandfather and happened to find him home.

"Hello," he started, "How have you been, and how is Grandma Alice?

His grandfather answered, "We are doing very well except for some minor medical problems, and we are all proud of you and how successful you are. Then Larry asked him about Bradley. "Well I haven't thought of Bradley for many a year"–and when he regained his composure, he reflected a bit on an age-old experience.

"Well, yes, I in fact went to Bradley for two years and then left to go to NYU and I remained in New York, where I liked it much better than Peoria."

Larry continued the questioning, "But what can you tell me about their basketball team? What happened in 1950 to that team, which I believe played City College in the finals of both the NCAA and the NIT?"

"Yes you are right, I haven't remembered this for some time. I was planning to go there, you know; the whole town were ardent Bradley fans. We loved the team, and they were winners day in and day out. In this particular year that you talked about, Bradley steamrolled the other teams, in fact, I believe we were ranked as the number one team in the country. Well we went through the NIT and met City College in the finals. They beat us and then we both got invited to the NCAA. And wouldn't you know it, we were up against City College in the finals again. But this time we knew we were going to win. I think we got cheated in that game when they should have called a foul, but City won again. I think they beat us by about three points. We were just heartbroken. I mean we were just that good, but I think when you get down to things, City was better coached. That Holman guy was a master and they moved the ball so well."

"So what happened to bring the team down?"

"Well, in the following year, a number of the guys were caught shaving points, and that was the end of the road. They lost three of their best players. I remember them quite well, Gene Melchiorre, Bill Mann, and George Chianakos. But they did not fix the championship games. The sad part of it was that Bradley took a number of years to regain their stature and, as you know, City College was finished completely after those guys were picked up for fixing games. It was really a sad time for Peoria, but I started Bradley when this erupted and I have to tell you that I broke down crying, it was so painful for me to have this wonderful vision of a fine basketball team and then to have the whole bottom drop out. Since that time, I lost complete interest in basketball except I have been following you and we are proud of what you have accomplished. Anyway, that is the story."

There was a moment of silence between them. Larry didn't know what to say so he just talked on. "Do you know what ever happened to any of the players?" "Well, not really, except for Melchiorre. You know, he was slated to be the number one pick that year in the NBA. He was a small guy, about 5'9" who could really play the pivot, but he was ruined. I think

I read something about him moving to Highland Park outside of Chicago, but I have no idea what has happened to those guys and personally, who cares?– because what they did was so terrible."

Larry thanked him and immediately had this crazy idea of getting in touch with Melchiorre and trying to find out what could have been in his mind to do this, especially when he had this amazing career ahead of him. But how could he find him, he wondered? He could call Bradley but he didn't want to do that so he tried to get his telephone number from the Internet and he found a Gene Melchiorre in Highland Park with the address and telephone number, so he called immediately. He wasn't sure what he wanted to ask him, but he felt as if he were guided by some unconscious motivation to uncover some hidden question inside him. Like, "What moves a man to do evil or destructive things especially when it relates to basketball?" Of course he had read about this stuff when it came to Wall Street but why in basketball? Just before he dialed the last number, he hung up the phone. "This is nutty, I don't know the guy and why am I going to bother him," and yet a certain mystery surrounded his need to uncover some hidden truth about people. Now he was driven to get to the bottom of this as much as he could, so he dialed again and was a bit stunned when someone at the other end of the line picked up the phone.

"Mr. Melchiorre," Larry felt the words dribble off his lips and then he waited. "Yes, this is Melchiorre." Larry went on, "My name is Larry Evans and I am the coach of the NYU basketball team." He stopped for a moment but Melchiorre said nothing, so Larry went on. "I have a grandfather who went to Bradley and his parents lived in Peoria, and I wondered if I could have a chance to talk to you."

"What about?" was the reply. Larry knew immediately it would be improper to bring up the scandals and Melchiorre could easily say no and he would certainly understand that; so he tried quickly to conjure up some other thoughts. He didn't aim to remind the guy of some painful memories, especially if he wanted to put them out of his mind. Then Larry hit upon another idea with which he was more comfortable.

"Well, Mr. Melchiorre, I come from New York and I have followed City College and I would love to be able to talk to you about the games you played against them in both the NIT and NCAA in 1950." Larry was proud of himself for being able to turn his question into something that he hoped would peak this man's interest.

"Why are you curious about these games?"

"Well, as I told you, I am a coach and I wanted to know more about Nat Holman's teaching ability. I believe he devised something called the 'figure eight' and I would like to know what it was like to go up against that."

"You know it was a long time ago, but I would be lying if I told you I have no memory of those games. In fact, I don't think I could ever forget them, and I would be willing to talk to you if you think it could be of any help."

"Well, look, I have this week off and I'm wondering if we could make it on Wednesday if I came out."

Melchiorre thought for a moment. "If you are willing to come out here I would tell you what I remember." With that settled, Larry got the directions from Chicago, which weren't very far, and they settled on a time.

Larry thought he would break out in a sweat but he didn't. Melchiorre would have no idea that he would want to delve into the sullen past of fixing games and then being barred from ever playing basketball again. He knew he would have to make a very cagey presentation but actually he talked himself into thinking that he would like to know something of Holman's coaching technique so it wouldn't be total ploy on his part. The last thing he wanted to do was to hurt this fellow's feelings or to bring up a time in his life that served to derail his future.

"It's funny how some people do things that change the course of their lives. Here he was in a good place at a good time and he wondered how different decisions he could have made would have set him on a totally different course, one that would be founded on success. Of course what Melchiorre did was so destructive, and he was sure that the guy never woke up a day in his life when those moments didn't filter into his mind. He could have been the number one draft pick and he lost it all, in some stupid adolescent move. And then he remembered Dambrot's remark and he said to himself, "I don't care how poor the guy was, what he did was to betray the very fans that looked up to him." But then he stopped himself, "Hey, I don't want to dislike the guy before I ever get to meet him."

The following Wednesday, Larry boarded an early-morning flight to Chicago, where he planned to rent a car and drive to Highland Park. He came aboard the plane and took a seat next to the window. He then found himself absorbed in what he was going to ask Melchiorre.

"What am I doing?" he confronted himself. "As I stop to think about this trip, why am I doing it? I don't know anything about him and I am not even sure I want to talk with him. He means nothing to me and what he did really repulses me, and yet I am on this flight. Well I should have put this whole idea out of my mind, but here I am flying to Chicago. But what the hell, it gives me something to think about. It's better that I told no one what I was doing; they could think it was plain weird and it might not put me in the best light."

Larry started to obsess about it. "What would Freud say?" he smiled to himself. "Am I after finding some deep unconscious elements that lurk within those who commit terrible acts? Do I really want to probe the man's psyche to find what could have prompted him to pull this kind of double-cross; and if I find out, then what? What would I do with this information? And why do I want to go to a place in his mind that may tell me nothing?"

One question followed another and then another until he had to stop to collect himself. It was taxing and debilitating but he kept going at it.

"Maybe deep down I want to understand what would motivate someone to undermine the game I love. And if this is on my mind, isn't it better to try to follow it as well as I can?"

Here is a sensational player who had such a gifted future and he shoots himself in the foot. He ruins the very thing that made life worth living. He was living his life, the game that gave him all his pleasure, and in addition he was a national figure. Everyone, it seems, knew of him; he played in the finals of both tournaments and he was watched by millions and was the biggest sensation throughout the state of Illinois, and especially in Peoria. Did he really think he could evade the possibility that no one would ever find out about it? Knowing how sleazy these gamblers were, did he really think they would leave no trace of what they were doing, that any investigator with a modicum of intelligence would not see the betting that was going on? How could he be that stupid, or was some other dynamic operating in his mind that was not so easy to detect? I think I am coming around to my motivation in seeing him. Maybe he could tell me about why someone would be so destructive when it came to the game that was so important.   ft side he attempts a lay-up with his right hand and of course the ball is blocked. Is he being destructive, or lazy? Or does he not want to succeed, as if there were a boundary that keeps him from triumphing? Could that be it? Here he was Melchiorre, who was on the brink of being the number-one draft choice from the NBA, and he literally throws it away. Was it too much for him? Was it a success that far surpassed what his father or other siblings could do? Well, I am going to have to be patient and supportive of this guy if I want to understand him, and what my need is to talk with him."

The plane set down in Chicago some two hours later, and Larry went to rent a car and took out his GPS and programmed the address. He drove out of the city and then entered the highway to Highland Park. When he arrived at Highland Park the GPS led him to Melchiorre's address. It was along a private wooded road on which sat a two-story house. Gene Melchiorre came out to greet him. He extended his hand to Larry, who took it and held it tightly for a moment. "Thank you, Mr. Melchiorre, for seeing me."

"Please call me Gene," he replied. Here he was, a short, pigeon-toed grandfather of 15 known by his many friends as Squeaky. Larry was led into the house, which was decorated by family photographs that adorned the walls and lay on top of the dressers. There was one drawing unlike the others; a 63-year-old comic book of a giant, youthful Melchiorre wearing a No.23 basketball jersey, a superhero in short shorts. Larry knew that he held the unusual distinction of being the only No.1 pick in N.B.A. history to never play in the league. After being chosen first by the Baltimore Bullets, Melchiorre was barred for life from the N.B.A. for his role in the point-shaving scandal of 1951. Actually, he and more than 30 other players from seven universities were arrested in the scandal.

Larry asked him how he was and what he was doing with himself. He told him about his day: he wakes up before sunrise, puts on gym shorts and Nikes, and goes downstairs via the electric stair lift. At 8 a.m. he drives about 10 minutes to his daughter's house for coffee. Then at the beginning of each month he gets on his computer and types out birthday cards for his grandchildren on a keyboard; and on Sunday nights he hosts a big family dinner at a local restaurant.

Then, remembering Larry's question on the initial phone call, he discussed what he remembered about the City College games. "We had already played thirty-six games over the course of the season and our coach Forrest Anderson opened the game with a surprise zone defense. He felt that we were too tired to play man-to-man for forty minutes. City took control of the game and they were awesome against our zone. And with nine minutes left in the game we switched to man-to-man and I just took over. We launched a full-court press and I stole the ball and dribbled ahead of the field for an easy lay-up. City hit some good shots and with about fifty-seven seconds left, the score was 69-64. And the next thing I remember as if it were yesterday, I stole the ball twice and the score was now 69-68.

"City tried to freeze the ball but I stole it again and headed down court, but Dambrot caught me at the basket and there was this collision. The problem was that no foul was called. Dambrot retrieved the ball and threw it to Mager at the other end, who laid it up and the final was 71-68. The game before this wasn't so tight and City won 69-61 and I fouled out of the game. The problem was that we were too exhausted and we couldn't keep up with them; but then with some time off between tournaments we were rested for the next games that we thought we should have won, and that a foul should have been called—but that's the way it goes. So City celebrated, but we still came back heroes. To answer your question about Holman, I think he was a great coach and the team really passed the ball and played with a real team effort. I would say we had the superior team, but City was just on a roll and they couldn't lose. Look at the game they played with Kentucky, where they won by, I think, over forty points. Can you believe my memory for all that?— but it was the highlight of my life."

Melchiorre got up and brought back a photo album. Inside were relics from his stardom; photos in major newspapers, his first-team all-American honor, a script for a television commercial that Melchiorre had appeared in with Joe DiMaggio. He went on to talk of his life, the son of Italian immigrant parents with a father that was barely 5 feet and his mother 4-10. "They thought I was too short to play basketball, but I developed an array of hook-and-scoop shots to outwit bigger, slower opponents. They gave me the name Squeaky after my voice cracked on the basketball court. You know, before I played for Bradley I spent 22 months in the Army, where I played basketball. In fact, when I came to Bradley, they called me the Midget George Mikan."

Larry felt that it was time to ask him about the scandals: he liked to talk and maybe he would be receptive to it. Larry asked him how he got through the scandals.

Melchoirre was taken aback. He hadn't figured that this would come up, although he had some idea that it couldn't be totally avoided. And on some level, Melchoirre enjoyed the focus of the questions that put him in a kind of spotlight. At least someone hadn't forgotten him. So he mustered his composure and thought for a moment. "You know I really am not prepared for that direction you are taking; but it isn't so painful as I thought it would be and I have really never stopped thinking about it. How could I ever put it out of my mind?– it was the worst thing I ever did in my life, and from time to time it comes back to haunt me; but let me get to it.

"I was interviewed in a 1953 article in *Look* Magazine. The name of the article was 'How I Fell for the Basketball Bribers.' This is difficult for me, but the story goes something like this. I met these gamblers in the hotel room and was told that point-shaving was widespread and had been going on for years. Players were using the money to start businesses after graduation. One gambler said, 'It's not as if you're throwing the game, all you have to do is win by more points or fewer points than the bookmakers think you're supposed to.'"

"And they assured me that was no chance of getting caught." At this point in the, it was clear that Melchiorre knew he was breaking the law, otherwise why assure him? "I admitted to accepting money but I didn't ever want to throw any games."

Larry couldn't control himself: "So why did you do it?"

"Well," he went on, "none of us had any money. We justified ourselves, I guess, by saying the colleges were making plenty out of us. We argued to ourselves that what we were doing was wrong, but not too wrong, because we weren't going to throw any games. I pleaded guilty to a misdemeanor and received a suspended sentence, but then I was barred from the N.B.A. for life."

Larry could see that he needed to talk more about it and ease whatever guilt he would have from over 50 years ago.

"For the next six months, I stayed indoors. When I was ready to go out it was not easy finding a job because nobody wanted to hire me. Finally, I decided to return to Highland Park, where I worked as a letter carrier. I was able to play semi-pro ball in Scranton, PA, but it was poorly run and that was the end of my basketball career."

"Would you like some coffee?" Larry shook his head and Melchiorre got up and poured two cups and brought them to the table. Then he went on.

"I felt terrible for the next few years, and I decided to see if I could raise a family. By this time, I co-owned an appliance store and a women's sportswear line, and played in a park-district softball league. When we got together after the game and had a few beers, we never talked about those bad times. I never would discuss this with my family either. I was able to buy my dream home here in Riverwoods, but then a few months later my wife and college sweetheart, Kay, had a stroke and was paralyzed on her left side. I became her caregiver but then she died last year. Now I live with my brother Deno. It's funny, but we are both hard of hearing and we watch the television set to closed-captioning mode. We're like an old married couple who bike all the time.

"All things considered, life isn't too bad. We play golf together many afternoons and this chance came up. A former Bradley basketball player, Fred Dickman, asked me to be his assistant coach for a girl's eighth-grade basketball team. I brought them cookies to every game and they really love me. And the best thing happened when in 2012, I was inducted into Highland Park High School's Athletic Hall of Fame. With that, I was honored during a ceremony and was introduced at halftime of a basketball game. It meant a lot to me. But now I don't follow the N.B.A. or college games – it doesn't do much for me and I don't ever watch an N.B.A. draft."

Larry could see that he didn't really want to discuss much after this, but, oddly, he went on. "You know all this trouble began when this crook gambler came up to me. He told me they called him Nick the Greek and the next thing you know I am in this room with these three gamblers who gave us this speech about how colleges were getting rich from us. And this conversation changed my life forever. Some say I could have been a legend. You know, Coach Adolf Rupp from Kentucky said that I knew every trick that can shake a man loose. I guess I made the most out of my life; but there is never a day that goes by that I don't have some memory of those times. It's just impossible to shake it." And with that Gene got up to indicate that the conversation had ended. "Thank you for coming, but I am getting a bit tired and these thoughts are getting to me. I guess I will never forget those times, but I have lived with it and not too badly, I would say. But I regret deeply what I did and have never stopped repenting for it."

Larry thanked him, shook his hand and then turned and departed. As he left, he thought, "He doesn't look bad for a guy who is 86, but then again, he must have been a superb athlete in his day." When he got into his car and drove away, he started to think what a splendid career he would have had as a professional. Height was not so important in those days as it is now.

When he got on the plane again, he tried to make more out of the interview. In a way he felt sorry for the guy, but he did have a loving family and had the comfort of his brother's company. Still, the one stage in his life where he could have excelled and become a nationally acclaimed athlete was taken from him. Yet, he said to himself, he has kids and grandkids and they are a tight-knit family. But he could never attend Bradley's alumni meetings, where he would have been toasted over and over again. But after all these years, people may not feel that sorry for him— their memories would have faded. Yet Larry couldn't help feeling sorry for him. In many ways, he has been robbed of many great moments in his life. Yes, he could have been a celebrity.

But then Larry asked himself, "Did I learn much more about what motivated him to do this?" And that answer would be negative; but he didn't think that Gene knew much more about his motivation; it had to be more than just a lack of money. Yes, Larry asked himself again, what would Freud have made of it all? Maybe he felt as if the school were taking advantage of him, which made sense if you factored in the monies that came to the school through basketball. But if it weren't for the school, how would Gene have achieved this prominence? So, in fact, shouldn't he be more appreciative of what the school had done for him, that enabled these players to reach the height that they did? "I mean," intoned Larry, "those games against City College were nationally televised so everyone in the country heard of Gene Melchiorre. Shouldn't he have been grateful about that?– or am I talking like a school official? But I really feel this way. Without these sports the athletes would be like everybody else on campus, but they are not like everybody else– they are the heroes who move our dreams. They can't walk into a classroom without everyone swarming all over them. But it's the colleges which are enabling this to happen. So where is the appreciation and why were they talked into shaving points so easily.? Do you think it was just that they didn't feel they were appreciated enough?"

As Larry went on, he became more agitated in his mind. "This guy Melchiorre comes to Bradley, gets a full scholarship, plays all these games with this high recognition, but still feels as if the school is exploiting him." And then Larry finally fell on the rewards of this visit. He said to himself: "A player has to feel as if he is doing as good a job as he can, not only for the school but for himself. He has to feel that what's important is how well he can play the game, and it has to be mostly for himself, even though the whole school is behind his winning., Of course they want him to win, but he has to feel that he wants it for himself. Yes, the school is rewarded with a winning team that the students can identify with, this spectacular team, and yet the player must feel that he gives his all to the game, win or lose, and it has to reside in him. Isn't this what Ayn Rand talks about in her book *The 'Fountainhead*? Yes, at times a player may feel he has let his team or school down; but he has to feel mostly what he may have done to himself. Those are the ingredients of a real winner. Michael Jordan may have played for the Chicago Bulls, but he really played for himself, and his investment was in himself to be the best player he could be and score the most points he was able. If he felt as if he were playing solely for the Chicago Bulls, he would compromises his, and that's when he might feel the team is exploiting him. This is not a good position to be in, and it really marks the difference between two types of people. Then again, there were so many who scalped points from so many colleges so that maybe the guys who were susceptible felt as if they were taken advantage of. But then there will be the Junius Kelloggs who would immediately report a bribe offer. He must be listening to a different drummer."

And by the time the plane set down in New York, Larry felt damned good about the trip. He felt sorry for Melchiorre and he wished he could have been there and counseled him about what he was doing, but that was an idle wish. So many futures and so many exciting possibilities were washed down the drain; and, more than that, so many students from City or NYU will never get the experience of watching a Division One basketball game with all the excitement, the tension, and the drama of seeing the game explode into one great spectacle.

CHAPTER NINE

Ultimate Quest

As Larry was sitting in his office going over some last plans about the opening game of the second season, the phone rang and as he picked it up, Marc Stein introduced himself. They had met before and Art told him that he would be following NYU for the *New York Times* and would appreciate talking to him after the game or even before, if he had anything to say about what he anticipated. The opening season was a long time off, but he had heard some good rumors about the team and would love to print a story about it. They made an appointment, which excited Larry.

Generally the team was getting along better in their practices; however, the blacks seem to hang out with other blacks and the whites including an Irish and German player, two WASPs who found solace in one another. [An Irishman would not likely be a WASP, unless he is from Northern Ireland]. That left the three from the Middle East, who had formed an alliance that created a puzzle for many people, but they became celebrities on campus. They were widely recognized and found themselves to be invited to all kinds of parties; and once Abdul got over his initial inhibition he became quite a ladies' man. The three Middle Easterners shared deep opinions related to the political realities and the historical significance of much of the conflicts that existed in their world. They would talk incessantly about occurrences in the Middle East, but without the rancor that found its way into other groups. They often got together on a Friday night and conversed about the events of the day.

Yossi came into one of these meetings with a great need to tell them the incredible news. "Do you know who wants to meet me?" he asked them. No answer ensued, so he blurted out, "Bibi in person, what do you think of that? Now I can say I have arrived."

"When is this?"

Yossi reacted excitedly, "Next week when he comes to the UN, they have slotted a time for me to talk with him. I just can't believe this, I am really popular not only here but in Israel–and I wonder how you guys would react if Abbas wanted to talk with you."

"Probably the same way,' said Omar, "except that Bibi can be a trouble- maker. He doesn't give an inch and many of our problems can be laid on his door step."

"Come on, we have been through this before, he has to get a coalition together, he can't just do what he wants to, and I think you know this, but that's not my point. I am feeling so great that he even wants to meet with me."

So, Larry's exhortation to him when they met in Israel was coming true. The three guys were making quite a stir in New York and became extra popular at NYU. Each one had lengthy interviews in the school newspaper and when they walked into their classrooms they were swamped with questions. And of course NYU was getting a lot of media coverage, which was both good and bad. There was much criticism about their expansion into Greenwich Village, yet on the other hand the city was appreciative that they now had a Division One team of which they could be proud. Often people quoted the New York Yankees and then New York University. It did add a glamor to the city, which had been without a class team for some time. Columbia couldn't give out scholarships, so they were continually hampered in trying to develop a class basketball team; and Fordham, as Larry well knew, did not have the interest as well as the motivation to bring big- time basketball to the city. So this left NYU, and they were going gangbusters in their third season with the Big Three, as they were called. The new stadium on the West Side fit in perfectly, because there was such a demand for tickets that they sold out every game. Everyone used to talk about how precious the tickets were for North Carolina or Duke, but the Violets were competing on similar turf.

The buzz over three players from the Middle East found its way to many national newspapers. At first there were countless questions raised about whether the three could really play together, and then there were questions about how they could have been recruited. Of course, there are players from around the world who go to American universities and they represent Europe as well as Asia; but there had never been players from Muslim countries and there had never been a team that featured an Israeli together with two Arabs.

In one incident that was reported, some faculty members from Yeshiva University were discussing the problems in the Middle East and then one told the others that NYU had a Jewish basketball center. "Impossible," said the other professor, how could that be?– and how tall is he?"

The other fellow shot back, "he is 6'10," and the other guy retorted, "that's a miracle," and then the other guy followed this up: "The real miracle is that he is playing with two Arabs who are 6'7" and 6'6."

Finally the other, looking shocked, said: "Now that is a miracle beyond belief."

Ellen started to enter more into Larry's ideas about the team. She would tell him about the trouble areas that she spotted and her thoughts about how they could be improved. On nights that Larry was busy, she and Sherman would have dinner. At first they talked about strategy on the court but more and more Sherman started to confide in her about the important issues in his life and she was so comforting to him, especially when they talked about women.

On campus, there were continual problems, some minor some not-so-minor. One afternoon, Omar and Abdul were strolling down one of the streets near NYU and Abdul excused himself for a moment to buy some gum. Omar was standing along against the wall when two guys confronted him. One guy said to him, "Why do you play with the Jews?"

The other guy added to it, ", are you a Jew-lover?"

Omar became a bit agitated; he reacted poorly to their anger. "What do you mean?" he asked.

"You know what we mean, why do you play with Jews when they are killing your people over there. Are you stupid?" Just then Abdul came out of the store and immediately sensed something was wrong. When the agitators saw him they decided to move, but not before one of them said again, "Don't continue this or you will be in trouble, I am warning you."

"What happened?" asked Abdul.

"Oh the usual junk that they spit out about why we play with Jews. This is the first time that this has happened like this on the street, and I hope it is the last." But Abdul reported it to Larry, who then thought it was best to bring it up before his players. So at their next meeting he talked about it. Yossi was stunned and hurt to think that in this sophisticated place, students would talk that way.

"Well," said Larry, "there is nothing you really can do about it, please do not strike back at these guys, otherwise it will be picked up for the wrong reasons. And the last thing you want to do is get into a fight, you must protect your body at all costs, we need every one of you in tip top condition."

And then they went on to discuss this in more depth. Johnson remarked, "You know they used to say this about us. How can you whites play with them blacks?– and the only way we could show them was to beat them and that's what we did. I have to tell you a funny thing I saw the other day. For some reason, Ole Miss was in town for some kind of reunion or game or something. Well, if you remember, Mississippi was one of the worst black -hating states in the Union. I think that the reunion had something to do with the football team and most of the players were black. How can you figure that one out?"

One other player piped in, "If they didn't have the blacks on the team they would lose most of the games. Even last Saturday, they had an Ole Miss team on television. At one point in the game, the entire team was black. I just howled at this and wondered how those Southern bigots could take it or accept it. So we have one Jew on our team and these guys are trying to make an issue out of it. I wish you would remember them so that we could go out and flatten their heads."

"Come on," said Larry, "you'll never convince them of the importance of playing together and forming one unit. And by the way, we have two Jews on the team, that is when you count me.

"Now I'd like to tell you a story. It's about this Rabbi Yisrael Mier Lau, who survived the Holocaust and is now the Chief Rabbi of Israel. On the opposite end of the spectrum stands the legendary Lakers Center, Kareem Abdul-Jabbar. He was born Lew Alcindor, Jr. and was one of the best basketball players of all time. In 1971 Lew Alcindor converted to Islam and changed his name to Kareem Abdul-Jabbar.

"These two men – one a Jew and the other a Muslim – are eagerly looking forward to meeting one another this July in Israel. You may want to know why. Jabbar is making a film about World War II and will honor the final wish of his father. Alcindor, Sr. had one dying wish. He requested that his son visit Israel and meet the little boy that he personally rescued from Buchenwald concentration camp and who had eventually became the prominent Rabbi Lau.

"Rabbi Lau said he clearly remembers how an African-American soldier during the Liberation picked him up, and told the residents of the German city of Weimar: 'Look at this sweet kid, he isn't even eight, yet he was your enemy; he threatened the Third Reich. He is the one against whom you waged war, and murdered millions like him.'"

"As someone who grew up in New York and who followed the Lakers, I never thought I'd see these two figures mentioned in the same sentence – let alone meeting in the Holy Land! After reading what Jabbar intends to do with his film and his visit, I look forward to seeing these two legends of their respective fields work toward bringing peace to the world."

After he finished there was a calm and introspection that came over the room. Everyone got the story, and they all seemed to grasp the point of people of divergent backgrounds who owe it to themselves to come together and work together.

Larry and his two assistants spent many hours poring over their forthcoming schedule for the Big East Conference. The schedule looked quite good with only a number of soft teams. However, they did get to play Syracuse, and a number of very good teams. The last thing Larry wanted was to emerge in his third season with a mediocre or losing record. With the guys he had assembled before him, he knew that he had a winning combination. All they needed was to play as a team and they would be off and running. They knew that they had the players in place, the strategies worked out, but this was in practice. The real test would be to play a first-rate team. And now the opportunity presented itself in the name of Duquesne.

As the first game started Larry began to feel exuberant. He could see that Duquesne did not look as if it were going to compete at a high level. He couldn't quite put his finger on it but he could sense it immediately. And the game became a blowout for NYU. They double-teamed their center, hoisting successful shots from all over the court. And they used the pick-and-roll effectively, and screened for their cutting players. You could see that in their practice, Larry and his assistants made provisions to construct a team that played so well together. So they ran the other team off the court. The other part that he observed was that Abdul was one awesome rebounder.

You can teach shooting selection, driving, and jump-shooting, but there is little way to teach rebounding. Larry realized that it is more of an instinct. Most players don't like it because it results in so many collisions and banging heads. But Abdul was fearsome; he reminded him of Dennis Rodman, who jumped for everything.

At the end, when they came back to the locker room, there was such an air of euphoria. Their first game and they had finally come together, playing with the kind of team work that Larry had wished for since becoming their coach. They met this initial challenge with the kind of vigor of champions. Larry could see how in their rejoicing they acted as if they were one unit – they all related so well to each other. He thought, "What a beginning!"

On the sports section of the daily newspapers, one declared, "NYU destroys foe," another wrote "NYU plummeted Duquesne," and finally, the last one said "NYU wins first game" Larry preferred the term "destroyed."

In their second game they displayed a real toughness. From the opening tip, Yossi looked like a kid in a neighborhood playground. He drained four threes. He went coast-to-coast, blowing past defenders, switching hands on the dribble, and finishing with a right-handed lay-up. Larry could see that his knowledge of the game when he didn't have the ball increased tremendously. He poured in a game high, 27 points. When the game was over, Larry assembled the team in the locker room and launched into a speech.

Considering the talent we have on this team, two victories do not amount to all that much but of course you blew them away. But, at times you guys looked painful. Then he shouted out to them, *Painful! Look, I have thought about this and listen closely to what I have to say. There are three kinds of offenses we can employ. The first one is the normal kind, we get the ball and move it up court at a normal pace. The second kind is that we get the ball and move it up court very slowly. This is when you may have a big man who ambles up the court, so that you have to wait for him to position himself in the pivot because the rest of the team is so much faster. Now for the third kind of offense, this calls for speed, the ball is rushed up court in order to throw the other team off their defense. But it is more than this, because you really need substitutes who can run and run and when they start to tire, you throw in some of the next team. In addition, you have to anticipate where the pass is going to go and then pinpoint that pass almost with your eyes shut. I was reading about such a team in the 40s. They came from St. Louis and were called the Billikens with a center whose name was Easy Ed Macauley. Their speed had not been seen before in Madison Square Garden and they defeated one of the top ranked teams in the country, LIU. This is what I would like to envision for us. I think in spite of our problems we can come away with a very winning season. And this is where more of the bench will get into the game. So what do you think?*

He then went on:

Very few athletes are born so richly talented that every action and instinct comes easily to them. Even those of us with great talent must fight against the softness of their bodies, the slowing of mental reaction, the dispersion of attention. And most of us must practice for scores of thousands of hours to sharpen their skills; most must painstakingly identify weaknesses and compensate for them; most must learn the humiliations and intricacies of team play, and of that fierce competition with ourselves in which we are measured against the achieved standards of our sport. I just wanted to get some of my thoughts off my chest

He looked closely at everyone and then continued:

All of us must every day face failure and defeat. Every game is a risk, a loss of face. In the thousands of practice sessions, in the countless series of injuries, frustrations, failures, and losses, we must be ready to face our competitors in the pursuit of winning. Every game is a continual proving ground as to whether we can take it as well as dish it out. We are here to form a brotherhood that will give us the strength to enter into each contest. In every game, one side is defeated and you know defeat hurts. And at times, the more talented do not always win. A game tests considerably more than talent. It really tests our entire life. To continue to win our games is to feel as though the gods are on our side, as though we are the darlings of fate. Remember the words of Vince Lombardi: Winning isn't everything; it's the only thing" It isn't the thought of lording it over number two or number three that brings satisfaction; in our hearts we may know that in some way our competitors are superior. But finishing first is to have destiny blowing out the sails of our ship. Let the other be better on the books today; but let fate bestow victory on us. And I want you to carry this message into every game you enter. I am saying this because our competition is going to get tougher after tonight.

The team sat there stone-cold, taking in Larry's words that commanded them to continue winning game after game. The team nodded their approval and they expressed a willingness to give it a yeoman's try. Some ventured an uncertainty as to whether you could really have two teams of equal strength, but they agreed to give it a try. Yet it never really came to that so they all knew how well conditioned they had to be.

He left them in the locker room to dress and then walked out into the night air. He looked around at the landscape of the Village and breathed in a deep sigh. He was fitting in just beautifully with the tumult and vibrancy of this area. Initially he was worried that it was going to be too hectic for him, but now he felt as if he thrived on this energy and excitement. This was the New York that you read about in the newspapers: every night there were tons of theatre, movies and concerts, and Larry realized that he really did not take full advantage of this. He needed to bring his cultural IQ up by many points. And he smiled because he was going to have dinner with Ellen, who always had a bubbling manner.

But if his first and second season proved to be a bit of a failure, this was beginning to shape up. The players learned their roles more effectively and they were patient and serious. And the team was getting their chemistry in place. Robinson was becoming one hell of a point guard that brought stability to the team. They began to demolish their opponents with their athleticism. Larry had chosen

his assistants very carefully, especially Sherman, because these were
the guys who would focus on each player's strengths and weaknesses.
In many ways they were the backbone of the team. While they may
have all been involved in recruiting, the assistants did a large part of
the grunt work, but he picked them because he knew they loved it.

NYU won their next game rather handily; the opposing team
was too short for the likes of Yossi, Omar and Abdul, but then Larry
realized that Johnson was 6'5" and Gilmartin was 6'4". They outre-
bounded them and rained in on three point shots and they came into
the second half with a 20-point lead. Their defense was impeccable.

Following this in the practice, Larry warned them that the next
game would be the real test; they were playing Syracuse, which was
ranked fourth in the country. They were big and imposing. Boheim
was an ace recruiter and produced winning teams over the years.
They won the NCAA tournament in 2003 with Carmelo Anthony
as the standout. But they lost to Indiana in 1987 by one point. Many
people felt that it was hard for Boheim to beat Bobby Knight because
he was an assistant to him and could loom as a father figure. But
there goes the Oedipus complex and its psychological analysis—yet
Larry thought that psychology should enter into any scrutiny of
winning and losing. It can't all rest on skill; otherwise what role
would tension and attitude play in the game? Of course, psychology
plays a big role. Watch a team that is up by 20 start to fall apart. Is
that too big a score to integrate into one's psyche, or does winning
by 20 points make a team feel they are destroying their opponent?
It happens in tennis all the time.

Well, Larry was not going to let his team lose because they
were fearful of these opposing giants. As someone once said, "If you
worry about losing, you can never win." In the locker room before
the game, Larry launched into one of his lectures:

*We are going to win some games and lose others but when we win
it is because you are going to have confidence in me and my system. By
being alert you are going to make fewer mistakes than your opponents.*

The quality of each of your lives is in direct proportion to your commitment to excellence. I think it is our obligation to develop once more a strong spirit of competitive interest and to be first. If we settle for nothing less than our best, we will be amazed at what we can accomplish in our life. In a larger sense, we are engaged right now in a struggle that is far more fiercely contested than any game. It is a struggle for the hearts, for the minds, and for the souls of all of us, and it is a game in which there are no spectators, only players, and it is a struggle which will test all of our courage, all of our stamina, and all of our leadership ability, and only if we are physically and mentally ready will we win this one.

The game did not go so well as Larry would have hoped. NYU was a bit sloppy and at half-time they were behind by 10 points. In the locker room during half time, Larry lit into them.

You guys were inept and disoriented. We turned the ball over 8 times, which led to their baskets. What the hell were you thinking out there? You were careless on defense, shoddy on offense, and at times you looked disordered. We are playing one of the great teams in the country, this game will give us our identity, and you have approached it in an almost amateurish way. You are better than this: I have watched you play better than this and it is not just another game; at this point, it is the game of the season. If we win this game we will show the world that we have to be reckoned with. After a disastrous first and even second season we were taken for granted, almost made fun of, we had trouble winning a game. But I want you guys to show them that we have got what is needed to be a first-rate team. I know this because I have seen it, but not with these turnovers. I am not going to single out any one player, we are a team and not individuals. So I want to see a different second half; otherwise I can hear the papers say that I was intimidated by Boheim. This is not what you want, so let's go out and show who the winners are, who the champs are, and who can play this game the way it was meant to be played. You guys are just too soft, just like Charmin toilet paper, so come out and play hard.

In the second half, NYU was a different team. They were hitting the open man, Yossi was striking in for points, and Omar and Abdul were streaming in for easy baskets. And when the defense took them too closely, Johnson and Gilmartin started to rattle in the threes. Syracuse kept calling for a time-out, but they could not contain the vitality and drive that came alive in the second half. When the game was over NYU walked away with an 8-point win. The fans went wild: they all knew what this game meant and what was riding on it. There was no mistaking that NYU had a tough and winning combination. Back at the locker room, Larry thanked them.

More than winning you showed who you were, you solidified your character, you overcame any doubts you may have had, and you paid back this university's believing in you because when we went to Division One we had to go there with more than a promise; we entered into a program that garnered great belief and hopes for this team. Now we have taken New York City by storm and nothing will stop us if I have your trust in our mission.

Larry assumed a look of determination and moved his hands in a victory celebration.

He realized that his hard work had paid off. Yossi was sensational at the center position. He played impeccable defense, set screens, rebounded, and drove hard to the basket. Uncle Sol was right after all, Yossi just anchored the team and when pushed became ferocious and aggressive. The other pieces of the team were fitting together like a beautifully woven tapestry. He realized that the ability of each player to try to make the next guy better had all the earmarks of a winning team.

The next two games were pushovers even though the teams were good, but they didn't have the height or speed that NYU was showing. But what happened next was out of the script for a semi-miracle. After their fifth game the top 25 teams were listed in the newspaper. Kentucky was first, North Carolina was second, and Louisville was third as Syracuse dropped to fourth. But lo and behold, NYU came up as the top twenty-fourth team of the week.

To even get into the top twenty-five would have been beyond Larry's wildest dreams. When Larry looked at this, he sat down and kept staring at it. A negative thought shot through him that it might be a typo, but of course he knew this was no mistake. When the fact of this got around, the student body became uncontrollable. Every T-shirt, hat, sweater or piece of apparel with an NYU logo was sold out immediately. The campus rocked with exuberance and the air was filled with the utmost passion and furor.

There was such a force that this team provided the school. It was the human spirit, nothing stills it, nothing fulfills it – true, straight, and well targeted, it soars like an arrow toward the proper beauty of humanity. Their athletic ability exemplified something of deep meaning –a frightening meaning even. Once they stand out as they do, they do not quite belong to themselves. Great passions are invested in them. Their exploits and their failures have great power to create exultation, or to depress. When the students talk about the team's performances, it is almost as though they are talking about a secret part of themselves, as if the stars above had some secret bonding intertwining with their own psyches.

Larry was elevated to a higher plane. He understood more and more the mythic line of basketball: a game of fake and feint and false intention; a game of run, run, run; a game of feet, of swift decision, instantaneous reversal, catlike moves, cool accuracy, spring and jump. The pace is hot. The rhythm of the game beats with the seconds, a rule to shoot in thirty seconds. Only when the ball goes out of bounds, or a point is scored, or a foul is called, does the clock stop; the play flows on. Even when a play is called or a pattern established, the game flows on until a whistle blows, moving relentlessly as lungs heave and legs weary ;it follows like a jazz ensemble that rocks.

The students who formed the major fan base loved the new pressing defenses, the sweat, the toll it took on blistering feet, the pounding up and down the floor, hawking, falling, leaping, tangling, pushing, shoving for position. The team could be seen like a single living body; the two teams clinging to each other up and down the court like giant wrestlers, locked in high-velocity and sweating contact at every point of movement. Warily, at times, the dribbling guards approach the other team's embrace; like arms, the defensive guards swing loosely right and left, circling before clapping tightly into the foe's line of movement. Each team is a mystical body, one, united. Enormous feats of concentration, enormous bursts of energy, vast reservoirs of habit and instinct are required. A part of our deepest identity is uttered in this game. Those of us are taught possibilities we might otherwise have never known.

Would NYU ever be the same again? The vitality was contagious, it permeated into the heartbeat of every student. The cheering at the games resembled religious chants, something spiritual and alive with desire and craving victory at all costs. It unlocked the appetite that was tranquil and stagnant in most of the students. Now they experienced a surge of excitement, the lid was taken off the unrest, the campus pulsated and the exhilaration seeped out into the atmosphere. What a great place to be! was a statement made by so many of the students. Now they didn't have to be envious of the big college basketball teams; it all had come home and weren't they proud to be there? "No, I don't have to go to North Carolina, I get my thrill right here."

Larry knew he had to counsel his stars before all this elation would go to their heads. Thank goodness I have Ellen and Sherman with whom to vent, I need them. But this didn't happen, because in their next game the team came out like mythic warriors, pouncing on every mistake and then bounding up the court to weave an intricate play for the score. By this time, tickets were impossible to come by and the stadium easily filled up for each game. Even on the road against lesser teams, they sold out their arenas. And the emails poured in. Larry opened up his cell phone to hundreds of messages. It was almost impossible to read them all. But then his eyes became riveted on one from Rick Pitino, who succinctly congratulated him on his success and ranking. In fact, the team moved up to 18 in the top 25.

But as we know, what goes up must come down, and the team experienced its first loss to St. John's. It was a tight game but they missed too many foul shots and St. John's was so hot that night that they seemed unable to miss their threes. It was as if everything they threw up went in, so that NYU had to keep coming from behind, which was not what they were used to. And in this process they became careless, with too many turnovers because they were trying too hard; and in the process they lost their composure. But losing is bound to happen, and the team took it in good measure. In fact losing may have been a mixed blessing because it exposed a weakness that they could address – the tension of trying too hard. And they reasoned that at least they had lost to another New York team. Now the season was drawing to a close and they had lost 3 games but won 25.

By the end of the season, NYU was on top of their conference and got an automatic bid to the NCAA tournament. They would have anyway, because they'd moved to 11 in the rankings. Now Larry waited to see how the pairing would go and what bracket they were in. When they printed out the pairings, he heaved a deep sigh; they were not in the same line as Kentucky, Louisville, Duke or North Carolina.

The first game was an easy one against a very weak opponent, but the next team they faced would be Syracuse. Although NYU beat them earlier, their team got stronger and seemed to coalesce toward the end of the season. Larry knew that this would be a tough one. He became almost bleary-eyed watching the tapes, going over the weaknesses and strengths. He became obsessed with the defensive alignments. He felt that Abdul was not that good on defense, but that Omar was a hawk when it came to guarding his opponent. And Yossi was a total phenomenon. The two forwards could hold their own and they just had to be on for the game.

To start the game, NYU came out and buried their first three threes. A huge student throng came down to the game and their shouting created a din in the arena that overshadowed everything that was taking place on the floor below. The game was tightly played and it came down to the wire. Syracuse was ahead by two points with 20 seconds to play. NYU brought the ball up, careful and determined. There was a hush in the crowd; a silence prevailed as the attention of the fans was focused on that last-minute play. Omar brought the ball past the half-court line and passed it to Yossi, who held the ball and then threw it out. It had already been determined who would take the final shot. It was a set play and Boheim was up for it. However, he figured it wrong – the ball went into Johnson behind the three-point line on the right side. He had a moment to set up the shot and let it go. As the ball arched in the air, everyone held his breath as the ball dropped through the net and NYU came out with a one- point victory. Everyone swarmed around Johnson, hugging and kissing him, and Larry ran over to him and put his arms around him. Now we were in round three.

The next game was difficult but they won as time expired. This moved them to Sweet 16, which was close, but they pulled it off. Next came the Elite 8, where NYU just swept the other team aside. They peaked at this point and then came the important Final Four. This was a tough game, as Florida had had a great season. They held the lead for most of the game. Larry substituted carefully; he needed fresh players at the end. The team just came together even more than before. Abdul was unstoppable, hitting on Alley-oops and hauling down rebounds. Their fast break was working to a point where they were unstoppable and they edged out a victory by three points. Larry was almost dumbfounded: he had brought the team to the finals of the NCAA. Who could possibly have even dreamed of this – it represented a different, higher stratosphere – a place in the heavens. Larry waited for the next game that was played after this, so that he could see who his opponent would be. Of course the team he constantly worried about that could be his challenger was North Carolina. The thought of playing against Roy Williams frightened him. And on schedule, North Carolina pulled off the victory with keen foul shooting and excellent accuracy from the outside . Now, Larry and his team had Sunday to construct and plan their game.

The New York papers carried the story on the front page. There was so much analysis about an Israeli and two Palestinians playing together. Their story reverberated around the world. Israel did not know what to do with this story, as the same would be said about the West Bank and Gaza. It was so out-of-line with reality that the writers had to think deeply in order to make a reasonable story appear in the papers. And more than that, it had to explain how these players meshed so well; what happened to all this animosity that people had read about? Could it just disappear into thin air, and why were these three players so different? Nowhere else could you find so much harmony, but that was put aside as all parties prayed for victory. Could they really pull this off even if they had come so far? Larry wished the whole school could have come down for the game, but of course that would be impossible. What happened in New York was unimaginable. The overwhelming need to provide coverage for the game led to greatly expanded TV broadcasting. Lincoln Center, where they had put up huge TV screens and hundreds of outdoor seats for the viewing of opera, now was set up to show the game on a wide screen. Many movie theatres, including the Ziegfeld, were charging a modest $5 admission fee for the game; and at NYU, a massive TV screen was set up in Washington Square Park to display the action and many fans went to their gyms, where the game was televised. And of course every bar in town would be packed to the rafters. The tension and excitement captured the entire city: it was now a New York happening, something the city hadn't experienced for some time.

Larry was asked to do a short interview for one of the leading TV stations. He entered the room and sat placidly waiting for the questions. In time, his demeanor changed and he became more excited. The commentator asked him how he felt about his team and his views on the deciding game. Before Larry answered, the commentator complimented him on the miraculous turnaround for the team and the skill involved in taking NYU into the finals of the NCAA after only three years.

Larry broke out in a huge smile and then answered:

Thank you for the compliment, and we all are so thrilled to be here and playing for the championship. I love this team and I love to see how they refuse to die. I love to see impossible odds confronted, or impossible dares accepted. I love to see the incredible grace lavished on simple plays— the simple flashing beauty of perfect form; and even more than this I love to see the heart of these players that refuses to give in, refuses to panic, seizes opportunity, slips through defenses, exerts itself beyond capacity. In Larry's mind, this was show-time and he told himself he was going all out for this TV presentation.

In all my life I have never known such thoroughly penetrating joys as playing with an inspired team against a team we recognize from the beginning had every reason to beat us. But will they? I love it when the other side is winning and there are only moments left; I love it when it would be reasonable to be reconciled to defeat, but one will not, cannot. I love it when a last set of calculated reckless, free and impassioned efforts is crowned with success. When I see my team play that way, I am full of admiration and gratitude. That is the way I believe the human race should live. When we actually accomplish it, it is for me as if the intentions of the gods above were suddenly clear as day before our eyes.

The commentator broke in: "These are really uplifting sentiments; do you usually talk this way or at least talk to your team in this way?"

Larry beamed.

Well I do share the sentiments I just expressed. Every team at their best loses sometimes. It does mean that losing is, in the end, one's own responsibility. There are no excuses. Winning does not simply mean crushing one's opponents but being the best one can possibly be – and conquering the fates and adversities that are stronger forces even than opposing teams. I think that winning is both excellence and vindication in the face of the opposition. It is a form of thumbing one's nose, for a moment, at the cancers and diseases that, in the end, strike us all down, every one of us. Maybe this is what Vince Lombardi meant when he said winning is the only thing - as an attitude, a desire, a spirit. Winning means being as perfect under fire as humans can be. Losing means somehow, through one's own fault, not having prepared enough. I feel strongly at this moment that my team is prepared to win. They worked hard for this moment in time. They trained while pushing their bodies to places they never thought they could get to. We are certainly going to give it our best and we pray that our best will in the end win. I have dreamed of this game my entire life. I never thought that I could get to this place– that I would be in contention to play in the championship game with one of the great teams and coaches of all time. We are prepared for this game. Thank you again for this opportunity.

They shook hands and Larry went back the hotel.

The night of the game was greeted with great eagerness and anticipation with North Carolina's being favored by 3 or 4 points. After the singing of the "Star Spangled Banner," the teams lined up to play. Larry had given his players a last- minute motivational speech.

We shoot the same percentage that they do: rebounds, assists and three-point shots are similar so what is going to do it for us is in our heads, the psychology of winning. You believe in yourself, then the rest is taken care of. We match their size, their height and speed, and in fact in some ways we outdo them. So I want you to go out there and show them what a New York team can do. We are here to take back our history: remember City College of New York won this in 1950 and there has been a drought ever since. Well tonight they are going to hear from us.

North Carolina controlled the opening jump, brought the ball up, and scored on an outside shot. Before long they scored a fast eight points; then Larry had to call a time-out to quiet his charges. Then NYU registered on the score board and the game went back and forth until half-time, when Carolina walked off with a twelve-point lead.

The second half opened with Carolina's shooting the lights out, scoring from every conceivable spot on the court. NYU kept themselves in the game with streaking lay-ups and well-executed picks. But tonight they could not match the athleticism of the other team and the score kept enlarging. With six minutes to go, Carolina had improved their lead to 15 points and of course the Violet fans started to seriously worry about their chances to win the game. One voice after another felt as if "We've come so far only to lose our moorings."

But then a strange thing unfolded before Larry's eyes. Where before Carolina had played with an effective team effort, somehow with their large lead they started playing less as a team and just passed the ball around. They lost their way having the big lead. NYU then scored a three-pointer, reducing their edge to 12. On the next play, Johnson intercepted a pass and sped down court for an easy lay-up. Then a Carolina player was fouled in the act of shooting but missed both shots, and Yossi got the ball low and barreled in to score. They were now behind by 8 points and there was another turnover that resulted in a Violet score, bringing it to 6 points. Another foul by NYU, but both shots missed. Gilmartin brought the ball up, threw it to Yossi, who turned to his right and then shot a pass on his left side to Abdul, who was streaking to the basket for a lay-up, reducing the lead to 4 points.

Williams called a time-out. Larry was stunned with the turnaround. He had witnessed this before but never with so much resting on the outcome. The large lead created too many problems for Carolina; they forgot what a team effort meant and they almost became listless. A long three caromed off the backboard that Yossi hauled down, and then he threw it up court to Omar, who took it to the right side and passed it to Yossi in the center. As some of the players moved toward him, he threw it to Johnson in the corner. Then a Carolina player ran to Johnson, who had that extra time; but instead of shooting, he pump-faked and got fouled. He then went to the line, turned to Larry to gain confidence, and quietly put in three foul shots to bring NYU within one point.

The clock was ticking with 55 seconds remaining as Carolina brought the ball up. Instead of running out as much time as they could, they took a shot precipitously that rolled off the rim into Omar's outstretched hands. He passed to Gilmartin, who slowly and carefully brought the ball up with 25 seconds still remaining. He ran off another 10 seconds, then threw it into Yossi who pivoted, moved slowly toward the basket, and then hooked it in. This gave NYU a one-point lead and a time-out was called. The fans in the arena were staggered as much as the players. Who could have predicted this? One of the leading teams in the country was now experiencing this kind of meltdown. With 9 seconds on the clock, Carolina brought the ball into the front court and called another time-out.

The game continued, and Carolina made one pass and then another into their center. He backed into Yossi turned and leaped up for the shot. Yossi anticipated this and leaped up behind him; and as he attempted to get the shot off, Yossi, with his outstretched hands, blocked the shot and pushed it as far back as he could. The ball was recovered by Johnson, who dribbled out the clock; and the scoreboard registered NYU's victory 62-61. Larry wanted to put his head into his hands because he was so moved, but he remembered the time that Jim Valvano won the final game with North Carolina State against Houston in 1983. Valvano became so excited that he ran and jumped around the court with such abandon. "This is my role model," he said to himself and then he took off circling the court and jumping up and down until he ran over to his team and hugged each one. What a stunning achievement and what an unusual upset. Then the two teams lined up to shake each other's hands. As Larry moved along the line, he spotted Roy Williams coming along the other side. His heart started beating faster, was it fear or elation? And when he faced Williams, he said quietly "Good game," to which

Williams responded "Great game." Larry grinned, turned his face up, and muttered to himself, "Hold my place in heaven."

And finally Larry had faced his last demon.

The crowd broke out into a massive chant that lasted until the presentation of the trophy. Yossi was named the most valuable player, Larry grasped the trophy for the winning team, and then the Violets cut down the nets.

People were stomping and shouting in their seats. Larry walked to the sidelines, where Ellen was waiting together with his parents. He grabbed her hand. He looked lovingly into her eyes and cryptically said, "I propose," and she replied, "I accept."

And the best thing was hugging his two friends, Phil and Paul, who couldn't contain their joy and exuberance. And then he reached over to pull in Sherman and the four meshed so well; and they knew what a championship team is all about. Larry looked at them and thanked them and then said to Sherman, "I don't think I could have done this without you; you really have given me the confidence I needed and the aggression I always wanted."

Back in New York there was pandemonium. The theatres let out, the fans from Lincoln Center emerged from their seats, and the customers left the bars. As thousands came onto the streets, the odd thing was that no one went home. They formed a massive procession and then walked down Broadway. Traffic was at a standstill as the crowd, picking up more people along its way, headed straight to Washington Square along Fifth Avenue to celebrate, to rejoice, and to commemorate the return of New York to world prominence. This was a team that would be long remembered, and here was a city that was home to this team.

This long convoy of people ambled slowly downtown toward Washington Square. There was a decided rhythm that sped the crowd along, with determination and a hunger that spelled victory and winning. And then someone broke into song and the song was "New York, New York." The rest of the people began to pick up the lyric and finally everyone was singing. An outsider would imagine that some religious apparition had made its presence. The crowd carried with it the dreams of the future, the hopes and vision of a better world, one that was instilled with enough energy to weather any storm. This was an upset that set the city on fire, that brought all different parts of the city, the religious and the ethnic, together into one massive entity. And all the parts wanted to feel this unity, a harmony and a love that fit together like a massive jigsaw puzzle. And when this puzzle all came together, there was an exquisite painting of the greatest city in the world and, for these moments, the greatest college in the world.

As they made their way downtown, the Dean, who was seated in his private office with some celebrities, realized that when the crowd descended on Washington Square, a prominent speaker would be needed to greet them. However, their coach, president, mayor and even governor were at the game so whom could he turn to? And there beside him was Barack Obama, former President of the United States, who had been invited to this intimate gathering and viewing. He turned to Obama with a longing voice: "Do you think you could stand on stage and bring some words of courage to this crowd?" All those in the room watched this mammoth crowd walking steadily downtown. Barack responded; "I see where all the heavy hitters are at the game and of course I would want to do my part with a few words." Obama was majestic, as he always is in talking in front of crowds. He went on to say:

The contest we just witnessed is a ritual conducted under the sight and powers of the gods. To have won this game must show that fate is on our side. It is not the mere game, not the mere pride, not the vaunting of self over others; it is the sense of one's inflation by power and now the victor has been chosen. The elation of victory must be experienced to be understood; one is lifted, raised, infused with more than abundant life. We need to praise our team, our coach, and our president. They have brought the blessings from the heavens above, who have imparted such

*love and appreciation on us, knowing what we went through to arrive
at this majestic place in history. Thank you and never let this moment
leave you.*

With these words the crowd started to disassemble, spreading
out in all directions and casting a canvas rich in texture and glowing
in color.

The next day the team returned to New York and witnessed one
of the largest ticker-tape parades that ever assembled before City
Hall. It was hard for Larry to come to his senses, but he did deliver
one hell of a speech, filled with his motivational tributes and his
sense of purpose and of winning. There were so many emails from
so many people: those that knew him when he was a mere child or
saw him as an adolescent and then befriended him as an adult. But
he scrolled down to see and hope that there was one email that would
give him so much pleasure. It was the voice of Pitino who wrote,
"Congratulations, you deserve it, you worked hard for it. The best to
you." That really sealed the victory. His parents were crying, feeling
so much joy; his best friends couldn't hug him enough, and all his
former assistants and coaches were there. And then he walked over
to Uncle Sol, saying, "You started it with that hoop you gave me and
I can't thank you enough."

He turned to Sherman who was sitting next to him: "Well we
did it; and I don't think I could have done it without you." Sherman
was touched and he responded in kind. "I want to thank you for
talking to the folks over at Hofstra. They told me that you promoted
me with high recommendations. Well I am going for an interview
in a few days and the way it looks, the job is mine. What do you
know about that?"

Larry started to laugh. He looked Sherman in his face: "And
now you are going to go at me." "Well," Sherman replied, "Maybe
not in the beginning, but soon you better watch out." With that
they both laughed and wrapped their arms around each other. And

in a while the proceedings drew to a close, but there was much celebration to be had.

The next day Larry was sitting in his office when there was a knock on the door. "Come in," and in walked Yossi, Abdul and Omar. They sat down and Yossi spoke first, "We have something important to tell you." In that moment, Larry felt a twinge of fear, thinking that they were going to tell him they would enter the NBA draft. But Yossi said quietly, "We've decided to come back next year and see what havoc we can inflict on this world of basketball." Larry muffled his tears, he was so taken by this. "I can't tell you how moved I am with the love and appreciation you have for me and the team." Yossi immediately replied, "Look, if Florida could do it under Donovan, why not you."

The Daily News headline read "NYU COMES HOME A CHAMPION." And in a matter of weeks the enrollment tripled.

In the meantime, Marc Stein at the *New York Times* asked Larry to write out something that he could print quickly, some intimate feelings he had. And here was Larry the winner who was getting married and had the whole world at his feet. He was staring down at Washington Square Park and the memory of an 8-year old kid throwing up this small rubber ball at a basket that hung over the door flashed through his mind. All he could say to himself was "I love that kid, he carried me along this wonderful road of triumph." He then submitted his text to Clive Barnes from the *New York Times* that would define his love of basketball. He vaguely remembered something Michael Jordan had written some time ago. This is what Larry had written:

Dear Basketball,

It has been almost 23 years since the first day we met. 23 years since I saw you hanging over the back of my door. 23 years since my Uncle Sol introduced us.

If someone would have told me then, what would become of us, I'm not sure I would have believed them. I barely remembered your name.

Then I started seeing you around the neighborhood and watching you on television. I used to see you with guys down at the playground, where we hung out a few times. The more I got to know you, the more I liked you. And as life would have it, when I finally got really interested in you, when I was finally ready to get serious, you told me I wouldn't be tall enough, fast enough or even good enough.

I was crushed. I was hurt. I think I even cried.

Then I wanted you more than ever. So I practiced. I hustled. I worked on my game. Passing, Dribbling. Shooting. Thinking. I ran. I did sit-ups. I did push-ups. I did pull-ups. I lifted weights. I studied you. I began to fall in love and you noticed.

At that time, I wasn't sure exactly what was going on. But now I know. I listened to you more, I tried to understand you and how to respect you and appreciate you. And then it happened. That night when we won the National Championship, you found me coaching the best team in the nation and we danced.

Since then, you've become so much more than just a ball to me. You've become more than just a court. More than just a hoop. More than just a pair of sneakers. More than just a game.

In some respects, you've become my life. My passions. My motivation. My inspiration.

So much has changed since the first day we met, and to a large degree, I have you to thank. So if you haven't heard me say it before, let me say it now for the world to hear. Thank you. Thank you, Basketball. Thank you for everything. Thank you for the education and the experience. Thank you for teaching me the game behind, beneath, within, above and around the game...the game of the game. Thank you for the moon and the stars, and last but not least, thank you for giving me NYU.

I know I'm not the only one who loves you. I know you have loved many before me and will love many after me. But, I also know what we have is unique. It is special. So as our relationship changes as all relationships do, one thing is for sure.

I love you, Basketball. I love everything about you and I always will. As I continue in my job as a coach our relationship will never end.

Much Love and Respect,
Larry Evans

EPILOGUE

FINALE: PEACE ACHIEVED

What happened next could not have been predicted. It could read just as well as something outrageous if it weren't true. At the end of the school year in June, Yossi, Omar and Abdul made plans to go back to the Middle East. They had visited their home few times during the years that they were there at NYU. They had been working on some plans that would turn the trip into a political adventure. During the time at NYU, they communicated with a number of organizations in Israel, the West Bank, and Gaza. There were groups there devoted to peace and reconciliation between the Palestinians and the Israelis.

When they arrived they visited their families first and then after a week started to put their plans in motion. This involved giving a number of strong speeches before as many groups as they could and then attempting to get as much publicity as possible. There were strong groups existing in both camps that wanted peace between them in the worst way; and of course there were groups who wanted them to disappear, so that agitation between the sides would be kept alive.

Yossi made the first impassioned speech. He stood before the Israeli parliament and spoke. "If the three of us could come together and win a championship, why can't the rest of our countries do the same thing? We have been together for almost two years, and the union has only resulted in a stronger bond between us. We championed each other, motivated one another, and created the best opportunities for each of us. I would like to have you see what we have done as a microcosm for our plans to bring peace between the two factions."

Next came Omar, who spoke to a contingent of his people: "We have much to learn from the Israelis. They can bring so much power and strength to our people. If we delay this process, then we are only depriving our people of the riches we can attain. I know many of you hate them because they took our lands, but remember it was we who attacked them not once, but three times, in an effort to destroy them. They have stood up to us and even developed industries for us. They left Gaza and we have let a terrorist organization take hold there. And what great harm would come if we recognized their existence even as a Jewish state. After WWII it was obvious that they had no place to go, they were almost eradicated in Europe and they came here; but they were here thousands of years ago.

We talk of the right of return, but realistically they could not absorb all the people that we would like to have return here. The Palestinians have lived in other countries such as Jordan, and they live like poor homeless souls. Our own people don't take us in and provide us with the most basics of survival. We can only improve our lives by coming to some kind of agreement with Israel. I beg you to take this position."

Then Abdul took the podium. "Initially I hated the Jews and when Omar invited me to come to New York I resisted, because I did not want to play with a Jew, someone who I felt oppressed my people. But we have been together for two years and there are only good things I can say about him. He has tried over and over to improve my life and make me realize that hatred can take a terrible toll on a country. I don't want to hate, and I don't want to obsess about revenge against a people I feel could be the best thing for us. On more than one occasion, Israel has attempted to improve our living conditions, and they are in the position to do that. I also beg you to come to terms with them. I would like to put Abbas and Netanyahu in a room together, close the door, and make sure they don't come out until a viable peace plan is worked out. Toward that end I would lend my entire support."

These talks were carried throughout the Middle East in all the newspapers and telecasts. Finally, after weeks of constant attention to this process, the two leaders started to come around. They had met before, but with a very hazy kind of mission. Now there was a seriousness to their discussions. Would this leave this rapprochement open as a possibility for the future? Could this herald the end of the conflicts between parts of the Middle East? Anything is possible.

The three players were hailed as heroes who were leading the fight for peace in the Middle East. When Larry read this in the newspaper he was so impressed that he decided to fly to Tel Aviv. He also wanted to get married there and see whether he could have any part in these negotiations. Everything good came out of the victory and the world could become a better place. And it all resulted from that 8-year old boy who had high hopes for his future; who wished for great things to happen and then worked to make sure they would happen. With faith, desire and commitment to an ideal all dreams are possible. How would you know?–well, just ask that kid.

Printed in the United States
by Baker & Taylor Publisher Services